The Big Blue

Evan Louis Herold

ISBN: 978-1-7966-0630-0

All this is love; and all love is but this.

- Rupert Brooke

1

Nick contemplated the woman leaning against the boat's railing. She held a drink in her hand, and at this time of night it was clearly half-empty, not half-full.

When Nick considered her, taking his eyes away from the distant bow of the yacht as it cut through the dark waves, he remembered the way she had been described. *Good Goddamn bones.* The first time he saw her she was very much alone, but there was something else besides her good bones and her aloofness to claim his interest. It was near the few shops and restaurants alongside the marina, and as she walked by his table, he had set his newspaper aside and regarded her with curiosity.

At that particular resort there was an outdoor café which Nick sometimes sat at during his occasional work-breaks away from the yacht. It was a typical occurrence to see a woman like her spending a few hours of her day slowly moving along the walkway and looking into shop windows, or running up enormous bills at the boutiques – although, usually, there was someone sent along to accompany such a person.

But on that sunny day, there she was by herself. He

noted her stunning appearance, and the way the light moved over her salon-dyed black hair. But then there was an odd slant that she gave to her arms and legs as she paused in front of a window. He recognized, too – with her nervous glances around - that she appeared to have larger things playing with her mind than mere window shopping. Surprisingly, the displays of rich and frivolous clothing hanging inside were only a minor distraction to her. Even from his distance Nick could see dozens of emeralds that sparkled on a dress behind the glass, but which clearly waited for some other patron.

Yet then her head turned a small amount in his direction (almost as if to view him head on) and it appeared she somehow recognized him. Then she thought better of actually looking at him in full.

Suddenly, she moved farther along the walkway (as if ignoring him) and toward the next point on her map, and left a trail of mystery in her wake. All that remained then were the usual experiences of such a seaside resort: the manicured flower beds along the walkway: the exotic sports cars crawling along narrow roads (and announcing their presence with burbling exhaust notes), and the ancient buildings and their pastel facades. And also, the many other people, tourists, and locals. But no one like her.

In truth, even after she eventually came onboard the yacht, and then spent many days around and amongst the other girls and crew, Nick had barely come to know her at all. Still, he chided himself. From the first he should have identified her as some sort of *Radcliff girl*, even if she didn't yet officially belong to that wandering tribe.

He had glimpsed her many times on the yacht, but never again onshore. Once, memorably, he had viewed her down in the yacht's galley while the chef operated the blender and filled the space with noise, and she sat on a chair nearby the counter. The chef chatted with the other girls in a too-loud voice (the topic was the best way to manage a three-day *dietary cleanse* by limiting one's intake to merely seaweed) and as the chef talked, he held his finger down on a button, and the blender whirred-away and mulched some richly green material. And she – oddly – positioned herself slightly leaning to one side, as if she were ready to run away and flee the entire scene at a moment's notice. It seemed she wanted to be *anywhere* other than where she was, and yet she stayed.

But then Nick glimpsed her other times, as he walked closely past her in the yacht's main hallway. She gave him a polite nod and a brief smile, as if the two of them shared some unknown and mysterious connection, the details of which were completely unfamiliar to him.

Now here she was standing just next to him on deck, and there was that half-empty drink in her hand, and they were wandering around a certain kind of conversation. It was if all those previous encounters were leading up to this. Her eyes were now frequently meeting his, and for some reason she was talking to him like the world was going to end this very night.

On this night he did know that Radcliff's warm bed waited for her down below, and that fact made every word hidden with some secret meaning. She leaned against the railing of the yacht – a different variation of the same uncomfortable position he had viewed as she stood and glimpsed inside the shop's windows days earlier - but this time the breeze played in the night air and then wrapped around her.

Earlier in the week they had pushed off and left port, and at the moment they were miles away from the coast and there was nothing else to occupy Nick's attention but her. (Perhaps she felt the same?) At night Radcliff's yacht, which was covered only with patterns from the boat's running lights, the moon overhead and distant stars, and the yellow glow of the helm's control panel, provided little for the eye to fall on, or be distracted by. Even the long and radiant wooden deck disappeared, and curved into a silent blackness. The boat and those people aboard her headed to the next resort on the list. And so between the two of them their conversation turned toward that unknown *end.*

"That's what you must figure out," she finally said, "Before it is all over...Before it ends...What are those millions of things you can't have?"

Nick did the math in his head. It was only three days since Radcliff's boat had pulled up its anchors and set course to travel farther north along the Italian coast. And by his count, she had apparently been on and off the boat four separate times before she made a decision to join them permanently (or some variation of that) and their pleasure-seeking journey around the Mediterranean. She was becoming a Radcliff girl. Nick reminded himself there was nothing unusual in this: She seemed to know Radcliff from some earlier encounters - or perhaps she simply made herself known to him, as was typical for the scene. That was probably after she made the *rounds*, and after she learned a thing or two about Radcliff and his little group. Girls like her were always on and off the boat, or somewhere else orbiting around, and soon Nick had made up his mind: She was a remote quantity of gorgeousness that he would eventually forget.

But she had made a choice. At some point she decided to fall into the circle on a more lasting basis and join them for a time, and for Nick, that meant relegating her to a far corner of his mind was going to become impossible.

At the marina he had watched with a contradictory mess of displeasure and expectation as one of the other crew loaded her few belongings onto the boat. In her possession, there was only a leather bag and a classically styled briefcase, seemingly from a different era. (As expected, she traveled light, and didn't bring much of anything at all along with her.) Nick watched as she steadied herself, demonstrating a casual familiarity with boats by using a grab-handle as she came aboard, and it was obvious she barely registered the significance of her decision. Thereafter she could often be seen milling alongside her new benefactor, or sometimes off by herself down in the cabin, preoccupied and reading a magazine. At those times she positioned herself with her chin awkwardly propped on the palm of her hand, and her legs sprawled out and on view.

But now here she was right in front of him, late at night.

She was talking with that sound in her voice and the end of the world – or something – waiting on the water and just beyond the black horizon. He felt a pull as they wandered around the uneasy topic of conversation at hand: The millions of things in the world that a person can have - and those that they can't... It was a conversation he would repeat to himself many times in the coming weeks. The most unsettling thing was the way she addressed him, as if opening your soul late at night in the middle of the Mediterranean was the most normal thing in the world, and he readjusted in his seat when she met his eyes. Again, the real question was why she stayed on deck here with him, when Radcliff's warm bed waited for her down below.

Nick focused on her, and then minded the boat as always. It was close to three a.m. and there was that romantic breeze blowing across the deck and playing with her short dress in that yellow glow from the boat lights, and her body was positioned with that same slant and slightly odd manner. Nick wanted to say – tell me about *you*. Tell me about that time I first saw you, walking alongside the shops and looking into store windows, and then you turned to almost face me. What was going through your mind, right then? Have you and I – *perhap*s – met before?

He listened as she slurred her words, thinking that it might just as easily be the lingering aftereffects of Moroccan hash oil playing with her voice.

"Do you – *Nick* - know what those millions of things you can't have are?" She took one last sip of her drink and set it to the side with a raised eyebrow and waited for his answer.

So there it was; her voice suddenly came to a point and said everything. His breath left his body. Maybe she did know him, after all.

Yes - She had heard his story, or at least the ugly parts.

Yes – She knew just how much he had lost and why. Her eyes regarded him now and looked for an answer. Clearly, she had heard some of the chatter about Nick, perhaps from one of the crew or other girls. The various reasons Nick called this boat home made for a stomach-turning cautionary tale; this was a particularly gossipy boat so the topic of Nick and his downfall was a favorite subject. Now the only question was how many of the ugly details about him - and his faltering life - made it into whatever version of the story she had heard.

Yes - He answered her in his mind. I know all about the things I can't have. Perhaps you would like me to list a few? A yacht like this; a lovely – but dangerous - girl like you; a bed that feels like my own.

Did Radcliff, or someone else, tell you my story?

That was what he really wanted to ask her. Did he tell you how I once had those things and now they are gone? Maybe on some afternoon while the two of you lay together under the sheets he told you all about my fall from the lush-life and into the gutter, just to caution you far away from me.

Radcliff told you all about the fraud that cost me everything, and might as well have destroyed me. He wanted you to see the sharp rocks that lie beneath the surface of the water. He wanted you to understand how they can tear a person apart without warning.

•

In the sun, the extravagant wood of the deck glowed and the immaculate white sails balanced and swelled-out against the wind. Despite his better judgment he observed her from afar on days when they pushed up the Italian coast and she sprawled about, along with the other girls on the forward deck. "*Good Goddamn bones*," was how Radcliff summed her up when he surveyed the flock.

Yes, Nick agreed, she possessed a fine structure on which to hang a woman, including high cheekbones, which made her seem all the more exotic and foreign. There were other expected physical qualities as well, which ran like a catalog of all things desirable in this clique: The hourglass shape, the rich looking hair – which in her case was an unusual jet-black color – and a generous amount of height and leg. Radcliff usually preferred his girls tall. And he liked them to *dress tall,* as well. That meant high heels, skirts, and sleeveless tops that showed long limbs and effortless style. Yet behind the scenes and among the crew that was a running joke: The only time squat and plump Radcliff measured up to them was when he stood on his wallet. *Ka-Ching!,* the similarly short-of-height cook might intone with a smile, after looking around to make sure the coast was clear.

Still, she was easy to recognize even from a distance thanks to the way she stretched her body out indiscriminately on a lounge chair. Next to her, sometimes, the blonde with the pug-nose reclined, and seemed effortless. But the jet-black-haired woman wore her lipstick a shade too bright, and her shimmery one-piece bathing suit reflected light from the sun as if it were a brash mirror. And every so often when the clouds shadowed the boat she wrapped a bright red beach towel over her shoulders like a funny little cape. In the breeze he caught tidbits of her voice and her words were tinged with an accent he recognized but had difficulty placing - Hungarian, he finally surmised.

Yet his practiced eye saw something more in the haphazard mincing of her appearance. There was something else in the calm abuses she was falling into, and the way she continually tilted her body as if she was on the verge of collapsing. It was *her* – that silhouette - but there was something catastrophically wrong. There was the feeling of a woman in shambles.

Her half-empty drink was now completely empty, and he rose to the occasion. "Would you like another? I can run below and get you something."

She shook her head "No"; perhaps her particular version of the world was indeed coming to an end. She was lost in thought and waiting for his answer - there were more important things in life than killing what remained of the alcohol. She couldn't let it go, for some reason. She wanted to hear him talk about the jagged rocks under the water. The things that had ripped him to pieces. The cautionary tale told to scare people like him and her straight. The fraud that had cost him most everything. "Nick, tell me, *please*...Do you know what those millions of things you can't have are?"

He shook his head. "I don't have the slightest idea." As if in comment, the boat pushed directly ahead, into the night.

She sighed and considered him for a moment. She knew a lie when she heard one.

With that she altered the subject. He noticed a different tone in her voice now and it sounded like a final coda at the end of a song. It was if she were telling him that their brief time together was soon to be over. He had failed her in some regard. The connection, whatever it was, was already fading.

"Nick, you are not the only American on this boat." She said this as if she were sharing an embarrassing secret; something that he refused to grant her in return. "When things get difficult for me I move around - I use my American passport. I was married once but we are not together anymore. Still, I keep the passport. And I suppose the last name when it suits me." Her eyes fell on him in a kind way, "It's one of those things people say I'm not supposed to have, but it's still mine anyway."

Suddenly it was over, she made to rise from her tilted position, and Nick stood to his feet to offer his arm. She was wobbly but uncaring and it made her all the more irresistible. Now, just next to her, within inches of her face, he again caught the scent of her hair in the air; although it was jet-black it somehow smelled like vanilla.

"I am done," she abruptly said, finally standing upright at her full length. "I think it is time to retire." Yes, he thought. You are being missed by someone, I am quite sure.

She then turned with a timid smile and headed down the stairs and into the interior of the boat.

He listened to the uneven *click-click* of her heels as she disappeared and sank down each step. And then he heard her stumble along the hallway towards the master bedroom, making it past Nick's bicycle that he kept strapped to the railing because there wasn't enough room in his own small quarters. From there she was then certainly through the last door and into Radcliff's enormous bed where she was never without company.

Alone, Nick breathed in the air and already began replaying their conversation in his head.

This night, there was no music or great symphony issuing from the stereo in Radcliff's bedroom from *afterwards*. After he was done with the girls. Typically, the music flowed underneath and around the door, and then followed down the hallway and made its way up onto the deck. And that music might thereby provide Nick with companionship. He could look at the yacht's instrumentation in its glow as he sat nearby – as if it would tell him anything unexpected - and then contemplate the forward view. But there was nothing else to share the scene.

He wondered over little details: A sideways glance, a pause that said more than it was supposed to, and an invitation from her that he longed for but dared not accept. As always, he kept his distance; he organized his defenses. He tried to pretend that he was simply the cool and remote captain of the boat, unaffected by her. He knew his place - and it clearly did not include a night with one of Radcliff's girls.

Still, he understood that beneath his composed exterior there was a flame that burned, and only a few people could see the light. She was one of those people.

Nick wished he could consign the whole horrible thing to the scrapheap of history. It was *all* constantly in his thoughts – even though he refused to tell her - he very well knew those many millions of things he could not have, at least anymore. Why did he refuse to open himself to her and tell her? Even just the small amount that she asked of him?

He turned the list through his head, yet again. There was the fraud that cost Nick everything: his home, his own beloved boat, and a future that seemed assured. There was his girl, whom he loved and whom he once imagined loved him (in her own way) in return. There was her beloved hand, which he wanted to hold, even if he was never entirely sure that she wanted to hold it in answer.

But there was also the horrible truth behind it all, and life as he learned did not always follow its intended course. Nick was supposed to be somewhere else. A different person. A different place. He intoned a name under his breath – *Johansen* – as if that brought everything into focus. The man that had changed the course of Nick's life.

It was like a shipwreck: big and tragic, and it just kept on happening until there was nothing to see. Nick's position, family empire, and wealth was erased in front of him. He watched it disappear in slow motion and was powerless to stop it, all due to his misguided trust and – *Yes* - greed.

But that was just the opening event. Afterwards there was the struggle to simply find his breath, and later to find a place to call home, no matter how miserable. At the time, it seemed he had nothing. He was sleeping on a floor in an abandoned house, and waking up with his cheek rubbed raw from the rough carpet. He was counting out pills, and trying to remember the magic number to finish it all. It was the disaster that was impossible to imagine but suddenly real, and after he surveyed the scene and pondered his options there was only one choice that made any sense, and so he made his escape.

Nick had bargained his way first to the prison-like existence of the container ship Athena, where he worked for several years. And from there he made his way to his current spot and window on the good life, here as captain of Radcliff's yacht. He decided it was a fair result after everything that had happened. It was a sometimes comfortable and yet a twisted existence, but considering the manner in which his life destroyed itself, the best he could hope for, just not the life he planned on. She – the Hungarian lovely - wanted to hear him say it, maybe somehow acknowledge that fact, but he refused.

Nick gazed out across the sea and took in the fullness of the starry sky and let it settle his thoughts. These were usually the times he took reassurance in the isolated life at sea and held the solitude closely. At these times he was a member of a congregation that spanned across the Earth and across history. And yet underneath it there was something missing - he was unfit for it in some way that he couldn't put right. In the instant when he breathed in that unlikely vanilla scent from her hair he wanted it back: everything that was lost to him. His old life.

He corrected himself: everything that was *taken* from him, and he would do anything to get it.

Again he plied that sour name in his head - *Johansen.*

Nick stayed on the deck another hour before ending his watch and handing it over to another crew member. He heard the faint sounds of the diesel motors slowly urging them forward. By the morning light he expected the boat to have traveled another forty miles along their route.

He moved to the same place the Hungarian lovely had occupied earlier and saw the view from her tilted position.

The sails were stowed away and overhead the single mast climbed an impossible distance into the air. He saw the spot where he had sat in front of her and smiled to himself when he imagined that he must have looked like an outsized child with his long legs bent tight and pulled in. He tried to figure out why, when her hair was so darkly colored and black, it somehow had that particular fragrance.

Vanilla, which to him seemed so *light.* How odd.

•

Nick sits in a beach chair, the kind of wooden weathered chairs that dot the coast like white splotches of paint.

He buries his toes into the sand, feeling the heat collect and then change as he pries further into the cold, wet sand below. In this small corner of the world there are only a few beaches that are *not* composed of rocks and tiny pebbles, and from his vantage point he can count three sandcastles being built by children in its honor. From the lifeguard stand an Italian flag rustles with the breeze. The sunlight is intense at mid-day and all the bodies surrounding them are decorated with sunglasses and wide-brimmed hats.

The beach population begins to recede in the interest of lunch. Umbrellas are lowered and towels are folded like party decorations being put away. But among his tribe there is no hurry to leave, as ever. Later in the day Radcliff has a table reserved at his favorite restaurant. In truth it is merely one of *dozens* of favorite restaurants scattered along their planned route this lazy summer, and so they remain on the beach and pass the time.

If she were here with them, lopping her conversation with that Hungarian accent and those odd slurring words, Nick would be happy to sit, talk and listen. But mostly just listen.

He wants that voice to again sink into his chest. He wants to smell that vanilla in her jet-black hair. But she is gone now and he is anxious to leave as well. He wants to get on with something – *anything.*

What are those millions of things I cannot have? He never gave her an honest answer, and if she knew better she never told him.

Among the bodies walking back for lunch are every type: short and squat, long and lean. In most cases, the barely-there swimsuits doing no favors; these are people for whom style is definitely *not* store-bought. For these people, the world has been about other things and now on vacation - with wives, with husbands, with girlfriends, with families - they demonstrate that cultured European love for a simple-life, rather than showy pretense. Nick watches as skinny kids are towed in-hand from the water by plump moms, and the children aren't afraid to use their superior dexterity to slip from grasp and prolong their fun a few seconds more. Bellies are displayed with pride. Hair (*and oh, is there hair!*) is found under armpits and across legs and in dark swirls on forearms, and not just on the men. There is a pleasurable ease in knowing everyone is looking and that no one cares.

But among Nick's group there is just one body type. The exception being Radcliff who lounges in the sun like a sea lion waiting for feeding time at the zoo. What must the vacationing beach-goers think as they happen to cross paths on their way back from the surf with this little plot of sand? There they find a single middle-aged lump for who the term *portly* might have been coined. And bizarrely surrounding him are three drop-dead beauties, and to the side there is Nick, all lanky muscularity and with a broad swimmer's back and shoulders. Together lounging on the sand like a cobbled-up family they must seem perverse and ridiculous. Radcliff perhaps enjoys this most of all: Seeing and *being seen* with his girls. Radcliff doesn't follow the typical summer-route (or social conventions) of his particular variety of man. He often prefers to slum it around the plebeians, and yet his story is painfully obvious to anyone with a hint of imagination. Radcliff is "one of those men": extraordinarily wealthy, happy to flaunt it, and always willing to exercise his money to get whatever he wants. And what about the girls? What is their story? Well, that is never entirely clear, even to Nick.

Nick sits with his chair facing slightly away from the others. It's his way of distancing himself and pretending his life is still somewhere else. To the side they are talking: "Pilates. Isometrics. Running. Low-carb. Botox. Uppers. Cameron Diaz. Tuna fish. Grapefruit."

The primary conversational beach-topics include exercise, celebrities, food and drugs. Over the weeks and months of this and other tours, every faddish new diet and exercise routine has been examined and analyzed from every conceivable angle. *Cleansing diets* are the new rage and each variation is filled with many opportunities for intense discussions. During Nick's first few weeks on the yacht he withheld his shock as the most gorgeous girls he ever met talked in nauseating detail about what they found in the toilet after an intense *kale only* diet. These years later Nick barley notices when their conversations dissect body functions.

And then there are the drugs.

At first Nick thought any number of pharmalogical combinations explained the odd manner of the Hungarian lovely. His working diagnosis: Quaaludes, vodka, and a dose of Moroccan hash oil mixed in for good measure. Over time Nick has developed a secondhand expertise in the signs and effects of over-the-counter, prescription and illicit drugs, and later capable in their procurement. Nick buys them for Radcliff, and Radcliff passes them to whomever. Nick studies the drug-enhanced scene and makes notes in his mental journal. Maybe, he sometimes thinks, it's his one way out of this place.

•

Nick is now only partly listening. The red, white and green of the flag are suddenly lifeless without a breeze. The kids have abandoned their sandcastles and within an hour the tide will be far enough in to swamp and wash away their morning's work. Will it be one big wave or several smaller ones that finally take down their castles? Nick thinks about how life changes; there is the ebb and the flow. And yet these past years his life somehow seems fixed in stone and impossible to change.

He remembers the container ship, the Athena, and his first leap away from the ruins and the fraud that Johansen wrought over his life.

There it was, moored alongside the dock. The ship was

impossibly large and solid as he walked towards it. The weight in his duffle bag – and the way that small load made him bend over and struggle - made him feel frail and fragile in comparison. Inside that worn bag, there were only a few belongings, which he had squirreled away and deemed important enough to take with him. Things that were useful; things that he needed. And there was one particular picture of his old sailing boat, and he and his old friends posed on the deck. He had placed the picture in the bottom of that bag and wrapped it in a shirt to protect it and keep it safe as a remembrance. For many weeks now, he knew the world was going to be a very brutal thing, which he was no measure against.

Up close, the container ship was unearthly. He was shocked to see the way the gentle swells of the water moved the hull, and the sluggish way it stretched like a sleeping giant against the restraints. He had bluffed his way on board thanks to half-a-lifetime's knowledge of sailing, but only into a menial position; he would be cleaning, painting, and doing whatever general drudge-work was needed. It was the absolute bottom of the barrel, but all he could hope for. In the aftermath of what he began thinking of as *the crash*, he had found a toehold, and he was able to earn his commercial shipping credentials and certificates, eventually.

Still, despite his years of experiences at sea, he knew almost nothing about these ships or the day-to-day work he signed on for.

Nick would always remember the view he had of that massive black hull every time he approached the Athena. Sometimes, as he walked along the dock and glanced over, he wondered over the massive steel plates that formed the body of the hull. The rivets were so big they seemed to come from some other universe where normal laws of physics didn't apply. Even months later, when he saw the way the hulking monster rocked gently, and yet so enormously alongside the dock, he stopped and starred. The ship pulled at the ropes and raised them from the water, and then extended and tested them seemingly past the breaking point. The ropes acted like dish rags which were being wrung out, and they gently dribbled water back into the bay. This was something entirely different. Each time climbing up the gangway was either like walking into - or out of – a prison.

No matter, he considered it an escape. The ship was named after the Greek Goddess of wisdom and justice, and she carried thousands of containers for the Mazer Line. Although it was a German company it seemed all of the crew, aside from the captain and first mate, were Filipino. In their version of Tagalog, they strangled her name – Athena - into "*Tina*."

The ship presented the world with a huge sun-faded logo on her smokestack and when she came into Singapore, Long Beach, or sometimes Hamburg, she was simply one of dozens of ships that day that looked like they had sailed around the world a hundred times before. From a distance, there was nothing to call attention to her or anyone who worked on her, which was the way Nick wanted it.

In fact, no one much cared what was being transported in the containers stacked ten stories high on her deck and deep into the hold, except for nameless people on both sides of the ocean. Whenever Nick was summed up to the bridge, sometimes for a work assignment, sometimes (he felt) just because he was simply a bizarre curiosity that others wanted to gape at, he would take long glances out the windows, far forward, and see the containers stacked like massive building blocks. Green, yellow, red, and blue. Near the front of the ship the containers were so far away they actually started to seem strangely toy like. And yet the ship's wake was forming and flowing out from both sides of the hull like the most powerful man-made thing he had witnessed. From above, he imagined, the wake would seem like a supernatural arrow in the waves. Occasionally, Nick would look out to the shore as the ship passed through a channel, and see groups of kids out on the edge of a breakwater, their bicycles leaned against concrete pillars or massive rocks. They would wave their hands as the ship passed by, perhaps hoping that the captain would let loose with a deep and epic bellow from the fog horn (which he sometimes did, to their amazement).

But beyond those moments of exuberance, the ship was just another behemoth that made the voyage across the Pacific every three weeks at twenty-two knots in every kind of weather, and with the routine of the rising and setting sun.

It was harder work than anything he had ever experienced. Often it was eight hours on then only eight hours off. Unloading and loading at port often meant extra time and extra money to settle the debts that were still on his conscience. There was no old-life to hang onto anymore. Nick had disappeared the moment he stepped aboard, and yet what of his friends and what remained of his distant family? Those ties he cut immediately and merely sent what money he could, whenever he could.

That was what a person did in his circumstance. You settled in the best graces possible and fell off the map, unless you opted for suicide in the form of two-hundred tablets of aspirin and a signed note. The thought had occurred to him more than once. There was no need for a will. He had nothing: the entire family fortune – *his trust* - was lost and gone.

He kept to himself; he ate alone; he stayed in his quarters and slept as much as he could. He wanted to drain away into nothing. It seemed there was always that overpowering feeling of shame and guilt for the way he had squandered, abused, and allowed his inheritance to be snatched away from him. The family empire (if he could find the courage to use that word) was built over generations, and through slow, hard work and self-sacrifice - and in later years (simply enough) with smart investment strategies. And then Nick became the custodian. And then it was all destroyed and lost. One-hundred and fifty years gone, in only a few months.

And always, there was that name – *Johansen* – to turn like a knife in his gut.

Nick awoke with the ridiculously cheerful ring for the watch change, and when he finished his mindless and routine tasks (maybe running that paint brush over that same place he had months before) he listened to the wind whistle in between and amongst the containers. He smelled the salt air attacking the metal of the ship and the acrid diesel fumes from the engine. He seemed to welcome the smell. It entered his nose and then traveled through his body; it rested in his clothes and in his skin, and in the morning he washed it out. He felt the vibrations of a ship at move and the water hitting the hull, and in bad seas the propeller arresting the waves with a massive shudder. He imagined all of that metal turning and moving, and then forcing them forward. He found something strangely gratifying and calming about waking-up in the aftermath of a storm and knowing that huge distances had been crossed in the night.

The sea *does* forget, he thought.

Sometimes he opened a map and charted the legs of

their crossing by using a sextant and considered the way the ship moved through the miles without need for a rest at a slow steady pace. But then miraculously once she was at port and unloaded and reloaded, she would set off in the opposite direction with barely more than a single day's break. It was tireless. In some sort of deference to the position he now occupied, Nick pounded out pushups by the hundreds whenever the need for flight took hold again, and followed that with pull-ups on the hot water pipe that ran by the galley. The exhaustion and fatigue rooted him in place. He found satisfaction in being just a physical thing.

The cook every so often watched him when he stepped outside of the kitchen to take his cigarette break; the cook flicked ashes into the wind and looked at Nick doing pull-ups as if he were looking at a fool.

Life was hard enough as it was, why add to the pain?

The paint on the hot-water pipe was soft and gummy, and one day when Nick dropped back to his feet in exhaustion, apropos of nothing, he raised his palms and showed the cook the white paint that had ground its way far into his hands. It was the first time Nick had shared a laugh with someone in more than two years. Later the cook asked the question – What are you doing here? – that Nick knew the entire crew wanted to ask. *You don't belong on this ship doing this shit-work,* was the inferred statement.

They were keen social and economic observers and recognized an outlier when they saw one. They wondered why he never tried to graduate to a different position or tried for any kind of promotion. They noticed his callous-free hands that soon toughed up, and his ancient watch that he fastened securely around his wrist and refused to part with, even in the worst of conditions. It was the way he shaved off his stubble every morning and the strange manner he folded his napkin at the end of every meal. It was evidence of the slow accumulation of habit and a character transposed from a bizarre different world, and which refused to leave.

Nick tried to answer: I've nowhere else to go but here. The only skill I have, which is worth something, is sailing. That was enough to get me on this ship, and this is where I'm staying.

•

The blonde with the pug-nose is talking. The voice breaks Nick's concentration and disrupts his memory. Nick's ears perk up and he is suddenly returned to the beach, trying to predict which of the coming waves will bring the first sandcastle to its knees.

"She was just odd." The blonde with the pug-nose is making a point, emphatically. "I'm not sure she even said more than a dozen words to me the whole time she was on the boat."

They are talking about *her.* Again, he can picture her. Sitting there with her chin awkwardly resting on her hand, while sprawled out and paging through a magazine. Her legs on display.

Or otherwise, as he first saw her: That slant as she distractedly looked into shop windows alongside the marina, and then that look she made towards him. As if she knew him. As if the two of them had some connection - and then she decided to ignore him, and leave him for another time.

Nick's back is to the girls, but Nick can imagine the manner in which they are nodding in agreement. Odd. Yes. He knows they are setting down their magazines and phones and considering the subject. Yes - she was just slightly wrong for the scene. Out of place. Radcliff for his part is unusually quiet on the subject; he doesn't even mention her *good Goddamn bones.*

"Where was she from? Slovakia or someplace in the boonies, wasn't it?"

"Hungary…She was Hungarian." Nick cannot help but enter into the conversation, though he has no interest in the back-and-forth that is likely to follow.

"Really?" The blonde with the pug-nose is doubtful.

"Pretty sure. It was her accent. Although she did tell me she had an American passport."

The group absorbs these pieces of information for whatever they are worth. Nick looks over his shoulder and notices that the brown-haired girl with the discreet dolphin tattoo on her hip has nothing to add on the matter; as usual she is lost in a quiet half-daze and Nick wishes they could all join her. She's back to her routine of taking Klonopin every morning, Nick decides. It's part of her breakfast again…0.50-miligrams of anti-anxiety medication as soon as she wakes up.

"What happened to her?" The other blonde with the less-memorable nose is suddenly involved now, and as Nick has observed on many other occasions, she likes to dig in places where she thinks she'll find dirt. "I got up the other morning and she was just gone…Packed-up and left the boat without a goodbye. And we were all going to do something to celebrate the solstice, *that night!* Quite rude, I thought."

And then after a brief pause and time to think, Radcliff enters the conversation like a tiger. His voice demands that the topic is now closed. "We've covered this before…She just wanted to go home," he says with the authority of someone who knows everything.

The others are silent now. She wanted to go home. As if such a place actually existed for a girl like her.

Nick hears the two blondes shuffle in their seats in protest and in doubt, but otherwise remain quiet. The brown-haired girl is deep in another place (she doesn't even stir) and Nick wants to wade into the haze alongside of her.

•

It only takes a few ounces of water in the lungs to drown a person. Sometimes people drown in only a few inches of surf, right on the beach. They make a mistake, and lose their bearings, and then an errant flow of water covers them.

The water inundates their mouth and nose. They suck in, they don't know to fight the urge to breathe at that moment, they can't resist the instinct. The panic sets in and there is no one around to help them.

And yet here are Nick, Radcliff, and the girls, and the other crew. They are all out on the yacht, surrounded with enough water to sink every person who has ever lived. Nick knows it doesn't take much more than a moment of terror, a wave timed just right, and an unfortunate swallow and then you are lost. At every moment, tragedy is right here, waiting.

Just a few ounces of water: That's less than you might be able to cup in the palm of your hand, and with that little splash down your trachea you could be dead. Nick constantly reminds himself of this fact. And, he thinks, what else would a person be then? A mystery, perhaps? Just a terrible little object. Something floating face-down in the waves. Maybe your arms bending lifelessly. Maybe shifting hideously in the water, without resistance or force. And yet looking around, the scene before them is absolutely stunning and beautiful. Radcliff does this at times. He brings them all to a halt in the middle of absolutely nothing.

The most recent resort is days behind them now. They made the beach scene, they made the club scene, and the girls shopped during the day and Nick acted as a mule, carrying the bags from store to store and gave moral support when the money ran dry. He provided Radcliff's credit card (marked Zzynex Holdings, Spa.) and sympathetically shook his head after signing the bill one final time. *Maxed out for the day*, he said, adding up the numbers and noting the security block had probably been activated.

They spent an away night in a five-star hotel and Nick watched the waves and the tide destroy the sandcastles on yet another beach and felt an inexplicable joy in the scene. Radcliff squeezed in lunch and dinner at four of his favorite restaurants at that particular resort, and later captured the spirit of the season by buying an appetizer of lemon chicken to feed the semi-domesticated cats that cutely *mewed* and congregated around one restaurant's patio.

Everything tended to blur together, strong impressions muddled within a fog. That was just the nature of their meandering trip, one which Nick had made many times before. In retrospect the only memory that really left a clear impression on Nick was a giant rotating sign they saw above a store. They were sitting at a café and the girls were taking a break from shopping. They were shooting the breeze in that carefree time-wasting way, nursing their Egyptian coffees, filtering the grounds between their teeth, and across the street was a sign for a rather posh drycleaner that read *Super White* on one side and then slowly turned to display *Super Bianco* on the other side.

The blonde with the pug-nose set down her cup, motioned to the sign, and with feigned ignorance said, "See...*Bianco.* That means *white*" - pausing a perfect moment - "And that's how easy it is to learn Italian!" She gave a self-mocking ditzy-grin to the group, and Nick answered with his own wide smile.

But now they are back on the boat, and Nice is only one day away. Water is everywhere around them, land is still nowhere in sight, and yet Radcliff needs more. He tells Nick to lower the sails and come to a dead stop, or at least here in the middle of the sea, to a drift. The seafloor here is thousands of feet below them and so there is no anchoring. The summer sun is beating down and reflecting back into infinity, and the tiny wavelets are metallic and the surface is a healthy blue, as if swimming in it has actual nutritional value.

There are a few murmurs of discontent from the girls who approach the cruise merely as a distance to be covered, and thus view such stops as an impediment to the real attraction, which is always the next resort on the map. But Radcliff will have none of that. He appears on deck in his matching pearl grey swimsuit and towel, just as if he were at a spa in Switzerland, and surveys the scene. Looking down into the water it is apparent they are as stationary as they can be. He sets his towel aside, grabs his sunglasses securely in his hand, and jumps from the rear-most of the yacht in one surprisingly elegant and confident motion, hitting the blue with just the barest splash of an expert diver, despite his prominent belly.

He reappears on the surface and shakes the droplets from his head and looks back up at the boat. This is exactly what he wants. He is treading water and the waves are calm and lazy rollers which pick him up a few feet at a time and then lower him back into a trough.

"How is it?" Nick stands on the edge looking down, his hands are gripping the railing strongly, as if he were contemplating an impossible acrobatic, overhead leap from the boat. They are miles from the shipping lanes and the day is sprawling and restful.

"Brilliant, simply brilliant. Come on in!"

Within a few minutes Nick is back on deck and ready for his swim. He checks around for a moment, noting that the chain ladder is indeed down and accessible, and then double checks that both the blonde girls will stay close by, just in case anything should happen. The ocean is quiet. The remainder of the crew are busying themselves below in preparation for the usual late-day feast. The girl with the discreet dolphin tattoo is probably sequestering herself in a room. Nick knows, of course, that he shouldn't leave the boat; its madness in a sense, but Radcliff enjoys subverting reality and Nick is more than pleased to join in.

He dives off with the same graceful swan-dive as Radcliff and hits the water with a piercing force that sends him deep into the ocean. It's a dive he has accomplish many times (and will continue to) but never before like this. There is the instant and shocking cold that envelops his body, and then the otherworldly-blue and weightlessness as he floats to the surface.

He takes a breath. "Perfect," he says to Radcliff who returns a genuine smile.

But in truth, there is something very wrong in the water, although Nick can't name the feeling. On the surface, the sun has warmed the water several degrees, but down by his feet, which he kicks to keep him afloat, there is an icy grip hanging onto his ankles.

To the uninitiated there is a difficulty in swimming through the ocean: there are waves that try and cover your head and constantly push and threaten, there is the saltwater that can sting your eyes and tastes ugly in your mouth, and there is the oddity of moving your legs and arms and finding that they do not propel you as you imagine they should. The standard reference points that a person might find at a swimming pool are nonexistent, and thus the ocean changes the way you think about progress and distance: it becomes what you know, instead of what you can see. Similarly, there is the possibility of encountering some random piece of debris floating and hidden just beneath the surface - waiting to either startle you, or cause you harm. But Nick is versed in all of this, and so he sets off to circle the yacht a few dozen times, while keeping an eye on the coming waves and letting them move him without fighting the strength.

It's a fool who overexerts himself in such a situation, and so he swims far below his limits. From this perspective mere inches above the waterline, the yacht is massive and immobile; it's the dark, royal blue of the hull that overwhelms, whereas standing on the deck, it's the white of the mast, boom and sails. Out here in the midst of the ocean it's suddenly the only safety in the world and as such there is an understanding that binds those on the boat, and those in the water: The ladder will be kept down; the engine will be kept off.

They all silently comprehend that a horrifying death is possibly just a single sick moment away for whoever is unlucky enough to be off the boat. In the middle of nothing, there is a trust that friendships and people are genuine.

•

Radcliff is doing mini-laps back and forth along the length of the boat. He is keeping his head-up and far above the water, and his sunglasses are on now and *very 1950's*. He seems to be no different than any other slightly-aged-uncle-type getting a wee bit of exercise at the neighborhood pool.

Nick pulls and reaches as he swims; he feels the fluid move around his body and between his limbs, and he losses count of his circuits of the yacht (as he always does) just as when they are anchored in a bay and he laps in a large circle. He finally comes to a stop near Radcliff, who has been resting, using his corpulence as a flotation device, and is talking with the two blonde girls who lean over the side and refuse to jump in – "We're scared of the sharks!"- they joke almost in unison. The mild wind pushes the boat broadside, and every so often Nick and Radcliff must swim forward to keep in contact, but otherwise it all seems disconcertingly normal, almost as if they were simply along the edge of a huge lake.

Radcliff is philosophical at such times, and Nick and the two blondes are his ideal foils.

"Do you know what the primordial elements of life are?" Radcliff addresses them as if sharing a great truth. Out here there is no sound, save for the slush against the boat or the stirring of water beneath a hand, and his voice seems to travel miles.

Nick shakes his head 'No', while the two blondes smile at *primordial.* They know they are an audience for one of Radcliff's sweeping proclamations. He is massively rich, charismatic, and so *very* confident, so he must know things (sometimes), they think.

"For the last – *oh* - few billion of years in which life has existed on Earth, there are two elements that have made life possible. Water and sunlight."

The blondes for their part are suddenly interested. Yes, of course, it's that simple. Despite all of the magazine science they have absorbed over the years, it's just two elements at the root of everything. At once they forget about proteins and acids, and all of those minutiae organizing themselves and producing life…and eventually cellulite and sagging skin. As usual, Radcliff provides answers to the big questions, and the answers are always charming.

"The sun sends out light, which travels trillions of miles in every direction, but only a very little of it reaches us. It's quite harsh out in space, yet when it reaches our atmosphere it becomes diffused and suddenly charitable - and then it strikes water. From that first moment of sun and water, life was inevitable."

Radcliff begins trawling towards the ladder and upon reaching it, makes his summation. "Those are the two elements that govern our planet." He begins to breathe a little heavily as he climbs out of the ocean, pulling himself up a few rungs, but manages a final burst: "And so I thought to myself years ago…If I am going to live my life right, I am going to surround myself with those two things!"

Nick waits as Radcliff scales the ladder, and as Radcliff gruntingly hoists himself back onto the boat, Nick follows him on board. Returned to the deck, Nick dries off as best possible with one of his T-shirts he finds laying about; his breathing is still labored from his swim and his muscles feel heavy with blood and effort. After a few minutes and a few words, both of the blondes and Radcliff gather themselves together and head down the stairs and into the cabin, and Nick is left alone topside with instructions to get back underway as soon as possible. The intermission in their journey is finished. From below, the galley brings up the sounds of preparations of their awaiting lunch, thanks (largely) to Santi, their expert chief. Radcliff - and so for the rest of them - always eats well.

The remaining saltwater on Nick's body dries in the breeze; it leaves a sticky tightness. He can feel it on his back, and where it has dribbled down from his wet hair onto his temples and cheeks.

Standing there, alone on the yacht, he has a glimpse of something. His eyes settle on an empty lounge chair, and there is a rumpled red beach towel which hangs over its side. A scent of vanilla rests disturbingly in the air. *Her.*

He tries to think philosophically: There will always be people sunk into his chest. And always there will be some vestige of them left behind. But again, he can't distance himself from a different world. It is starting to approach him.

The feeling is swirling and the sea is stretching out into absolutely nothing. The boat is waiting for him to take charge. Far past the horizon is Nice, which Radcliff has talked-up the last couple of days, and now everyone is ready to be there, *already*. Nick takes his place behind the wheel. He banishes a thought: Someone else is standing beside him, tilted against the railing of the yacht.

A single person is all that is needed to operate the boat, as per Radcliff's spare-no-expense design brief. Nick pushes the button for an electric motor which raises the foresail; this catches and fills with air and slowly brings the boat parallel to the wind.

Terrified by something he cannot name, Nick raises the mainsail with another simple press of a button. He cannot turn his head and look beside him, for fear of what he will see. Even now, in the blinding beauty of a sunny day, a feeling – a grasping horror - comes up to stand next to him.

The electric motor whirs gently and a huge triangular sheet of fabric that, supposedly, is the largest such sail on any yacht currently in the Mediterranean raises, flutters and catches the wind in full.

Overhead the great boom swings wide - violently - until it is caught by the rigging, which helps channel all of that force of wind into forward motion. Thus, the entire inhabitation of the boat, and all else aboard her, move towards their destination.

2

Radcliff likes to say that the yacht is not a boat, it is an *event;* Nick bristles every time he hears this description. He wants to correct Radcliff: It is you and your band of schemers, schmoozers, and sophists that are the event. The yacht is just a stage.

But now here they are gliding into Nice and there is truth in Radcliff's words. Nick often imagines the view from the green and rocky hills that border the ocean as the yacht parallels the land and makes for the harbor. It's a view he has seen many times, and he has even glimpsed this very boat as it glided on its sails towards one of the smaller bays that lie nearby. Along the coast there are beaches, marinas, villas, orchards, gardens, hotels, cafes, shops, plazas, fountains, and every aspect of resort life imaginable. It is all resplendent, and he knows that – amazingly - even in this jaded environment conversations will *still* stop, fingers will point, and life will take a brief pause as the boat comes into view.

There is a sense of relief and excitement as Nick calls down to Radcliff, "We are here…," and yet a weight settles into him. This is the epicenter of his miscarried life. It's the same ugly epiphany he has known for years that rests like a lead weight in his stomach, where it will stay day and night. Nick knows why that sensation suddenly makes its way straight into his gut - *Johansen.* This is his backyard. It is *that* particular man who is almost certainly here - the man that reordered Nick's life - and now all of them are wandering in, seemingly without a care in the world.

Radcliff wordlessly climbs the stairs from below and then positions himself next to Nick and views the scene. A rare onshore breeze for this time of day pushes them ahead quickly, and with the sun high overhead in a cloudless sky, Nick is sure Radcliff will expect sails-up until the last moment, which is all movie star perfect. If *she* were here with them, lounging and sprawled-out with that red towel hung around her shoulders like a funny little cape, he would indeed find it an especially wonderful view. But without her voice – just her feeling - there is something very wrong.

Still, they cruise into the bay like champions returning from a quest: The girls are up and down and gathering themselves in anticipation of paradise as well as lazy visits to spas and shops, while Radcliff raises his binoculars to his eyes (with a motion loaded with significance) and notes the other yachts and cabin cruisers they will be joining. Nick knows there is a slight chance that he will spot one particular yacht – it is a gleaming white thing and impossible to miss – but he is thankful that the boat is likely berthed in a different marina, a few miles away. Either that, or it is perhaps on one of its many journeys around the Mediterranean. For Nick, it is that particular yacht that is loaded with significance, yet for Radcliff, it must only be another item to compare himself to.

In his usual way, Radcliff is taking stock of the company they will keep. Scattered across the bay there are the usual suspects: cruisers with helipads and swimming pools, and then the others, which are barely worth his attention. To the side is one of the many *Quay Queens*. To Nick's knowledge, it has only spent two weeks out of its ten years since launch actually 'at sea.' He has watched it depreciate season by season, and soak up labor, for no other reason than for someone to say "It's mine." Farther away are the braggart yachts, which are little more than a collection of hotel rooms that happen to float. These boats are the mere lifestyle accessories for the know-nothings, which Radcliff frankly *hates* for their insincerity. Then, there are the handful of boats owned by genuine patrons. They are used as intended, and have resumes that stretch around the globe. Over the years, Nick has ingratiated himself with the harbormaster (which was admittedly an easy thing to do coming from Radcliff's grand yacht) and has learned much about the comings and goings of the motley crowd.

"Hmmm…Looks like Roger is in town," Radcliff states to himself, more than Nick. "Looks like his boat is about due for an overhaul...I swear I can see rust flecks on the railing even from here." (He pauses for affect.) "That poor man is just like his brother, and just like his father! I'm telling you, DNA is destiny, the unlucky bastards: They are all doomed." Already, Nick can imagine his work calendar filling and begins to see his days ahead as more and more encumbered.

Radcliff's boat has three regular crew other than Nick. They are the ones who between them share the drudge work and he is sure they are breathing a thankful sigh at the news they have arrived in France. It's a much needed break: the cleaning, the dishes, the cooking, the non-stop organizing and catering to whims and wants takes its toll. It's all of the invisible labor that supports the business at hand. That is just life on a boat, never mind the luxury. Everyone's quirks can turn into aggravating traits and it's very easy to read the irritation on the maid's face whenever the pug-nose blonde makes her daily call for her breakfast. Each morning she wants her usual bowl of cornflakes with just a hint of nonfat milk, and along the side she expects to find her most critical demand: *THINLY sliced peaches.* As always, her Scottish accent underlines the specificity of her requirements.

It's true, the space closes in after only hours at sea, and there is a simple joy when the staff alight on land. They know they can simply walk straight ahead for as long as possible, and are free from the chores and breakfast preparation, noted to the last inane detail, until they *about face* and return.

There are no berths available in the marinas and even if there were only a few would accommodate the yacht, simply because it is far too large. But that suits Radcliff fine. He doesn't want to mingle closely with the others - he has plans.

The sails are quickly pulled down and they coast in on inertia, old school, like a clipper ship. Nick drops the rear anchor to slow them; the enormous metal tarantula crawls down through the water and then eventually reaches the sandy seafloor, where it drags and slows their progress. Once they are motionless, he then tidies up the boat with the diesel engines on the edge of other yachts, cruisers, and hangers-on that are likewise scattered in the bay. As usual, they will join the fleet, as per the running agreement Radcliff has with the authorities. Nick then drops the front anchor and pulls and imbeds it into the seafloor with an electric motor that gently *whirs* and does the work of several men.

Once this is accomplished there are only the odds and ends that remain. Nick goes through his mental checklist; his job is nothing but lists, he sometimes thinks. First up, the crew that he oversees: the entire time they are at sea, they continually talk about boyfriends and girlfriends they have on the side in cities around the world, but the first thing they want when they arrive at port are free cards for Internet cafes so they can get on Skype and call home - the people that really matter are waiting. Santi, the chef, is particularly adamant that he must contact his boyfriend back in Argentina the first moment he steps on shore.

In the quiet Nick can hear conversations in the cabin below. There is laughter and suddenly people are animatedly talking over each other. Radcliff sets the binoculars down after one last survey of the surroundings and heads below deck, as if seeking to corral the high spirits toward his ends. Soon he is on his phone and Nick knows it will only be minutes until a skiff appears to carry Radcliff and whoever else to the marina, documents and customs check, and from there they will catch a few cars to whatever hotel has been arranged. There is luggage to be dealt with and then Nick must help with the transfer of Radcliff's base of operation.

They are tentatively scheduled to stay in Nice two weeks; it's roughly the halfway point of their meandering run and Nick allows himself to wallow in the sour sickness while he again considers the otherwise ideal surroundings. It is July now, and at this time of year he knows who else makes the sunny region of France his home.

•

Nick forces his bike uphill. He stands on the pedals and they turn as he concentrates on the road and he follows the climb. After a long few days in Nice, Nick has earned several hours of freedom away from the yacht. It's his first real break - and he needs to make the most of it. This particular time in Nice, there is no interest in marking his time at cafes or otherwise flittering away the hours and recuperating in whatever way he needs.

As he turns the crank of the bike, there is only a narrow shoulder to escape if a car or truck wants to jostle for space; the lanes are big enough for barely one vehicle and the drop-off to the side is sharp and steep. Every so often he comes to a curve that provides a view of the bay and coastline, and from this geographic height there is a sense that he is surveying the world from an eagle's perch. There is the temptation to stop, catch his breath, allow his legs to recover, and let the sights of the French coast weave their way into his soul, but a glance down at his watch tells him that time is short and so he pushes harder and breathes deeper and the bike carries him that small bit faster. The backpack strapped to his back makes a dull thud against his body and the weight of Radcliff's prized high-powered binoculars is always apparent as a lump between his shoulder blades.

He does this for just a few seconds of relief, as he has many times before.

There is a small dirt path. It's a foot trail, barely used and threatened by overgrowth - bushes and trees nibble at its edges thanks to recent years of apparent abandonment – with only an occasional person rambling down its length. From his elevated perspective on the road, Nick can barely see it as he rounds yet another corner. These days, the path doesn't even quite reach the road. Unusually heavy spring rains have washed leaves into piles and clumps that further obscure the little trail. But, there it is – he finds the dirt impression, and lets out a deep breath. He must dismount his bicycle and lift it over a short rock barrier that borders the road. He carries his bike on his shoulder and stumbles along the path.

Finally, he finds his place under a tree in an olive grove, with a panoramic vista of the sea. For anyone else, the scene is a million dollar view. Today, he stops and gazes: the waves are behaving strangely, like they are wild and moving corrugations on an icy green-blue field. He knows in fact the water is actually quite warm, and it seems the land itself is pulling the distant ripples toward him.

He waits in the shadows, catching his breath and allowing the effort of the ride to dissipate, and then with his naked eye (eventually) he sees him – *Johansen.*

This part is always the same. Nick has done this for years now, ever since the crash and whenever he is near Nice during the summer, which is often. The day is bright and beautiful, and naturally Johansen is out on his yacht for his regular mid-morning cruise along the coast and out to sea and back.

Right on time Nick sees the sharp hull cutting through the waves: the sails are full and proud, the boat tilts on its side as it catches the wind, and Nick brings the binoculars to his eyes for a closer look. The yacht is a large white thing – not nearly as big as Radcliff's but just as remarkable - and clearly visible pacing back and forth along its length and giving orders to his crew is Johansen. Sometimes there were a few girls on board, and sometimes there were not. Sometimes there was a very small tender, or skiff, attached transversely to the stern. It was brought up, out of the water, by cables and an ingenious track system, although sometimes Johansen apparently just left the skiff in the harbor and ran his boat clean.

And apparently, even if there were hundreds of electric

motors and servos to run the rigging and manage the rest of the boat, Johansen still preferred to oversee a large crew and have them do his bidding. Nick knew that whenever Johansen set out on one of his many pan-European jaunts, he often sent his yacht ahead to meet him; Johansen wanted it available for pleasure cruises or entertaining. Presumably, this happened whenever Johansen's new (or ongoing) *arrangements* demanded his personal attention, and he presumably left the bulk of his crew at home at such times and sailed it just by himself or with a few others.

Nick smiles; he can imagine the voice of Johansen and the very commands themselves. That was how they first met, after all. Johansen was a sailing man and Nick was a sailing man. Back then, he was half-a-world away in California.

On that particular day Nick was just helping out; he was on a boat, acting as a crew member, and providing that needed extra hand. For Nick, it was simply gratifying to be there holding a line, listening to the supernatural effortlessness as the boat sliced perfectly through the water, as if he were on his own (much more modest) boat. It was like experiencing music that didn't rely on electronic amplification, like listening to an acoustic guitar that was strummed beautifully, and the chords were naturally carrying into his ear. Silence. Music. Every so often Johansen's confident voice issued a directive and cut the peace with a clear order, and people responded. Nick was on a vessel sharing his love for the sport and a joy of life. At the time, those little experiences meant everything.

Things are different now, however.

Through the binocular's lenses, Nick imagines he is looking at the surprisingly compact figure through a sniper's rifle scope. A huge distance is miraculously reduced to mere feet and he can see his quarry's hair rustling in the wind, watch his mouth voice orders, and then Nick contemplates the softness of Johansen's forehead. Nick imagines his finger, squeezing a trigger. He pretends for a few moments that with good aim and a little luck he could get rid of that silver hair blowing in the wind and find relief for that feeling in his stomach.

If he had first met Johansen on the street, or more likely in one of the marbled bank lobbies found in Zurich, and guessed his profession, Nick might have thought he was nothing other than a retired athlete. He would have imagined Johansen as an occasional ski instructor, who earned his keep by tutoring the moneyed classes on the slopes of the Alps. Johansen, then as now, moves with a kind of easy physical grace, despite his age, and he wears his deep year-round tan like an old pro who can still outrun everyone else on the mountain. He seems the very model of a European gentleman: socially adept yet reserved and self-effacing. He seems like someone you could trust your life with, after a time.

But then Nick inevitably catches sight of the two body guards that stand next to Johansen on the deck of the yacht, or so he always assumes that is who they are, because they seem to protectively bracket Johansen everywhere he goes. Again they place themselves close by, even while he is out at sea on a morning's cruise and he is clearly untouchable by anything other than a meteor falling from the sky.

The two men are not tall, and do not appear particularly intimidating looking, thanks to round faces, narrow shoulders and doughy physiques, all of which in Nick's mind makes them even more lethal. Because that is the essence of Johansen's nature: Absolute and unexpected savagery.

The sea is now changed, and that particular color of blue-grey which makes it appear to be a rolling band of steel (and the olive trees that surround Nick) seem to be the only movement and life on the planet. The white yacht fades in the distance, and Nick sets down the binoculars and rests in the shade beneath one of the scraggily trees. He props his back against the trunk as he looks out across the coast.

Far below he can hear the waves breaking on the rocks, and the sound is a hypnotic and repeating pattern that keeps him locked in a daze of thoughts. Instinctively he turns to catch a glance of his bike, checking to make sure it is there just beside him, weary that even here (seemingly miles away from another person) there is still a risk of theft.

But Nick is alone. There is no doubt about that. It is the same spot, the same view, the same feeling as last time and all the times before that. He waits and wonders; he retraces his steps. He does the math and comes up with the same answers

•

Johansen followed the old con artist's code to the last detail, he just ran his operation on a much different scale. He never operated in his own neighborhood, which meant all of Europe was off limits, and so he purloined elsewhere, restricting himself to North America and to the Pacific Rim, or so Nick always guessed. He never gave a hint of *wanting*. In fact, he gave and gave. Johansen shook your hand and looked steadily into your eyes. He wanted to be your friend. It didn't take long until he invited you over to the clubhouse, which was nearby and just alongside the marina. Once there, both of you perused the overpriced menu. Both of you scoffed a little at the names of the daily specials – *the Seafarer; the Whaler; the Shackleton*…Ridiculous. He laughed out loud with you and ordered drinks for you and some of your acquaintances that happened to mill about. The hackneyed nautical décor hanging on the walls and the affected gentleman's club trappings of the environment suddenly seemed *okay* - and actually, somewhat comforting.

Later, he invited you onto 'his' yacht, which he had leased for several months, as a man like him was prone to do as he traveled the world. And in so doing, he casually displayed the advantages of his wealth, and as you talked, he suggested that such privilege and symbols of money were truthfully unimportant to him.

He wanted you to know a few things.

Johansen wanted you to know that he quietly disdained the gaudy trappings of fortune. Honestly and truly, he cared about *people.* He always made this sort of statement with a steady gaze. (Still, the way he said the words and spoke the ideas made it seem as if he had said them before. And maybe before in a *very* similar situation.) He said that he cared about people living to their potential.

And, he said, if that happened to include vast amounts of money, so be it. If he caught your gaze at just the right time, you were predisposed to believe all of it.

He introduced you to his business associates on the phone, and he met you at magnificent restaurants and celebrated the anticipated accomplishments of your future life, and always urged you to look forward. "Look up – Look forward," he literally said, as if you were otherwise buried in something unworthy of your fine character, and needed to be reminded of everything else that was possible.

He put his trust in you, as well, until the last moment.

And then it was difficult to understand just what had happened. Even years later when it was obvious - that a person, a family, a business, had been defrauded - there was a lingering bafflement that such a man as Johansen could really do such a thing. He seemed so genuine and so likeable. Always, there was that steady gaze and unfaltering handshake. You were flattered by his attention.

Johansen operated by guile, not by force, and that was what made it particularly brutal, because afterward there was nothing to say, "That was the moment..." Nick understood these years later that it was up to both the villain and the victim, acting in concert. The first time Nick shook Johansen's hand and felt the roughness on his skin and a lifetime's embrace of actual physical work in his firm grip, Nick knew he respected the man. Later, he also came to understand that it was *all* a manipulation. And yet Nick was a willing participant in the crime.

Johansen played on your vanity and greed. He subtly exposed and nurtured those selfish, horrible instincts, and by the end of it you were his accomplice in the fraud. The shocking part was that it didn't take a particularly long time. Mere weeks, in fact. He had help too, in the form of a complicit industry that hid its skeletons far from view. An *extra twelve percent per year* in the Caymans seemed almost too good to believe, even if it did mean running afoul of the IRS and every better aspect of a person's cautious nature.

In the end, of course, it was too good to be true.

Johansen wasn't even there to witness the final cut. That was when Nick signed the last document and gave up the last account number. Instead, he sent one of his minions who

Nick barely recognized; someone who flited around the corners of Johansen's grand design. He was strangely named Mr. Samson, and he possessed great bags beneath his eyes that made him ageless – he might have been thirty, or sixty-years old. He was an irritating, disingenuous, little man who didn't want to rush the last piece of the puzzle; he walked around Nick's spacious house and admired the art hanging on the walls in a completely insincere way and pretended to have forgotten the most important papers, and then he inexplicably pulled them from his briefcase. He talked with a British accent that seemed contrived and exaggerated, as if he heightened his inflections and cadences in an attempt to charm all of the ignorant colonists that he was forced to interact with. But he was nothing but a simple salesman sent to close the deal.

It was all perfect and plain to see these years later. The frustration Nick felt was meant to urge him on, and most importantly, disregard the actual documents themselves. Of course, Nick didn't actually read all of those papers. Of course, Nick jumped over the imaginary hurdles erected to make him feel as if *he* were the one in charge and *he* was the one that simply wanted it done. Anything, so he could "look up; look forward," he reminded himself. So he could be rid of the annoying man who was picking up a sculpture and offering his opinion of its artistic value. "Out of my house," Nick wanted to say. "It's time for me to relax and think about the *small* fortune I am going to grow into a *huge* fortune."

Because Nick had done the computations, he was at ease and pleased with himself; he had studied the numbers and projected his wealth far into the future. With Johnsen's help, he had plotted the new yield curves on a spreadsheet: they curved dramatically up, like a ski jump, compounding and multiplying incredibly. It would become, eventually, an astounding empire proudly handed down to future generations of his family, whoever they might turn out to be. They could do *good* with the money; they could be secure. It would be enduring. A legacy.

But after the calls went unanswered and then the very phone numbers themselves were disconnected, Nick started to understand the real nature of savagery. It was an aloneness.

At first he thought it was like a vicious animal ripping at his stomach – the softest, most vulnerable part of his body being torn and pulled apart. He pictured the violence like it was happening to somebody else: he saw the jaws lowering and then the way the animal's teeth pierced into the victim's skin. He saw the way the viscera split like meat being cut by a butcher's knife. There was nothing to stop it. What could he do? He was mere flesh, while they used these sharp instruments.

The few documents he had to make his claims were almost worthless. He kept them in a beige folder that was unnervingly thin. There were sheets of paper with impressive, and sometimes flippant company names, and wonderfully intricate and sophisticated corporate logos. Or on other pages, logos that looked like they had been designed in all of ten minutes with readily available clip-art. He faxed them to lawyers, to the SEC, to bank managers and administrative assistants.

Occasionally the more blunt voices on the other end of the phone would drop the formality and wondered aloud if indeed anything illegal had actually transpired. Nick's allegations concerned respected members and institutions of their community, and in any event it was out of their jurisdiction. In Nick's case, unfortunately, private offshore accounts were in the domain of the hosting country. Nick foolishly saw the papers he kept as a little nest, which he could mold into some sort of defense in an effort to protect himself from the inevitable onslaught of the end.

But it didn't matter. He had given up control; his money and assets were no longer his.

He had signed the papers and moved the funds of his own accord. Those were, of course, his signatures. Johansen didn't even do the favor of leaving a tidbit in Nick's checking account, as if the very last drops of dollars were what Johansen *really* wanted. Nick could fly down to the Caymans - if he had any money for a ticket - and run screaming into the bank's lobby and shout and accuse till his voice went out. He had the SWIFT codes and routing numbers and names of people and businesses. All of them were meaningless. They would look at him in embarrassment as if he were a lunatic, and then literally throw him out on the street. He could prove nothing, and even then so what? Nick knew it was hopeless; the money wasn't even there anymore - within hours it had surely been moved and changed into some other instrument and was plainly far away and suddenly untouchable.

Nick learned this much. It was funneled into corporations and holding groups, which were literally nothing: they were empty offices and mailing addresses. Perhaps an agent, some unimportant and nearly anonymous man from the U.S., presumably showed his face once a year, and signed some papers to prove some minor points of legality. That particular man was the one person who served as the face for an entire convoluted scheme, and who made his minimum required appearance by law at unknown intervals, and who kept the whole operation ostensibly legitimate. Whoever that man was, his name or face or identity, didn't actually matter. He was just one more insular and insulating step, all so Johansen could keep the system working, and continue his version of business as usual.

Nick's mind ran at night as he lay in bed with nothing but his own thoughts for commiseration, and the days on the calendar counted down until his home, his life elsewise, was no longer his. There was nothing to do. Attorneys would not talk to him after they saw the full picture and impossibility of the situation. Regulators and oversight offices sent him away when they saw Nick's complicit fraud and impropriety. He imagined the terror as a mouse faced off against a simple house cat, which had corned the little animal, and then played and batted it about. Of course, after the cat was bored with the one-sided fight, it opened its jaws to finish the entertainment. That was just what cats did.

The torture wasn't about physical pain, which Nick could cope with. It was about the helpless lonely way he scrambled for the remains of his life. Those pathetic phone calls. That rooting that he did through the beige folder, hoping for some piece of overlooked evidence or life-saving tidbit of information. And, of course, finding nothing. All the hours passing; the calendar counting down until he had no home. No place for a bed. A realization that he didn't need to pay the utility bill for his home, because by the time they cut the services, he would be gone. A desperation – looking for answers, finding nothing. Yelling at the top of his lungs in an empty room. It was the struggle that exposed his insignificance; his feeble position against a much larger foe that would always prevail.

•

As the sun passes over the resort towns of the Côte d'Azur Nick works the pedals and fights past traffic, as tourists slow down to take in the sights and stop at the shops and cafes. In a different time Nick might have been one of them, plugging along the French coast in a rented car with friends and family gathered around him. But today Roman ruins, magnificent entrances to villas and seaside communities are obstacles to be surmounted. He needs to get back to Radcliff's yacht; back to whatever waits for him.

He coasts through villages and catches his breath; he views shopkeepers through their store windows and sees his own reflection mirrored back. Nick wonders, if over the years and the many trips he has made through the country on his bicycle, they have come to recognize him among the usual faces of the summer season. If so they probably think of him as nothing more than an amateur athlete in training. Sometimes he slows down and comes to a stop. He rests on benches alongside the roadway and later troubles a café attendant to refill his various water bottles, and they are always happy to help. It's easy at such times to pretend that the world is moving forward, just as it should.

However, Nick has an urge to make one of his old side trips. He wants to head inland and towards the town of Grasse. Up ahead, there is a spur in the road, and all he needs to do is turn right instead of continuing along the coast.

Further on that spur and another twenty miles is a valley. It's a difficult bike ride to get there; he will have to battle more hills and traffic. But finally there is an orchard of sorts.

Even from miles away that particular plot of land is

obvious: it fills the landscape with a perfectly manicured assortment of trees and fat shrubs. A stone wall is visible from a high point along the road and marks the perimeter of the property. On many occasions Nick has stopped his ride and caught his breath at that point, while pondering the significance of the view. It's the lion's den - it's where Johansen has his summer villa.

•

Even years before Nick found a place to call home with Radcliff and his yacht, he had the dubious pleasure of that ride and that view. Nick's schedule provided him weeks between contracts on the Athena, which meant he had time to wander around and pursue his vague hope of revenge. It kept him in some sort of limbo.

Nick knew that heading inland on his bike to that particular spot gave him a different kind of respite and set his mind in a different direction. The exhausting effort of the journey gave him moments of insight as he split his concentration between the road, the pain in his muscles, and his predicament.

Nick, after all, understood important things about Johansen. Nick had resources to consult and his intelligence to urge him on, and floating around in Nick's head was a vague hope of settling the score. If not exactly getting his family's fortune back, then at least doing *something.* It wasn't easy to find Johansen's French residence, and Nick learned quickly that Europeans protect their anonymity much more vehemently than people in the United States. But eventually he asked the right question of the right database and there it was: an address speaking to him from a computer screen.

He learned a lot from that address and from that small but critical piece of information. As he pushed the pedals and turned the bicycle's crank and constantly circulated that tidbit of knowledge through his mind, he came to a conclusion: Johansen didn't need to hide.

The voices on the other end of the phone were speaking to him, again.

Johansen was respected. This was just the way things were. Johansen was part of the establishment; he was a pillar of the community. Nick dug through newspaper archives and public records. Johansen had entire wings in hospitals named after him; he had his picture taken while eating lunch with finance ministers, and he donated to political entities around the globe. He wasn't, in fact, a shadowy figure dodging the authorities. They welcomed him in, and they embraced his reputation.

Nick was shocked. He glimpsed into that grey world of hazy legalities, tax dodges, and outright fraud and found, now years later, that it was merely ordinary.

•

In June for several years, Nick marked time as Johansen opened his villa for the season. Despite the hazard of being found lurking on the fringes, and despite the ugliness the proximity of Johansen drove into him, Nick made the journey on occasion. He rode his bike slowly by the main gate and pretended to be a tourist awed by Johansen's huge estate. Days would pass and with each one he took another chance and slowed his bike and peered as far as he could into the inner sanctum. He sometimes stopped and rested and observed with a detective's eye the details of Johansen's world at work.

Changes like clockwork marked Johansen's imminent seasonal arrival to his corner in the south of France. Nick would first see the cleaning ladies arrive in their crisp white uniforms; then the gardeners in their dusty work shirts. Within a week the man himself and his entourage would arrive as indicated by the dark Mercedes sedans parked along the drive.

That was when life entered its summer routine. Nick took his several weeks break from the Athena. He had time and enough money - *barely* - to stay in Europe on the cheap and slink around the coastal towns and villages. He took the train down from Hamburg. He knew he looked strange amongst the usual types: He was an outsized American traveling alone, and dressed not as a tourist but some wandering jetsetter in his *old-life* clothes, yet with only a few dollars in his pocket and a posh bicycle amongst his meager luggage. He was too far along to be a college kid winging his way around the country. He was too young to be a man-of-means carelessly wandering. He didn't make sense, and with every stranger's look into his eyes he felt they knew his entire ignoble story. Prying older women were direct in their inquiries: Why aren't you married? Where is your family? They scowled with his evasive non-answers. They recognized him for what he was.

He found a dirt-cheap room in Marseille, and each time as Nick pushed the weekly fee across the front desk's counter, the manager's eyes crawled over him with an entirely predictable and doubtful expression. Upstairs, in his temporary abode, Nick regarded the purple neon sign from the all-night pharmacy across the street. It beamed-in an unhealthy light, even when he pulled the flimsy curtains closed, and that made the stains on the wall even more obvious.

Nick always set his bag on the narrow bed, and he always noted the way the mattress collapsed under the moderate weight. He washed his clothes in the little porcelain sink that jutted out from the wall, and then he hung his clothes out the window to dry. It was just like the natives once did ages ago, and just like the obnoxious and shouting couple that lived down the hall still did. He made the decrepit little room at this particular *pension* a home for as much time as he could.

He kept hidden in crowds of sunseekers and in families of pale faces vacationing from England. He nursed and stretched his cups of espresso in outside cafes, often glancing away from his newspaper in hopes of an occasional sighting. For Nick, it seemed Johansen was everywhere. When Nick opened the Financial Times and read stories of collapsing businesses, burned wealth and improbable new empires emerging from some grey dusk, behind them all he imagined one name.

It eventually dawned on him that Johansen would likely have a boat nearby as well, and Nick made the rounds at marinas and ports along the coast. Johansen was certainly an excellent man behind the wheel of a boat; it was a genuine passion of his, Nick intuited, and one of the few pieces of information he learned about Johansen during his financial courtship that was actually true. This was the French Mediterranean, a place far away from Nick's old home in California, but harbors were the same everywhere.

It didn't take long for Nick to find one particularly striking white yacht; it didn't take long for Nick to notice its regular morning cruise out to sea and back; and it didn't take long for Nick to see that it was guided by a familiar figure –

someone at an advanced age. This was someone with a mane of silver hair that was obvious even from a great distance as it rustled in the wind.

It didn't take long for Nick to stake out a lonely olive grove with a panoramic view of the sea.

From the very start he would sit there glaring through the binoculars and imagine he had the power to fix a rifle at that target and pull a trigger. He would remove that forehead and tuft of hair every time it sailed past with a perfectly aimed bullet. In his mind, he heard and felt the loud shot and recoil from the gun, and somehow imagined the metal projectile crossing the distance and splintering that forehead like a battle axe.

He imagined the two body guards looking helplessly back at the cliff face and seeing the sun glisten on the reflection of his sniper's scope - but for just a moment. That was before he packed up his gun, rode away on his bike and started his new life. The vision, at heart, was as if the mouse could somehow out-power the cat.

It didn't take long for Nick to fall into his routine as Johansen's clandestine shadow, but after a while the impossibility of his waking dream did take some kind of a toll on his life. It wasn't just limbo that his state-of-mind kept him. After all of the time and ugliness that had coursed through his veins, it was difficult for Nick to pretend he had a chance to get back what was stolen from him. His hope of doing *something*, was just a dream. Any variety of anonymous revenge felt hollow, even if such a thing was possible. He was a different person now, and the world was changing as well.

He was coming to realize that years later he wasn't connected in the same way to all of those things and all of those people that were once the center of his existence. That particular old life was now fading away in the distance. There were now hints and lines on his face that hadn't been there before. By memory, he could no longer walk through his old home and find every point of consequence. There were corners that he had forgotten. There were feelings but no longer certainties. That part of his life was now gone forever.

He pushed the pedals of his bike, rode through miles of country. He felt the pain in his muscles and the complete exhaustion's attempt to overtake him. And then he pushed harder. He went through hills and coastal villages. And all of this was nothing but other peoples' existence, which he felt a stranger to. He couldn't even pretend to be a wandering tourist. He was just *here*. Some person, at the moment, on a bike, and then later, he would be some person working on a boat. He wondered if anything, anything worthy, was replacing his old life, or if this existence was all he could to look forward to. He knew it wasn't enough.

3

Nick rests in his little room on the yacht. His legs ache from his ride and he is wondering if for once he should dare to go into the city, find a spa, and pay for a professional massage. The boat is almost imperceptibly rocking and lulling him into a sleepy mood of indecision. Still, his door is partly open and he can suddenly discern the stirrings of someone rummaging around in the galley. Whoever it is, they are riffling through cupboards and pulling out items.

Radcliff has fitted a big bag of potato chips with something he found in London, what he calls a Moo-Clip, and that's what it looks like (a cute, smiling, little plastic cow) and that's also what it sounds like, as Nick hears the electronic *"Moo…Moo…"* The sound is emanating from the galley as someone grabs the rustling bag and undoes the clip, and digs into the chips. This time of day it was likely the brown-haired girl with the discreet dolphin tattoo on her hip; she began stirring only in the afternoon when left to her own devices and she always awoke starving.

Across the land, Nick thinks, this hour should be the dedicated *quiet time* in resorts and on boats. The sun is providing its lasts rays of light and anybody who was out working, or even lounging around all day, is weary and frazzled from the heat. Nick lies in his narrow bed, his feet are hanging over the end, and he listens again for the tell-tale *"Moo…Moo…"* as she returns to the bag and then the almost sweetly innocent "Crunch…Crunch…" as she crunches on the chips some more. After a few minutes of this she scavenges in one of the refrigerators for some leftovers. Soon she will become bored and then make enough effort to get decently dressed, and then he is sure she will wander around looking for someone who can deliver her to the right hotel. At the moment she is the only non-staff person on the boat, and that never works for her in this cloudy and irritated state.

She calls Nick "Sweetie" when she peers around the entrance to his half-open door. "Do you have anything, Sweetie? I'm having a tough time getting going."

Nick ponders the question, briefly. His siesta is over. She wants some sort of stimulant; that's what her *anything* is. "Radcliff has some Dexedrine," he stretches and rights himself on his bed. "But you'll have to wait until we get you over to his hotel."

She is annoyed but compliant. They both know she has been to the hotel several times in the last few days, but she never really paid attention to how to get there, or even bothered to learn the hotel's name. It's just a fog she wanders through. She prefers the boat because of its isolation and distance from anything resembling a normal life. She sleeps when she wants to, she takes the drugs that she wants to, and interacts with people at her convenience. Radcliff is the only light that guides her; his voice (sometimes booming) is the only thing that prods and pokes that brain in sufficient quantities. Her dullness mutes most things to a low-level background hum. Cab rides or any kind of complicated directions are definitely outside her capability.

Nick grabs her hand and leads her up the stairs onto the deck and she squints in the afternoon sun. "Buggers…Let me get my sunglasses." She haphazardly looks around for direction and then goes back down below while Nick readies the little skiff that is now tied to the yacht and is used for these types of back and forth errands. When she reappears five minutes later she looks more awake and has a designer bag with her, as if she is going shopping. At such times, no person could guess she is anything other than a perfectly *together* and desirable woman, never mind the facts. They set off across the marina and reach the dock, and then she waits for him to offer his hand again as she steps ashore; "Can you take me all the way there, Sweetie?" She only calls him *sweetie* when no one else is around and she wants something.

Radcliff barely notices when the two of them enter into the hotel suite. Signs and signals like this are not reassuring for her long-term prospects as a girl on the boat. Radcliff, however, is preoccupied with other things. He is meeting with his version of an Event Planning Cooperative.

The two blonde girls gather close by him, showing him lists and photocopied papers and receipts. Radcliff is growing weary of email, phones, and electronic gadgets. He only wants to view and shuffle around physical copies these days and so the table is covered in papers - he thinks the Chinese and NSA are listening to his conversations and reading his secrets, and he is probably right. At the end of the week the yacht will host a party and he likes to check up on the progress and review the details as the night in question grows near, but mostly he likes to bathe in the warm glow of people doing work for him. Sometimes he pauses, as if contemplating the flurry of activity, and studies the faces of either one of the blonde girls. They are similarly bent in concentration. To his credit, Radcliff often seems most happy when other people spend his money and exercise their imaginations for the greater glory of hedonism.

The two blondes ostensibly earn part of their keep by helping to organize and prepare for such large-scale social events, and they are giddy at the idea of playing wife, hostess and manager. It's as if they are saying, *See…I have other talents too.* Nick once noticed that the pug-nose blonde filled out her entry visa with big proud letters using the job title 'Sommelier' (or Wine Expert) under 'Occupation.' She also has started wearing reading glasses at times, which Nick is convinced she really doesn't need, because they give her an undeniable sexy-academic look.

During a lull in the activity, the brown-haired girl with the discreet dolphin tattoo leaves Nick's side and walks over to Radcliff's position, where she leans over slyly and whispers in his ear. Without breaking pace or looking askance, Radcliff points to the bedroom and says "dresser drawer" and she pats a kiss on his cheek and walks towards the room.

"Don't forget…when you're up and ready afterward," Radcliff states authoritatively, "I'll need you to sign a few things for me."

Yes, the brown-haired girl with the discreet dolphin tattoo is now apparently also acting as a player in Radcliff's low-wattage financial subterfuge and fraud. Radcliff of course runs a tax dodge (at least one, and probably many others, like all of *them*) and Nick, embarrassingly, is also a pawn in his scheme. Nick does a certain amount around the periphery for Radcliff, and then Nick pretends to not care. He tells himself, it's the price for his weakness he continues to pay.

Yet the brown-haired girl's presence in these matters is certainly either a mark of Radcliff's financial brilliance or financial lunacy. Nick half expects her to offer a droll *thank you* wink or a conspiratorial look over her shoulder as she makes for the Dexedrine, but she keeps her eyes on the door, pushes through into the bedroom and doesn't give away a single ounce of her focus.

Times like these are when the two blondes can demonstrate value beyond mere companionship and beauty, and they unquestionably make a special effort to seem involved and managerial.

"You know," says the blonde with the less-memorable nose, "I still need those cabinet dimensions from you, Nick." The blonde with the pug-nose pushes her glasses farther up on that same adorable nose, and perhaps wonders if she has anything to add on the emerging cabinet situation.

"Yes," he answers, cheerfully. "I'll call you with them as soon as I'm back to the boat."

He does his best to sound pleasant and reasonable, despite the triviality: The evident critical question is whether or not the cabinets in the yacht's galley can accommodate a new and much larger punch bowl - otherwise an alternative needs to be arranged, immediately. Such questions are things women-who-do-lunch concern themselves with, the girls imagine, and they want to graduate to that important class. Surrounding them is an entire segment of society that occupies their time with the opening and closing of houses over the seasons, managing domestics, perusing interior decorating magazines, writing gushing "thank you" cards, creating wine lists, and selecting ostentatious punch bowls. It must seem wonderfully satisfying from their playful distance.

But Radcliff's soirees, like the one they are planning, also hold a danger. (Hence, Nick thinks, the reading glasses; the heightened sense of dedication they are trying to present.) There will be other girls. There will be excellent opportunities for Radcliff to comparison shop. The blondes are savvy and experienced in such things. They know they need to be on their best game; they must be friendly and welcoming because it reflects well on Radcliff, but protective and wary of outsiders looking to hitch a ride because they have a lot to lose if they are supplanted in his heart and mind. Surely they could find another patron (eventually) but they have a good thing going here.

The good news for them is that the unexpected departure of the Hungarian girl with the *good Goddamn bones* seems to have given them a bit of breathing room and space for maneuvering, or even deepening their positions. After Radcliff managed to shut down discussion about her with his abrupt countermand, no one dared mentioned her again. Gone "home" is gone for good, apparently. But Radcliff's guiding philosophy is one of *more*…more sex, more girls, more travel, more experience, more life as he lives it.

They know Radcliff: whatever void is calling to him, he fills.

•

Radcliff always throws a great party. They tend to be reliably unhinged, with enough implied and actual debauchery to attract true connoisseurs of nightlife, or whatever he happens to be propagating at the time. Word goes out among the cognoscenti and they respond. That was half the reason Nick found his way onto the yacht the first time.

Outwardly, the parties appear stately and predictable, if also completely absurd. The day before Radcliff has aprons of lights hung along the mast and rigging of his yacht, so on the night in question, as the guests arrive in motorboats, it appears they are being brought to an enormous summertime Christmas tree in the bay, surrounded by a divine glow.

On the deck they are greeted with all the conventional trappings of a holiday party, though the only thing they are celebrating is high living itself; ornamented tables are overloaded with food and deserts, and there is a clear invitation to indulge. There are several bartenders seconded from ritzy local hangouts and they are always happy to stay busy and keep the drinks flowing. Every so often another *pop!* signals the next opened bottle of champagne. Below deck at the front of the boat Radcliff keeps the good wines, and he always insists they are stored sideways until the last moment, so the corks stay wet, and a knock on the passage door nearby opens another room where someone dispenses even stronger medicine.

When more guests discharge from yet another motorboat they are pulled onboard by whoever preceded them and greetings go around so that it feels like everyone knows everyone else. Once they are on the deck and find their bearings the lights overhead draw eyes towards the heavens, as if the yacht is actually a cathedral. Moving fore and aft, navigating through people and obstacles, the boat seems enormous and each section of the yacht is its own occasion.

Isolated on the prow of the boat it always seems that

people simply want to sit and stare back at the dark and bright city, which is initially a disconcerting experience – like seeing the world in reverse and from the outside in. The appearance is like viewing your own house at night with the lights on inside: Through the windows you can see the familiar furniture and pictures on the walls, but from some stranger's perspective. Elsewhere, on the water and in the sky, the world is simply black, as if boat is the only place that appears welcoming or with the imprint of humanity.

In the rearmost of the yacht people are loud, buoyant, and jostle for space. They touch shoulders and put hands on backs to press through tight spaces and they keep their drinks out before them as they steer around the maze, while those that stand on top of the cabin looking down want to lean against the railing and watch the scene develop under their noses. They nurse their drinks contemplatively, and it is from this perspective (on high) that allows *people watching* at its finest. Voices filter up and a skillful ear can make out conversations and watch the subtle interplay among groups. Here a person is elbowing for attention; there a person is retreating into a shell, and to the side a grand master holds everyone's interest - that is Radcliff, as always.

Inside the yacht, submerged within its walls and hull, they talk reflectively, aware of their own voices in the confined space. The rooms and halls are less spacious than might be expected because the ceilings are just a touch too low and there are only a few windows to breathe with the outside world. The air conditioning is kept on and it always seems refreshingly chilled and tranquil, as if this is where the catacombs are found. In this space people renew old acquaintances and the extroverts among the groups make new friends easily. In other corners people draw backwards and some just drift away.

Radcliff walks the boat constantly – up and down - shaking hands, owning the greeting completely and then suddenly disengaging himself. He studies people in momentary snapshots of life and makes sweeping assumptions about their past and future, some of which he knows will come true. Those who are new to the boat want to wander and explore. Their mouths gape at the sheer size of the thing; they need to stop and point and take hold of another person with whom they can share their amazement.

Mouths form words: "One-hundred million?"

Heads nod in agreement: "pounds, dollars or euros?"

"I heard pounds, but who knows?"

Inevitably, their gazes go upwards with the Christmas-like lights and trace the nearly eight-story height of the single mast. Incredibly, they are inside the Christmas tree! Those few that are impossibly cool to the scene allow that – *Yes* – it is magnificent, but also wonder if the boat does anything other than host lavish parties.

There are always discoveries and many mysteries. As Nick walks the halls and rooms below, he hears broken bits of conversations: French, English, Italian, and sometimes German. Whatever happened to old what's-his-name? The answers filter in and then another curiosity holds attention.

There is Radcliff talking, and then another older gent bursts into a genuine laugh. He shakes his head as if imparting a hard-learned lesson.

"Shoe size!" Nick hears this over the top of everything else. "*We all talked about it.*" The old gent is smiling as he elaborates, recounting a story he no doubt saves for rare occasions like this. "That, my friend, is the first thing you learn running a shop on High Street: all women lie about their shoe size. It's not their dress size that's really sensitive, no, it's their shoe size. And they all lie about it - and I do mean all of them."

Radcliff for a change is legitimately engaged by another person's proclamation; he smiles and is on the verge of a full-fledged guffaw.

"A beautiful, I mean absolutely jaw-slackening, woman sits down. And – now, this is a daily occurrence, mind – I'm looking at her feet and know full-well that she is an easy seven or maybe eight. But no, she's insisting to me she's a five. So I go back and get her a pair of sevens no matter, and when I slip them on her feet I don't tell her the size. She stands up - and oh you should see the expression on her face! She walks around and admires herself in the mirror. She does the shoe-dance. Naturally she's ecstatic, because she thinks she's just fit perfectly into a pair of *fives*."

Radcliff barely contains himself now, and he allows a chortle to clear his throat.

"So of course, she takes them. I ring them up and never mention the real size, but why should I? She's happy, and I just made a sale. I tried to get some of the manufacturers to stop labeling sizes. I said 'Look: I'll sell an extra twenty pair a week if they can't see the number!'"

They are now both shaking their heads in unison at the thought. Radcliff loves stories like this; it confirms what he thinks he knows about women and their vanity, and perhaps by extension that rest of the world. Nick is caught by Radcliff's eyes and he is beckoned over, in good spirits. Introductions go around and Nick is urged to pour on the charm. Nick knows at times like these he is kept around for a reason similar to the girls. He has acres of sophistication and breeding; he's here because it reflects well on his employer.

Radcliff is now in full-swing and is generously ordering more drinks for the small circle of his suddenly close friends. A bartender is in Radcliff's outside-voice distance, although they are most certainly *inside*, and a booming sound covers the boat: "Hold the tiki on that drink. No umbrellas or ornamental fruit. And definitely no bloody tiki torches to light my nose on fire!" Radcliff turns to the older gent, changing topics and drinks. "Ever had a swig of ouzo? You should try some. But for the love of God, make sure it's the good stuff." And without waiting for an answer Radcliff soon has a glass of the good stuff in his hand and it is passed around for everyone in the circle to take a small taste. "Nick, you found this in Cyprus, didn't you?"

"Oh, yes," he answers willingly, as the glass is passed to him. "I think it is served mostly as an aperitif, but this will do nicely." He raises it in a half-salude and toast to the company around him and takes a sip.

"My first time to the island actually, but I loved it. And yes, I will have to pick up another bottle of this next time!" They all share a laugh at Nick's mild jest and the topic slowly turns to the Greek islands and Crete in particular, a place Radcliff is suddenly adamant they *must* somehow reach come September. Someone chimes in – Aren't you worried about what's going on in Athens? The demonstrations, the riots, the economic – what would you call it? - upheaval? Radcliff waves the worry away: In his mind, that sort of rough business doesn't touch the islands. They are in a different world.

But inside, certainly, he must feel self-conscious about parading around as others retch and struggle. His face dims for a moment as a cloud descends, but then it is all back to business as normal.

After the party, you either clean up the mess, or move the party somewhere else. Radcliff always attempts another approach: he does his best to never let the party die. Nick sometimes plays a game with himself, guessing who among the crowd would want – or rate – an invite to whatever comes next.

Radcliff has a circle that orbits around him, as do other men of his ilk. Most everyone knows everyone else it seems, and there are many regulars that hop on and off the merry-go-round whenever it pleases them. The yacht is simply one place that they happily land on a holiday for a night like this, or even for a few weeks out the year. Nick thinks about the Hungarian girl and her little red towel for a cape, and that horrifying smell of vanilla, which even now in his haze wanders around the boat and touches his nose in some other form.

She was with them for mere days, and yet Nick never seems far from her reach. And maybe's Radcliff's reach, as well.

Names are thrown around and Nick files them away in his mental catalog for whatever advantage it might give his life at some point in the future, but as of yet there is little reason to bother with such details. His story seems fixed in stone and he is quietly resigned to the predictable next day, week, month and year that is surely coming for him.

4

Radcliff stands on the top of the cabin looking down on the deck. He's looking at the remains of last night's party: deck chairs are overturned, glasses, and plates are littered about, and bits of clothing are draped over the railing and piled up wherever, and certainly some of the refuse has spilled overboard and by now has floated away. As if in comment, the hyper-clear morning light of Nice makes the cube-shaped buildings that surround the marina look like they joyously sprang from a Picasso, and more inviting because of it.

For its part, the wooden deck of the yacht is beaming with sun, and yet there is an interloper: A man sleeps on his back, and he is clearly dead to the world. Radcliff stares at this unwelcome remnant. The sleeping man is positioned as if he was shot in the head last night, but has yet to be pushed off the side of the boat by someone trying to cover their crime.

Radcliff considers the scene and the unlikely corpse, which he cannot ignore, while Radcliff's belly protrudes from his unsecured robe so that it can apparently grab some much needed Vitamin D from the morning sun. "I think we killed that bastard last night," he intones to no one in particular, trying to fix just what to do with the body. "That boy is dead, dead."

Radcliff's hands scavenge around in his robe's pockets for something and finding nothing, he moves his attention to the debris nearby. A woman's sandal is now at hand, and he throws it directly at the body, which it hits on its second bounce. There is no effect to the impact, and the sleeping man continues to sleep and take up space.

With a scowl and "Hmmpht" Radcliff turns to descend back into the catacombs of the yacht and from there to direct the cleanup. Soon afterward there is the faint sound of a blender from the galley, and Nick knows that the new girl, Blake, is already ingratiating herself with Radcliff by making him some sort of a hangover-cure fruit drink. Only a few minutes earlier that morning he heard her voice filtering up to the yacht's deck, and he instantly knew that she would be joining them for the foreseeable future.

There she was, suddenly in the midst of everything last night. He remembers the details: the way she brushed her hair from her forehead in a self-conscious gesture, the way her numerous silver bracelets made a little jangle when she briefly took his hand in greeting, the way her cheeks creased as she smiled with laughter. There were no hints of Botox lingering in her animated expression. When they stood next to each other she let her hips rest lazily against his side, and he registered the woozy feeling of her body's warmth as it transferred into him.

Nick walked away from her as soon as he could manage. He abruptly excused himself as if there were immediate needs of the boat that he had to attend to.

And yet even with his back turned, and dozens of steps

away, he still heard that voice traveling alone above the surrounding din, though he was sure there was nothing special in it. The voice didn't slur with a strange sense of the end of the world, and it didn't hit him straight in the chest with a vague Hungarian accent, and yet there it was asking him to listen.

•

She wasn't like the other girls. And she certainly wasn't like the girl with the *good Goddamn bones.* Her name was Blake. "I was named after a character on a soap opera," she guffawed to the approval and laughs of others. Nobody could tell if she was merely joking or telling the truth, but it didn't matter. They stood in a circle trading quips with other semi-blitzed starlets and her hips rested against his and the world went off-center. After weeks in the summer sun her fair skin had changed a shade darker, and hints of freckles speckled her arms and cheeks. In a scene crowded with salon-approved blondes and brunets she threw her striking red hair into the fray with a simple, short style that was the height of fashion. Before long he assembled her story from others and she supplied the missing bits herself.

Of course she was an American (that voice of hers couldn't come from anywhere else) and the rest of her story was just like he imagined and a variation on a something Nick had heard dozens of times before. She apparently had an urge to travel and see the world. She was an art history student working on her graduate degree and taking advantage of a scholarship to study overseas but somehow she lost track of time in Paris. She fell in with a few jet-setters, trust-fund babies, and others burning through their allowance money, and well…the rest was typical.

Her version of a family put her up and took her along with them on their slow migration across Europe, from Swiss chalets in the winter, and eventually to French and Italian beaches in the summer. They spent on her and they attached themselves to her. They introduced her to their circles and gave her a glimpse of a different and careless life. School and art history would have to wait.

Nick wondered how long it took before she realized that there was an expected exchange of goods and services that accompanied this new life. She was trading on her spectacular looks and that dazzling light that shown around her. He wondered if already she had fended off hasty engagements and arrangements. Men like Radcliff - they wanted to cage that light and focus it on themselves. That was until they got bored with it, and looked for another. It spoke to some need. It's mine - *she's* mine.

And yet Nick wanted to take her apart, piece by piece. It seemed the alcohol was making him see things, and strangely familiar forms were moving just outside his perspective. This girl – Blake - was somehow prodding him, just like *her*. It was the feeling that wandered around the rooms and that came to an abnormal standing-slant against the railing on the boat. He wanted to begin a dissection that left everything exposed and kept nothing to the imagination. It was those damn sunglasses pushed into her hair, he decided. They were completely unnecessary; the hour was late after all - so what was she doing with them still perched like that, as if she had just dashed out the door for a lunchtime date? It was as if she had been out and about all day, just wandering around Nice, and now at close to midnight she had yet to admit it was just an act. She hadn't *just happened* onto the yacht. No, there was always a plan, Nick thought: there was an unmentioned purpose to her appearance here. Ulterior motives ruled the world.

It was impossible to imagine that she had just thrown something on in a few minutes and gone out with her friends on a whim and somehow found herself here, hours later, which tonight must have been ground zero for a girl like her. She most definitely *had not* simply bounced and bopped around Switzerland, Italy, and the south of France without a care in the world. That sort of life *cost* in all sorts of ways. Even simple rooms in resorts were an easy two-hundred euros a night this time of year. No, in truth someone had been taking very good care of her. And now here she was, apparently ready for the next leg of her adventure.

She smiled naturally, except when a picture was about to be taken, and then she made an awkward self-conscious pullback of her jaw that brought about a double chin and an open mouth that bared her teeth. That peculiar, strange expression was the only crack in her armor that Nick could see. He noticed there was a slight change of skin tone on the inside of her upper left arm; it was a faint birthmark that showed as if it were a little tea stain. He felt sure that if he could see whether or not she had tried to cover the mark with makeup, then he would suddenly understand everything there was to know about her.

They talked and caroused. There was a goofy, unmoderated side to her just underneath the polish that came through when she laughed. Already some of the other girls were looking sideways at her because she was enthusiastic; she made exaggerated movements and often took up more space than she needed. Her hands rested on her sides at times, calling attention to her shape, and he caught sight of almost too much leg as she moved one foot in front of the other. He thought back to another beauty that had captured his imagination, complete with her careless movements and her somehow odd manner. *That* beauty once rested haphazardly on a lounge with a beach towel across her shoulders - and near this very spot. That particular lovely had been on the verge of something. Now this one - she was at some particular point in her life as well.

He wondered at Blake's overfamiliarity with her surroundings and he watched when she placed her hand on the back of a man's shoulder as she made a conversational point. Nick scoffed to himself as he viewed the recipient of her slapdash touch - he was a typical patron of the scene. He sported the archetypal manicured stubble on top of a deep fake-and-bake orange-tinted tan; it was a look that Nick associated with Moroccan rug traders in the medina, as well as little *club boys* that congregated around black BMW's with dark windows.

Suddenly, and just as carelessly, she removed her hand and she left the rug trader. Her hand pushed away a strand of hair from her forehead, and her gaze was somewhere else. She craves novelty, Nick thought. She is fickle with her affections, and she is aware of her effect on men. His ear was caught by surprise thanks to the sound of her many silver bracelets resonating with the smallest clink as she shook his hand in a belated greeting. He instantly matched the warmth of her hips, which had moments earlier rested evocatively against his side, to the feeling of her fingers as Nick clasp her hand for a perfect moment. *"That's what you must figure out,"* someone once said. *"What are those millions of things you cannot have?"*

With a few abrupt words to the conversational circle he turned his back and walked away.

The night was still unfolding and the boat couldn't feel any smaller. Some of the more overt girls had decided to shed a layer of clothing, and flimsy jackets and tops were now resting on seatbacks. Empty glasses littered the deck and the haze of cigar and other smoke wafted in the air. Nick made his way forward with a particular expression stamped on his face, walking between people and the party's flotsam on the deck. To see him now was to see a person in that brief moment after being punched in the stomach, when the pain decides if it will just wash away or stay and multiply.

He found the pug-nose blonde looking bored, crushingly beautiful, and in need of company. On a night like this her reading glasses were nowhere to be found. She brightened with his approach and then she waltzed to his side, and after looking around to make sure Radcliff was somewhere else and out of view, caressed his hand meaningfully with hers.

Nick felt that pain stay and multiply.

•

Nick's room on the yacht is the most densely inhabited space Blake has ever seen. Books are stacked high and are also wedged between the few pieces of furniture. Pictures crowd the walls and maps are spread across his desk while notebooks and sheets of paper line its edges. Every inch seems occupied. There is an open closet that is nearly overwhelmed with clothes, shoes, coats, suits, hats, and anything else needed to outfit a life at sea or on land.

Blake notices one framed photograph hanging over Nick's bed. She examines it closely and sees a modest sailing boat, and on its deck she sees a handsome assortment of people standing in a group. In the center of the picture she spots Nick, nearby to a smart yet strangely plain-looking woman. Looking closer at the details, the two of them appear to be on the threshold of holding hands, but yet not quite to that point. The sun is setting in the background against an orange sky, and for the entire world it seems to capture an idyllic existence, except for the awkward near-intimacy of Nick and this woman.

Clearly the photograph is more than a few years old, and Blake wants to ask; she wants to know. But as she glances in Nick's direction, the expression he returns to her says everything. Some things she will let alone.

Last night Blake watched Nick with an enquiring eye. He was preoccupied. He was uncomfortable. She saw how he suddenly rushed away from their conversational circle like a magnet was pulling him elsewhere. At the time, she imagined it was because he was irritated and angry, perhaps because of a problem with one of the crew or the boat.

It seemed appropriate enough for her to mistake Nick for someone else. Nick was easy to categorize as a particular type of man, and it was easy for her to suppose he was just like someone of Radcliff's ilk - between his confident manner and his sometimes impatient behavior. She supposed Nick was the owner of the boat and also possessed that easily irritated attitude towards things that he managed or owned. Over the years, she had learned much about that particular attitude, which is endemic to a certain type of person, and her mistake was common. The judgment was one that people made often about Nick, but her error didn't last more than a short while.

In fact, many times people notice how Nick fusses with

the boat just like a proud father, checking and re-checking minor items. He winces when a sharp sound suggests more than a mere glass has dropped and broken, and crew members respond to him as if their jobs depend on his happiness. He looks the part too – aside from his relative youth. Or, more accurately, looks the part - others might *hope* owns such a magnificent thing, rather than the sad reality that is almost always the case.

It was the blonde with the less-memorable nose that told Nick about Blake mistaking his identity.

The blonde with the less-memorable nose found Nick at the close of the evening. She was drunk, at the very least, and her personality was turned to its most voluble setting. She saw Nick standing amongst an assortment of people; they were genteel and boisterous, and eye-catching, and slightly gruesome people. The party was on its last legs and she saw an opportunity and disengaged herself from her group of admirers and she approached him with that swaying hip-walk, which made *all* eyes gather in her direction, and then she unexpectedly bent in and whispered in his ear: "Some redhead was asking about you…"

The blonde with the less-memorable nose spoke those words in a manner that left no doubt as to their significance, which was one of her specialties.

"I straightened her up, however. She got the *Nick story, completely*." She said this and pulled back from his ear, so that she could make note of the look on his face and study the damage she had inflicted. Immediately, Nick remembered one particular time, in which he had inadvertently walked into a room upon hearing his name quietly – mockingly - mentioned, and viewed her performing for an audience: there she had been. She had the empty pockets of her pants turned out and on display, and a grossly exaggerated sad-sack clown expression on her face. It was as if to say in clear terms: What a pathetic and *literally* poor loser we have amongst ourselves. Nick lost EVERYTHING. Because he was stupid. And because he continues to be a titanic loser. And then she met his eyes, and didn't flinch.

This time Nick pulled back, knowing exactly who and what she meant.

In an instant he wondered just how much of his sordid story, his absurd cautionary tale, was disseminated and evaluated during her *straightening up* with Blake, even if it was only a matter of a few well-chosen words and disapproving scowls. (But surely, the blonde couldn't resist retelling the worst parts.) The details concerning the redistribution of Nick's wealth to another, even more wealthy gentleman, always made for an entertaining and illuminating few minutes of conversation. He thought: Now someone else knows about the rocks underneath the surface of the water. Good for them.

So here is Blake again, the afternoon of the next day. She's standing in his little cabin, looking at him while trying to avoid his eyes, searching for clues in the apparent wreckage of his life and that picture hanging on the wall. It's as if she can't quite believe Nick and his state - or maybe she merely needs more of the story. He managed to lose *everything*? His family's entire estate? Surely that boat in the picture as well. How many millions? How can such a thing happen? In his mind, he answers her: Greed, weakness…he doesn't know how else to reply to her.

Blake wants some kind of confirmation of the disaster, or perhaps some juicy details to fill in the blanks.

Maybe she wants to know the sordid facts and all about

the sad little moments of desperation. He wonders: Should I tell her about the last time I was at my bank…the journey to my ill-gotten residence - my little toehold? Maybe I should tell her about my vomit in the sink, and that unforgettable smell. Or perhaps those two hundred pills that waited in that particular medicine cabinet in that particular house. He remembers: It was as if those pills were placed there just for him to consider at that exact point in time, and served no other purpose.

Silently, Nick appraises himself as a freak of nature. He again imagines the blonde with the less-memorable nose standing there with her pockets turned out, but what upsets him most is the sad clown-like expression on her face. He's a pathetic animal, on display for others' astonishment. A man who doesn't belong. The illusion he sometimes maintains of living a decent life is easily shattered.

Blake takes her eyes off Nick, and off the picture of his one-time yacht. She smiles politely and simply asks if he will be accompanying them later on…They are all going east along the coast to see a property Radcliff is considering buying.

"Real estate is *nuts*, right now," she says, as if she has intimate knowledge of the ups and downs of the market, and Radcliff, the keen investor, is smart to jump on beachfront property.

"No," Nick shakes his head, and returns his version of an unflappable and polite smile. "I guess I'll be sitting that one out, today."

She is gone as suddenly as she appeared, and Nick, among other things quickly understands that apparently he has an opportunity this afternoon to do what he will. The herd is going to be off the boat, following their noses to other places and real estate adventures, and so he can easily justify a respite of his own. If Radcliff and his growing entourage are headed east this afternoon, Nick thinks, maybe he should take a few hours for himself and head west. He can do that pretend thing. He can pretend his life is somewhere else. He can pretend he is just a lone tourist with nothing better to do than worry that he is lost and off the beaten path, which is well-worn by decades of conscientious travelers. He can hop on a bus, play the vagabond for a while, and meander around the land and let the *day-after* headache working its way to his frontal lobe dissipate in the sun and air.

He recalls a small and decrepit nightclub several kilometers in from the coast and far enough away from the usual route that even on-season it struggles to make the rent. If it is still there, having survived Europe's own ongoing financial concussion, it makes a fine destination as it doubles as a little café – complete with other miscreants for customers - before the night rolls in. Last year, he even managed to procure some tranquilizers there for Radcliff, thanks to a character he struck up a conversation with.

The boat empties as Radcliff and company depart.

Nick hears the motor of the skiff start and rev, and then it dissipates in the distance. He imagines Radcliff and his growing team of accomplices facing forward towards the docks: surely they are all glamorous and at ease with their lives, with the wind in their hair and prosperous clothing trembling as the air buffets around them. Nick waits another hour just for good measure, announces his departure for a made-up "must-do" errand to the crew and then makes his own exit.

•

As Nick waits for the bus to show at the stop, he jangles some change in his pockets and evaluates the roadside scene. More and more he wants to be off the boat. Even the benches for public transportation have a bit of design flair in Nice, he surmises, and he settles into the contoured seat. He has a view of palm trees, gardens, and a stone retaining wall, atop which a street zig zags up to yet another level of the city. It all seems astoundingly clean, opulent, and yet classic.

Nick listens to the traffic plod by and smells and deciphers the contradictory scents of the landscape: the diesel fumes, the salt air, the smoke from restaurants…and then the rich clean scents from further inland.

Almost unbelievably there are also the faint remains of urine from drunks relieving themselves in the gutter, and further away garbage that has set just a bit too long in the summer sun, which is making its presence known with a sweet-sick odor. Never mind the manicured image, this is the confluence of a busy resort town with a big city. He also smells the unmistakable, hideous stench of vomit somewhere nearby (certainly that was a special gift to the city) and due to excessive drinking by someone the night before, as well. Perhaps, one of Radcliff's patrons couldn't handle their alcohol after their boat ride back in? It wouldn't surprise him in the least.

As he waits for the bus, he thinks about that acidic, horrible smell. He breathes it in. He lets the smell permeate his body and he thinks about the picture hanging on the wall in his cabin. It's the same picture of his one-time yacht, which Blake fixed her eyes on, as if she knew something. Surely, that extravagance is one of those millions of things he is not allowed to have.

The smell of vomit rests in his nose and lungs and it runs through his veins. It found him, like the smell of diesel smoke from the container ship.

He thinks: Sometimes your worst moments will never let go of you. He remembers one particular day that might have seen the end of everything. He remembers counting those two hundred little pills. Nick remembers the way they looked, as if they had waited for him to gather them up and then tally them out.

Yet sometimes, he knows, your worst moments are also your best.

•

On the countertop were white towelettes stacked perfectly in a neat little tray. The little towels were soft looking and had a perfumed scent, just like the kind flight attendants used to hand him from baskets on transatlantic journeys. Nick grabbed one of the fluffy squares and used it to wipe his face and mouth, and then he stood up straight, and looked in the mirror. He saw his reflection starring directly back at him, and surrounding his image the cool grey-marbled bathroom, and then to the side the doors that opened into the bank's *Reserve Lobby*. The third-floor lobby was a part of the bank separated for certain privileged clients and only accessible by a key card, something that only a few possessed, and now he thought that, too, is gone.

The stench of the vomit he had just left in the sink's basin rose up to his nostrils. He ran the water to flush the rest of the foul yellow and orange liquid down the drain and found another towel to dab the droplets from around the edge of the bowl and then he polished the surface, leaving the sink as perfect as he found it. He waited for a moment, listening to the sound of the air conditioning, feeling the time tick by, and surely the door would open and a security guard would embarrassingly ask him to please leave the premises or use other demeaning words to the same effect.

But instead the world continued on, and now it seemed it merely wanted to ignore him. Nick gathered himself and walked out the bathroom door and found the elevator, and for the last time hit the button for the main floor. Cleaned out, he thought. I'm cleaned out.

The street was different now. If he was feeling lazy or even a little drunk in the middle of the day after a lunch-time Martini (or two), he would have hailed a cab and thought nothing of it. Either that or he would have walked the short distance to where his car was parked and he might have driven the half-hour home, or maybe taken a detour to a coffee shop or stopped by his tailor to see if his new suit was ready. But this time was not the same: there was no car and no home and certainly no suit waiting for a final fitting, and so he considered his options. He started walking south simply because it seemed the smart direction to head and begin whatever came next.

There was a storage shed several miles away. He had borrowed some money and paid a year's rent on it months ago when he still held illusions of the future. It looked big when he first ratcheted up the door and looked inside, but as his trips to the shed became more frequent and he emptied in it as much of the contents of his house as he was able, it now seemed almost tiny. During the last week he could barely muster the strength to get out of bed, and thanks to the helpless panic and feint jabs at a solution that ended up going nowhere, he had neglected a few remaining items in his house, which somehow seemed the final betrayal to himself. But at the moment he thought different: that lapse of effort now meant there was enough space in the shed to lay down a few pillows on the concrete slab and make a bed for the night.

He walked along the sidewalk, disregarded the traffic and considered the world around him that he was suddenly a stranger to. No person might suspect that a plan to spend the night sleeping on a concrete slab was flashing through his mind even at this time, because through it all, he still looked the part of a man in charge. He'd always (or at least for the near-term) have his looks - his *stature.* It was a word an old girlfriend once intoned to him, as if that one sentiment answered every question about his character and appearance. He smiled to himself with a frown, yes – *stature.* That item was due only to good bones and a good structure, which he simply lucked into by the accident of his birth.

Abruptly his stomach turned again and he had that awful feeling, and then he was nothing but a passenger in his body as the acidic contents of his stomach began spewing out wherever it wanted. He felt his midsection convulse and nearly too late he thought about the vomit hitting his shoes and pant legs, and with a moment of panic and insight he bent forward and away.

Between an elementary school's parking lot and the sidewalk he found a long strip of well-tended grass. It was beautifully dark green and lush, and he crouched down, oblivious to the disturbing scene he was making as traffic roared past, and also to the children now looking through the school's windows. Nick pulled a fistful of grass lose with a strong *rrrrip*, and used the blades to wipe his mouth and cheeks, and then spit out whatever leftover taste he could. That made it a little better, but next morning his clean-cut face would show a day's hair growth, his clothes questionably dirty and used, and his shoes worn down and scuffed another fraction from all of the walking, his eyes a little hungry. It starts fast, he thought.

He walked and walked and changed directions three times before ending up on the doorstep of a one-time friend's house. Apparently his friend had somehow moved away and neglected to tell him, and yet it didn't surprise Nick in the least. As he knocked on the door, he noticed the casual disregard of the house: the dying lawn, and the untended shrubs. Liter had blown in and collected alongside a fence. This place had the whiff of failure as well.

Friends, onetime girlfriends, and his remaining distant family were now shunned by him thanks to his reordered-world…and they shunned him back. It was the cruel embarrassment and the irony of the situation: The one time he needed them, he refused to ask. And so – unknowingly – almost all of them carried on as if Nick was unaffected. Only a few offered their help, which he almost entirely refused.

He knocked on the door one last time and pondered the evening landscape of the neighborhood and the quiet scene, and wondered if he was now officially a pariah. He was glad the door remained unanswered and pleased with the newspapers and notices that had piled up on the front stoop, which seemed like their own counterintuitive "welcome" message. It took Nick thirty seconds to find a small basement window to break, and then he crawled in, without apparent alarms or notice from neighbors.

It didn't feel like breaking and entering. It felt like he was a hyena scavenging. The house was nearly empty, save for a few boxes and some leftover detritus of life. The water still ran. The phone hanging on the wall still had a dial tone. The air was unsettlingly calm and unmoving. For some reason there was a half-eaten donut left on the kitchen counter. He didn't dare turn on a light and test the electricity - perhaps even that was still on? - for fear of attracting attention from anyone nearby. Instead he found a plastic cup, ran the tap for a long while to let the rusty brown fade out and then drank what felt like a gallon of water. He sat on the floor and thought and listened, and eventually fell dead asleep.

In the morning, Los Angeles looked better. His neck hurt and his cheek was scuffed from the carpet, but that was hardly worth a thought. Perhaps for the following nights he could search for something to use as a pillow. Through the second-story window he had a view of the pollution that was settling into the basin of the city. He knew, with the summer heat that was sure to arrive, the air was only hours away from becoming choking and caustic. Already it was the color of dust and gasoline fumes, but there was a possibility circling in his head. At least, he thought, he had a plan. He would be walking again through that air and alongside that traffic, measuring the remaining dollars and change in his pockets.

•

The feeling from last night's drinking is moving around his head, and fortunately the bus arrives at the stop, seemingly just in time. Nick boards, escaping that faint smell of vomit in the gutter left from some drunkard, and his circling memories. He parses out the fare and then finds a window seat in which to contemplate the passing scenery. This is certainly *not* one of the many tourist-buses running the circuit along the French coast; it is without an open and exposed upper deck, and without throngs of tourists snapping pictures and buzzing happily. Instead he finds a small crowd of ordinary sorts. They are reading newspapers, glancing at their phones, and just trying to get somewhere in the easiest and most convenient way possible.

The route takes him inland, and often the coach struggles as the road climbs a hill, and then there is another stop and more people are on and off. There are palm trees and gleaming residences, mostly small apartments and tightly packed condominiums, as land is at a premium here, after all.

The route goes farther. There is slowly the recession of charming views and the rise of commercial and economic reality; he sees some minor industrial operations and dozens of enormous petroleum tanks, which are bordered by ordinary painted brick walls that still look somehow special and characterful.

This is his stop, if his guess is right and his memory intact, and it is marked by an old tree stump that has yet to be removed. Out of the bus now, he dons his sunglasses and heads straight for his goal; the scene is familiar, and yet he can't quite be sure he is headed in the right direction. There are a few locals ahead and they amble along with that same restful cadence of people on vacation and with time to spend. He imagines them as ducks walking along a lake's edge looking causally for a bite to eat.

He turns a corner and peers around a building and finally finds his little dive, masquerading as a café until the light fades. There are several more hours' worth of this sort of ambling-afternoon business, and he sets himself behind an outdoor table. After a long while the bartender arrives, clearly pained that he must double as a waiter at such times, and takes his order; Nick hopes the food will somehow calm the throbbing in his head. He counts the various drinks he consumed last night and losses track around the "seven" mark.

The entertainment for the day is clearly viewable across the street. From his seat outdoors Nick is able to watch the comedy of errors as a group of children attempts to resurrect an old motor-scooter. It is a grey, worn thing, propped up on a bent kickstand, and with a torn seat and missing fenders. He smiles as he sees that the children's good intentions have gone slightly awry. Apparently their efforts to replenish the oil in the motor's reservoir have instead doused the sidewalk in a thin coat of the rich and brown liquid, which is exacerbated by the water they have decided to squirt everywhere via a garden hose in an effort to clean it up. Within a few minutes the oil slick has quadrupled in size, and several of the kids are running into a nearby yard and back, giggling and yelling. Nick watches, as someone's neighbor, grandmother, mother, or aunt is shortly on the scene and her rising voice and hand gestures make an impression. Old papers and bits of cloth are put to use by the kids, and with a flourish of apparent indictments from the supervising adult, the incident is shortly on its way to a partial resolution.

Nick smiles to himself again, as if he were the one learning the lesson about oil and water. *That*, he thinks, was a memorable demonstration. He wonders if he will be able to accurately recount this little vignette once he is back on the boat. And then he subtly sighs, as he knows the only person he wants to share the story with is the striking redhead - Blake. Even now, with only the barest of words between them as of yet, there is some connection.

He sees, too, that the wandering life and his sometimes pretend and backwards looking escape, is falling apart. That pretend life is surely one of those millions of things he cannot have anymore.

He wants to tell his odd Hungarian lovely, he knows something now. Travel, and the religious experience of it, only matters when he has someone beloved to share it with.

•

Downstairs in the abandoned house, the air was still unnervingly calm and silent. He again found the half-eaten donut sitting in the same spot and with the same couple of bites missing, as if someone had forgotten it or simply lost interest in the last half.

Nick tapped the item with his finger, feeling the stale hardness, which had replaced the once soft consistency, and then brought his finger to his lips and tasted the sugar. He smiled sarcastically to himself as he fashioned himself a Hollywood-styled Native American tracker, trying to determine how long it had sat there, and by extension how long it had been since someone else had been in this house. He took a hesitant chewy bite of the donut and swallowed, and then another, and with that it was gone. He needed calories. Already he was thinking in terms of basic needs, and so he drank as much water as he could, and he made use of the bathroom; the storage shed was at least fifteen miles away and he saw no other way to cover the distance than by foot.

The sidewalks were intermittent. Sometimes they were needlessly wide and perfectly formed, and other times they just ended and left gravel paths alongside chain-link fences, and that was when he knew he had left the suburbs and entered the city.

Walking under bridges and beneath overpasses he smelled the especially foul remnants left from vagrants and saw the timid graffiti left from boys with only a single spray-can of paint and a few seconds of time or courage. Both seemed to mark their location in the world as a feeble warning to outsiders. He found areas hidden away that had clearly served as someone's home for the night: He saw the remains of old cigarettes in very strange, ordered small piles, and empty bottles and packaging from food. And most telling: cardboard boxes that had served both as a covering, and as a bed the previous night.

When the neighborhoods improved again and warehouses were replaced by strip malls, he found a fast-food restaurant and dropped inside. In the restroom, he again measured himself in the mirror. He didn't like what he viewed: his face was showing burn marks from the sun and seemed puffy; his eyes looked tearful from the dust and pollution; his collar was smudged. He knew his walk was now more of a tired lope. He wasn't built for this. He was using muscles in a manner in which they had never been used. He saw that his unearned *stature* was already beginning to crumble and be exposed for what it was. Just another fraud.

He cleaned himself up as best possible; the cool water on his face helped and the gritty industrial grade soap smelled like detergent from an auto shop, but did its job. He gathered some paper towels and cleaned off his shoes – two hundred dollar leather shoes that were nearly worthless as anything other than lounging accessories. He re-tucked in his shirt and once back into the dining room made a quick scan of the surroundings and found a used but empty cup alongside a newspaper. Nonchalantly he gathered the items up and filled the cup over and over with Root Beer from the serve-yourself drink station. He sat and paged through the newspaper. He knew the stories had no relevance to him anymore, but the act was mindless and soothing.

Nick pulled his wallet out and counted the dollars. He could come up with thousands - tens of thousands - selling the contents of the storage shed. *Yes* - he always had that as a last ditch effort. In the meantime he had fifty-seven dollars, an assortment of useless credit cards, and a half-filled punch card from a coffee shop. In a worst case scenario all of that might have to last a couple of weeks; he couldn't yet see hocking the family silver down at the pawn shop. Even a bus ticket seemed an indulgence and an insult to *something*. He couldn't quite figure out what that something was.

The storage shed was located at a facility that apparently didn't accommodate people who arrived by foot; the gate out front was supposed to be triggered by the weight of a car and the code on a keypad. He had one, but not the other, and so he climbed the fence and walked down the aisles while expecting an interdiction by a security guard or an employee that was sure to have seen him on the camera by the entrance. He was left alone, however, as he again ratcheted up the door to his shed and smelled the familiar, faintly musty smells of his books, furniture, rugs, artifacts and odds and ends gathered from so many trips around the world.

He found a duffle bag. He found suitable clothes. He found a coat. Already, there was a layer of dust on everything. He found a framed picture in a trunk from not so long ago. It was a picture of him, and his one-time love, standing amongst others and peculiarly not quite holding hands on the deck of his one-time boat. The sunset in the background played on the image; it made the scene and everyone in it glow in a heavenly light. On the reverse side of the image he knew he would find his handwriting. During one of his panic attacks, he had grabbed the picture in a fit, removed the back, and used the reverse side, as if it were a scratch sheet of paper to take notes when nothing else was at hand in his torn-apart home. He knew (covered up by the picture's backing) there were hastily written and barely legible names, phone numbers, and bank routing information. At the time, as he wrote the information out, he had noticed the weird incongruity of Johansen's horribly misjudged names of holding companies and offices.

These companies were the distant outposts and tools of Johansen's machine. One was named "Ice Station," and Nick remembered rattling out the name with his pen just as the inevitable demise became unquestionably clear.

Johansen was surely unassailable if he could be so coy and almost frivolous with his empire and its various designations. Nick felt that very moment yet again, and he thought for a few seconds and then made space for the picture in the bottom of the bag; he wrapped a shirt around it and buried it safely beneath everything else. He didn't expect to return here for months, or maybe even for years. The picture was the one memorial of his former life that he allowed himself.

The phone booth alongside the storage facility's office lacked both a phone and a directory. The metal wire used to secure the hand piece dangled metaphorically; it was a dead device but now something Nick needed more than ever. Cellphones were taking over the world, and no one but people like him who couldn't afford them seemed to care. Once inside the office, the manager of the facility eyed him suspiciously. He noted the duffle bag and looked twice at his I.D., but graciously offered to find - online - the information and phone numbers Nick needed upon verifying that he had indeed prepaid for twelve months of storage. The manager mused: "Most people just land here for a few months, or for a few decades it seems…nothing much in between."

The manager wanted his story, that much was obvious. He was trying to pry into this strangeness that Nick had become. Nick was now that rare sort of person who showed up on foot to a storage lot, and scrambled over the gate to rummage through the piles of his former life. Nick gave his best deflecting smile and concentrated on the task at hand. The computer worked its magic and the paper ran through the printer.

He had printouts with phone numbers and addresses, suddenly. It was a start. There were names of certification organizations, shipping companies, and container transport lines, and places and people to call; at the top stood the name of the ship, "Athena". He carefully folded the printouts, placed them in his pockets like they were the most valuable thing he had ever owned, said a generous "thank you" and allowed his proxy assistant to get back to his daytime TV. The curiosity of Nick left unanswered.

•

It was doubly hard walking back. There was the weight of the duffle bag, which he moved shoulder-to-shoulder in order to ease the fatigue, but now the absurdity of his non-shoes left their mark with blisters and biting pains on his feet. With the final few hundred yards back to his new home as a squatter, he broke into a wounding gallop but felt sure he would turn the last corner and see police cars in the driveway. There would surely be search lights and crime scene evidence men scouring the lawn but the house stood in the half-light, unchanged and abandoned, same as when he left it in the morning.

The newspapers were still on the walkway and bleached from the sun and flat from the rain. The weeds were staging a comeback between cracks in the cement. A neighborhood kid rode an old banana-seat bike down the street, popped a wheelie and barely gave Nick a glance.

Nick again crawled through the window he had broken out, pulling his lead-weight bag behind him. He waited and listened, as if that moment of quiet would enable him to hear the neighbors calling 9-1-1 to report his crime. But again there was nothing but that eerie silence: an abandoned home, and he as its only scavenging occupant. Nick could barely believe the water still worked. The phone still had a dial tone. The electric surface on the stove glowed hot. He could cook a meal, if he had anything to cook, or anything to cook it in. These were signs hinting at a possible turn in his fate; they felt like chances and favors that he didn't deserve.

He considered the cardboard boxes he had seen earlier on his long walk, which were used by someone as bedding and covers at some point in the past, or maybe even tonight. He thought about the way they had been trampled and adopted as blankets; he thought about the trash and debris of empty bottles and the cigarette stubs, which were piled into a tidy little group. They marked one person's weak hold on life. He fought back a tear and then the feeling took over. He walked through the house and sobbed.

In the bathroom, the medicine cabinet held some extras: Band-Aids, mouthwash, and several old bottles of pills.

He found a large bottle of aspirin and pried off its cap; it seemed the bottle was just waiting for him to do that one thing. He poured a small amount of the contents into the palm of his hand and guessed the number, and then he poured the rest onto the counter and stopped counting when he arrived at two hundred. That was the magic number.

He ran the shower and stood wearily under the water and let it do whatever it was capable of doing for him. He left the two hundred pills lying there on the counter, like a loaded gun. He eyed them every few seconds through the blurred haze of the old and mildewed shower curtain. This is it, he thought. Survival.

5

The girls are congregating in a tight little bundle on the deck of the yacht. After lunch Radcliff had made an obvious demonstration of affection for all of them, with gentle pats on the back and a kind word or two. Just like a patriarch who is trying to integrate a new kitten into a household already full of pets, children, and relatives. Now the girls are arranged around the deck in symbolically significant positions; their deckchairs are all facing each other in a clear effort towards relationship building and encouraging conversation. Still, the two non-stop blondes cluster together, slightly apart from new arrival Blake, and the brown-haired girl with the discreet dolphin tattoo is to the side and sedately quiet, which apparently suits everyone just fine.

Radcliff reclines and enjoys the scene, allowing bits of chit-chat to filter into his periphery. He is in his swimsuit and slathered in a particularly pungent concoction, which was designed by leading white lab coat people to rejuvenate the body, and which makes use of copious amounts of a uniquely smelly Asian fruit that was perhaps better left undiscovered. They are now miles out at sea, as evidenced by the deep and long rollers, and it is apparent that Radcliff is far into the *He who shall be bronzed* phase of the day.

Nick is minding the wheel of the boat and the scene nearby; his eyes are moving between the distant front of the boat as it cuts into the horizon, and the curious *blah* expression found on the tribe's most drug-addled member.

But who needs the dazed brown-haired girl when the Two Blondes Show is on? The pug-nosed blonde stands to her feet, looks at her compatriot and makes a timid hip sway in an attempt to mimic the dance she saw some time ago at a club. "Will you show me that little move?" She is asking hopefully and with genuine befuddlement.

The blonde with the less-memorable nose plays her usual role: "No."

"How can you be so mean? I'll be your best friend."

"Well, okay." The blonde with the less-memorable nose relents, stands up and stifles a little smile. She gets into character and then dazzles with a goofy-sexy sway that keeps rhythm to music only she can hear. The blonde with the pug-nose joins her, apparently to music with a different beat, and she tries her best to follow the unselfconscious movement of her new best friend.

Nick observes the routine with the rest of them, amused and smiling, and suddenly decides to offer his rendition of *The Girl from Ipanema* as musical accompaniment to the dance, which he loudly sings elevator-music style. Nick's eyes catch Radcliff in a rare moment of guilelessness; Nick judges Radcliff's bewilderment over a different generation by how wide his eyes open, and then how far his eyebrows begin to rise as he watches the show.

To the side of the stage Blake is looking on, taking notes, laughing and clapping in approval. Any other up-and-coming

Radcliff-girl would have joined the goofy-sexy dance routine to flaunt her wares, but Blake is content to *not* be the center of attention for the time being. Blake is clearly with them and part of something new; she's headed in a different direction than she was just a few days ago, and that is all she asks for now. Radcliff, as per his modus operandi, has changed and expanded his plans. The Greek island of Crete has been nagging at his loins – or so he says – and therefore Nice is in their rearview mirror. They might have continued on to Spain, or spent more time gallivanting around the Côte d'Azur throwing parties and spending money, but Radcliff has picked his latest female trophy and wants to abscond with the loot – or so Nick decides.

•

The problem is that the island of Crete is a huge distance away. As it is, the late summer winds blowing off the North African coast are starting to drive massive waves that traverse the whole ocean and tax the resolve of everyone to remain pleasant and sociable. To reach their next destination they will have to make it all the way down the length of Italy, and around the tip of the boot – and once near Greece, the winds are still huge, drying out the hillsides and often driving brush fires that travel miles in a single day.

A plan-B is therefore developed: Nick and the crew will take the boat alone to Crete; Radcliff and friends will be dropped off tomorrow at Genoa and will fly the rest of the way. Radcliff, naturally, has many close relationships with people who own private planes for just this sort of travel emergency, and who also *love* to be of service. Radcliff muses that such generosity also helps to justify the aircraft's yearly expense, and besides, if you've got it - flaunt it. Especially to your friends. This makes everyone happy, as the girls simply can't take more than two days at sea without turning bitter.

There is also the question of managing apprehensions. Hugging the coast, is reassuring to those weary of boat travel, and the understanding that some piece of land is just out near the horizon ties them to something safe and solid. But out in the midst of the sea there is simply nothing to hang on to. Radcliff's yacht, which seems so imposing and stalwart cruising around a bay, is nearly inconsequential compared to the forces that can be marshaled against it out in the deep blue ocean. Even now to the inexperienced, with the sails completely full, the yacht seems to tilt many degrees more than is prudent. Waves muscle along the side of the hull and the front of the boat makes a queasy figure-8 when viewed against the horizon. It's working, pressing on, despite the violence of the water. It sometimes seems that a complete disaster is only a single step away.

Nick needs the distance, however. It will give him some space and relief as well, but from Blake, the girl that is suddenly always *there*.

The tribe loafs around the rest of the afternoon (as if in polemic opposition to the work of the boat) and talks about Greece, and then they reminisce about Nice and then about the beachfront villa they toured with Radcliff just days earlier. They share the usual comments and thoughts, but the star of the scene is suddenly sitting on a low table right in front of them, thanks to Santi, the chef.

On the table is an enormous, perfectly sliced cheesecake with a side of blackberry sauce that probably tastes heavenly. The cake is much too large for even four times the group, and their entire conversation slowly turns into an attempt to reject the existence of this item. Who among them (except for Radcliff) will succumb and devour this calorie-leaden temptation?

The blonde with the pug-nose states: "I thought the villa had an absolutely gorgeous garden," while her eyes coldly examine the entirety of the cylindrical desert. Subtext: "I'm NOT eating any of that bloody cake."

The unexpected disjoint, reversal, and separation in the meandering journey has clearly tweaked Santi. He is feeling the pressures of his position as Head Cook (and as an expendable member of the crew) although he never states this explicitly. Santi, like the rest of them, sees how carefree Radcliff is with his travels, and he knows Radcliff is equally carefree and careless with people. Santi once told Nick in his broken English, that when Radcliff ventures out of his office and comes into the kitchen to taste the food, *"I'm scared. I'm always scared."* Nick could understand that sentiment.

A typical day finds Santi often untroubled, but then suddenly morose. He stands at the stove with his hand resting on his hip, the other hand slowly stirring a pot, and he stares down at the food in the time-honored manner of chefs everywhere. But often it seems there is a sadness; a bridge that cannot be built. He laughs and takes great pride in his work, and although he intellectually understands the social-private dividing line between himself and Radcliff's guests and girls, he is incapable of accepting the reality of it. Thus, he over shares much of his private life and feelings with anyone who seems to empathize with him. People like Nick. During the time on board Nick has read between the lines and sized up Santi: He is far too gentle a soul for this kind of posh-vagabond life.

This behavior, the kind of emotional weight that Santi

carries with him, irritates Radcliff and everyone knows it. Still on this particular afternoon the melancholy has manifested itself in the creation of this wondrous cheesecake, and as soon as Radcliff happily disappears below with two slices on his plate, Santi appears ostensibly to collect reviews of his work.

Santi hovers around the group and then accepts the invite to stay and talk, which he shortly bends into a sharp self-critique of his declining personal appearance and fashion sense. The blondes jump to attention with the prospect of a pet project. The blonde with the pug-nose even finds her glasses to don and fiddle with, for that extra amount of concern and sincerity. He is worried that his *amazingly incredible* boyfriend will not want to be seen with him when he gets back home to Argentina.

Santi tells them: The last time the two of them talked on Skype, he went so far as to choose a rundown Internet café that *didn't* offer video cameras on their computers. He can't even stand to look at himself, so how can his boyfriend abide the same slovenly visage? Even worse he despairs is that his profession as a chef demands that he eat all the time, and so he gets *gordito* he says. He pokes at his belly. And then he wants to eat more, because *of course he does.* It's a vicious circle.

The blonde with the less-memorable nose is offering her ear and shoulder to cry on, so that she can surely *also* collect dirt and compromising data for future use. Sometimes, too, she offers her seasoned opinions regarding personal style.

"Is that all that's wrong?" she asks, as her voice filters a catalog of other issues likely crippling Santi at the moment. She circles around him like a hawk that is curious about a wounded animal. The scent of emotional pain is in the air.

Nick imagines Santi slumping further into his chair with the thought of the many other things in his life that are simply wrong. And indeed soon he does slump even more, and with an air of resignation. The blonde with the less-memorable has scored a victory.

Meanwhile the blonde with the pug-nose joins the fray and talks hopefully about the *amazing* boutiques on the islands of Crete and Mykonos and in the hotels they will soon be visiting. For unknown reasons, she makes air-quotes with her fingers when she says the phrase "resort wear."

Santi is justifiably concerned that these shops mostly cater to the very style vacuum he suffers from. "What is wrong with me? This is clothing for old ladies," he waves his hands up and down to draw disparagement to his current ensemble, which did in fact have some cross-generational confusion. "I need something more me. I just don't know what that is."

He tries to cheer up: "I will try and be better when we get to Greece. You can all take me shopping, yes?"

Both of the blondes agree enthusiastically; it's a project they can get behind, but Santi is looking plainly at Blake for help as he says his words. Clearly he wants guidance from her most of all. In this world, appearance counts double. And there she is, wearing an unpretentious little dress that wonderfully splits the difference between effortless and formal. Her usual silver bracelets are occasionally clinking in the wind as she moves her arms, and as always her red hair and short cut offers a hint of challenge, and yet frames her face perfectly. She has style to burn, and Santi recognizes her sophistication.

Nick makes a mental note, as the two blondes register Santi's deference to Blake. Yes - she is a different kind of girl. Nick sees that the seeds of discontent among the newly augmented group are already being sown.

•

The push along the Italian coast is even more trying than Nick imagined. It is certainly a good thing that Radcliff and the girls are elsewhere, perhaps ensconced in a hotel (which is not heaving and rolling in the waves) and covered in pristine white sheets. His mind wanders to Blake and Radcliff together, and he can't stomach the thought. The seas are high; the boat is lonely; Nick must stay focused for eighteen hours out of every day as they push down the coast. He trusts Santi and the other crew to watch the boat while he sleeps, but every hour he has an alarm set to wake him up and go topside to check on whoever is minding the navigation, radar, helm, and he scans the horizon – just to be absolutely sure.

He sets his head down on the bunk, his feet sprawl over the edge, and his covers are nothing but a mess of uselessness, and then it seems only minutes later that the irritating electric tone of his alarm is bringing him up from a sleep at the bottom of the ocean.

He dreams over and over about a time many years ago when he was swimming far out at sea and he literally swam straight into a dead puffer fish. He was lost in the repetitive and mindless motion of his swim (kick, pull, breathe) and then suddenly the fish was right in front of him, bobbing up and down in the wavelets like an alien hybrid species. He caught a brief glance of the fish: it seemed half-porcupine and half-small buoy. The fish's poisonous spines were right by his face and even long deceased, they were still effective.

Before he had time to react, a wave pushed the carcass of the animal straight into him and it stung his cheek like the worst jellyfish attack he had ever felt.

At the time he wondered: What if the spines had struck his lips, or even his tongue? As it was, his cheek swelled up hugely from an allergic reaction. If the spines had hit his mouth perhaps he would have found it nearly impossible to breathe. Perhaps that would have been the end of him. He would have struggled for air and then drowned in a panic, thanks to a dead puffer fish.

He swam back to shore. He received a few injections and pills at a nearby clinic, which quickly addressed the swelling and which seemed to fix him up fine, but he was changed after that. The ocean is *also* trying to kill you, he thought. And you won't know how until it is too late.

Topside, he wanders the length of the boat, making cursory checks of lines and equipment. With a constant strong wind from three-quarters behind, the boat can easily pace most freighters and other commercial ships. It is simply *that* fast in ideal conditions. Out far on the horizon, perhaps thirty miles away, the grey form of a container ship is merely a tiny bump on the planet's surface and appears to lead them down the coast. Hours have passed and it has neither faded away nor grown larger.

If he ever leaves Radcliff's yacht, and someday he must, this is how he wants to remember his time.

•

There was no doubting Crete's geographic kinship to smugglers; on the map that Nick studies the little island appears to have thousands of natural harbors, most of which seem to be tight coves pressed into scraggily hillsides and cliff faces. Perfect, if it were three-hundred years ago and you were trying to evade detection and hide your boat and contraband, or perhaps, even so today.

Radcliff has found one of these hideaways, which is bordered by a postcard-perfect village. As Nick approaches on the yacht, he can see the immaculate whitewashed buildings radiating up against the rocky slopes like an amphitheater. The cove is especially deep. It's the same V-shape that continues down and down, under the water. He consults the charts and references the sounding equipment that describes the seafloor beneath the yacht. Even at low tide, the boat will have dozens of feet below it. There are shrubs and trees making a claim on scattered tidbits of arable land and they add dabs of dark green to the mountainsides. Much farther and higher away, he catches a glimpse of a few of the many hundreds of windmills, which are found all across this and other Greek islands. Through the binoculars, he studies them. This particular select group of windmills appears to have weathered the eons.

It is midday and the sun is at its brightest, the water is at its most inviting deep blue, and as the anchors let go on either end of the boat, the rat-a-tat sound surely carries several hundred yards away and into the village, announcing *the arrival,* if there were any doubt. Santi and the other crew are on deck, waving to shore, trying to pick out if that plump form in a swimsuit is indeed Radcliff. The handful of people on the beach all look more or less the same from a distance.

"Oh, yes, right there." Santi is pointing now. "Two blondie type girls. There is that mound next to them with the red shorts." His voice crests with excitement, "I was thinking we had the wrong place, maybe. It is very small, here." Nick secures the boat in place for the time being.

Nick, too, is in his version of an aged-uncle sensible-bathing suit, and he dives off the stern in a barely-considered athletic jump, and swims to shore. The water is surprisingly warm, and as always the first few strokes of his swim are strangely effortless and then slightly difficult as he keeps his head up higher than he might normally. The memory of the dead puffer fish, bobbing lifelessly in the waves, is still running through his mind. As he makes it to shore he sees Radcliff walking down the beach. The sharply rising sand and the incongruent view through the water towards the floor at Nick's feet makes him stumble as he plods ashore.

"They don't even have a dedicated skiff, or transport boat here!" Radcliff seems both pleased and surprised, "You'll have to wrangle one up from someone, it seems." Already Radcliff is tasking him with the usual encumbrances.

Nick shakes the water droplets from his hands and then clears his face, trying to find his bearings. This is the first time he has stood on land for many days and he is wobbly. The beach is only somewhat solid but unmoving, and he is fighting the sense that it is turning and undulating, as if he were drunk. He scans the scene for any signs of a tall curvy redhead in this moderately populated stretch of paradise and finds none. From a distance, the blonde with the pug-nose waves her arms and hands with an exaggerated greeting, and Nick returns her "hello" with a small salute.

"By the way, how long are we staying here?" Nick asks this for many reasons, one of which is to gauge how invested he should be in managing the back-and-forth of Radcliff's dual life between land and the boat.

Radcliff scrunches up his nose in a sort of thinking expression and then decides. "Oh, a few days, at least. We just set ourselves here this morning – been on Mykonos. Brilliant!"

Nick runs Radcliff's pronouncement through his filter, which he uses to gauge the likelihood of another spur of the moment end-run to another point on the globe. Radcliff is a true Brit: Everything is "brilliant" and the word has lost all significance due to its overuse; it does seem, however, that Radcliff is genuinely enchanted over this little spot for a change. Perhaps he has found yet another favorite restaurant somewhere nearby, or maybe something (or someone else) awaits him.

•

The hotel is modest by the group's standards. The brown-haired girl with the discreet dolphin tattoo on her hip is particularly irritated about the lack of space and the squeaks in the wood floors. As Nick carries a load of more bags up the stairs he can hear both the squeaks from his heavy footfalls and the complaints from down the hall. Now at the open door he peers inside, luggage hanging from his shoulders and in his hands; he pushes into the nearly crowded room. He catches Radcliff's eyes which motion to a pile of other luggage in the corner, and he makes an effort to avoid Blake's gaze as he stacks more on the small mountain.

"See, we need extra room," he hears this from today's most vocal member of the female quartet.

Radcliff makes a grimace face, which carries around the group, and this achieves his desired goal: the quietness of the girl with the discreet dolphin tattoo.

"They are full up, Love," he adds with a bit of his own irritation, just to make his point all the more clear.

Nick smiles to himself. How things change. He remembers years ago, car shopping with Radcliff and the girls. On that day Radcliff made a scene and dismissed the smaller body style of a new Rolls Royce merely because the very same girl sat in the back seat, flopped and lazed just a bit too much and barely brushed her knees against the luscious colony leather seatback. Her expression of extreme displeasure at her brushed knees was replicated via Radcliff's scathing words to the salesman: "It simply will *not* do. It's far too small!" These days, Radcliff has had enough of the addled royalty routine.

The blonde with the pug-nose interjects herself into the awkward silence that is creeping into the room. She knows how to cheer things up: "We hired a couple of cute little runabouts!" She is smiling and bubbling with energy. "We can drive over to that town…the one with the shops." She looks around for approval. "Oh," she says, just realizing the extra-amazing possibility of her plan, "we can bring Santi along and get him some new clothes!" She claps her hands in a rapid mini-burst of enthusiasm. Radcliff is not entirely amused. "Fine," he says. "But I think I'll sit that one out."

Clearly he needs a bit of peace and quiet, or perhaps a nap after this crew, and he pulls a couple of credit cards from his wallet and hands them to the blonde with the pug-nose. She kisses him on the cheek and gives him a love squeeze on the arm. "Oh, Nick," Radcliff says, adding as an after-thought, "I have a little extra errand for you. Go with them and find a bank with a decent safety deposit box." Radcliff marches determinedly into the bedroom and returns with what looks like a pillowcase filled with small books.

"It's all of their damn tablets, mobile devices, and what have you." he says, removing the mystery. The girls are not pleased, judging from their looks. "The phones are no use in the village, anyway. The shadow of the hills blocks the towers, or whatever." The girls' frowns are not deterred, but Radcliff is clear: "Hell, the CIA was bugging Diana's mobile all those years ago. I don't even want to guess what they're doing today. I'm done with it."

Nick takes the surprisingly heavy pillowcase, and Radcliff removes all doubt as to the mission. "Use your own name, pay with cash. Rent it for at least a few weeks."

As if attempting to end the scene before their patriarch digresses into an antigovernment tirade, the other blonde with the less-memorable nose now moves into the bedroom, and pats the side of the bed enticingly while eyeing Radcliff. He catches her drift and smiles approvingly. It seems she will be taking a lay-down as well, and will not join them on their shopping adventure either.

•

The little cars that the blondes hired are a couple of old Fiats, with two doors and four tiny seats and matching red paint, and are more or less perfect for combing over the island's tight roads and dealing with the narrow parking spaces. But when the brown-haired girl with the discreet dolphin tattoo turns the corner and sees the cute little red bumps, she has but a few words: "*You have got to be joking.*" She rotates 180 degrees with a huff and heads back to the hotel. Nothing seems to be going her way transportation or accommodation wise. Next, Nick thinks, perhaps the medications will somehow be lacking.

But the rest of them are more than game. Santi joins Blake in one, and Nick pilots the other with the remaining blonde girl as a passenger. She insists that they lead. She knows exactly the first shops she wants to hit, and so they set off across the island. The manicured road is a sharp contrast to the rough and often inhospitable terrain, and though they have seen this sort of scene before, they still marvel at the rugged view.

Nick leaves them at the first shop and wanders the town's center on foot looking for a bank. He carries the pillowcase over his shoulder and nearly gets lost a few times as the whitewashed buildings close in around the streets and meld into the pathways, leaving only enough room for pedestrians in a maze of up and down, and left and right. He sees a shopkeeper sweeping out his entranceway, and then the shopkeeper continues sweeping into the very street itself. No wonder the *whitewashed everything* seems so pristine.

The bank he does find is apparently closed for a few hours in the middle of the day, and he thus turns his attention to a prosperous looking hotel he happened across minutes earlier. With bits of common English and gestures on both sides, he arranges for the pillowcase and its contents to be left in the hotel's safe for a small fee, plus a generous tip to the staff. No passport is required. "I remember you," the desk clerk assures him with a serious countenance and atmosphere of professionalism, not in keeping with the rest of the transaction.

Nick finds the group again in another shop a few doors down from their initial prospect. Inside, he sees that Santi is dying for attention and Nick observes as Blake goes to his side and evaluates his new look in the mirror with him. She knows how to make people feel indispensable.

She straightens his collar and pulls the fabric to feel its weight and durability, and to smooth out any wrinkles. She suggests that a good tailor can recut the waist, but it is otherwise perfect. Blake even offers to make the alterations herself, if Santi doesn't mind helping her to unearth a sewing machine, which is supposedly buried in some storage locker back on the yacht. He is smiling and beaming; his short, stocky body seems to have grown a few inches in her presence, and the silhouette and colors of his new clothes are more subdued and more mature. He says, "I'm going to be myself, just *better*." The blonde with the pug-nose is scouring the racks and has created a pile of other must-have clothes for him.

They traverse the town, bags in hand, and take breaks in the shadowed portions of outdoor cafes and down their drinks and then poke at salads, which are inundated with olive oil. Weathered and ageless men with dark skin and light-colored clothes, and tattered espadrilles on their feet, sit and talk alongside the street. They occasionally look over at Nick and the prettied-up tourist girls, and then go back to whatever topic was held at bay. Blake pushes her sunglasses into her hair in the same fashion Nick first noticed that first night on the yacht many days ago. It's one of her signature moves. On a nearby table, Nick finds an ancient and well-used tourist guide book lying temptingly open, and he pages through it.

Discovering a particular picture and section in the book, Nick mentions that he wants to see some of the old windmills up close, just like the ones on the hillside reasonably close to the cove where they now make their home.

Blake nods her head in approval, "I'd like that too," she says, as they avoid each other's eyes.

•

Without a phone to provide a distraction, the blonde with the pug-nose is perhaps more gossipy than usual. As they walk from shop to shop, she also clearly appraises this interlude away from the others as an opportunity to educate Blake as too the *real* history and a makeup of their small group. The blonde with the pug-nose is often very sweet and sincere. She is nowhere near as manipulative and Machiavellian as others that have come and gone, but as she talks, Nick wonders if she is also attempting to establish herself as the queen bee in their cozy cooperative.

She tries at first to apologize for the brown-haired girl with the discreet dolphin tattoo. The case to be made on behalf of the brown-haired girl goes like this: She was sent through the wringer. She is a veteran of all sorts of bad things. Of course she is difficult to get along with but she isn't entirely responsible for her generalized bitchiness. People should know: There are extenuating circumstances. Nick has to laugh, and yet he also tends to agree.

When she felt like talking, the brown-haired girl with the discreet dolphin tattoo uploaded long and involved stories into the collective hive mind of the boat. More than any of the others, it was obvious the brown-haired girl had thus far lived the most extreme slumming-princess life, for better and for much worse. She had been a *Grid Girl* for a large Italian retail company, which the blonde with the pug-nose says, was less wonderful than you might imagine. The car races were long and loud and not very interesting, and the crews on the teams didn't have any extra time to spend taking girls out on the town and weren't much to look at either. They herded the girls out in a mass before the race, and then they were all supposed to stand around and smile, holding umbrellas to shield drivers and others from the sun. Apparently, she couldn't smile that long, the blonde says matter-of-factly.

The blonde girl with the pug-nose likes talking about how the brown-haired girl really liked talking about a nameless Egyptian who took steroids. Or more accurately, he *received* them, straight into his body. His butt cheeks to be perfectly accurate, but only after the nameless Egyptian forced the brown-haired girl to learn how to needle his fleshy haunches with the syringe just right. The bizarre part was that he refused to lift weights or otherwise exercise to capitalize on the benefits of the drug coursing through his veins. He developed acne all over his body; he was depressed and then suddenly angry and somehow felt invincible; his genitals changed shape and by the end of it he needed a testosterone injection just to perform a perfunctory act of intercourse. And that, of course, was horrifying in itself.

As per usual when the blonde girl with the pug-nose recounts the brown-haired girl's story, she is needlessly vivid and clear regarding the use of needles and just how *exactly* a person gives a genital injection. "It's just like this," she says, making use of her fingers and showing the correct angle of attack on the male member. And then she pushes down on the plunger of the make-believe syringe, and concentrates on the act, as if she really had done it herself and wanted people to learn this life skill.

Apparently, the nameless Egyptian barely spoke to the brown-haired girl, and when he did he demanded answers to questions he suddenly *had to know*: "Who was on the phone with you yesterday? Tell me!" She spent her days frightened, or bored to death. She watched TV and waited to go and do something, or mostly she waited for someone interesting to stop by and entertain her. Her drug use, Nick always guessed, started simply in this vacuum of life. Yet as far as he could tell, she didn't take "fun" drugs. Klonopin was for people with serious anxiety issues. Her dosage dulled and diluted experiences into a plain bland sandwich. For her, this indeed became some sort of weird and twisted world.

As they walk, Blake falls slightly back and keeps pace with Nick. She too has stories, she says, but not much along those lines. Genital injections were definitely out of her milieu. She laughs that Radcliff has surreptitiously named the girls according to hair color, "I'm Red *One*," she offers and wonders jokingly, if that means she is the very first of the redheads. About herself, she is more guarded. "I've had a pretty normal life," she suggests. During one summer as a teenager she worked at an older couple's house, she says.

"It was actually more of an *estate,"* she corrects herself. That was a rare thing in her neck of the woods. "My family was *not* so well off..," she says, hinting at something she won't yet discuss.

On the estate there were gardens and lawns that needed constant weeding and manicuring, she says. There were little projects like repairing fences, and a sprinkler system that always seemed to spring leaks. She and another girl helped out several days a week. They arrived early and worked hardest before the sun got too far in the sky, and by noon they were ready to call it a day. "Sometimes I'd come in for a break, just to get out of the heat." Nick can see that she is remembering, as her smile grows.

"They had this great old place, far too big for just the two of them, but it was important to keep it up, I suppose. Keep up that whole life. I can't imagine how horrible their air conditioning bill was during the hottest months. But –

wow! - it felt so good to come into that cool air and that wonderful house," she smiles and laughs.

"They would always bring us some drinks and sit and chat. I liked it best, though, when I was in there alone with just the wife. She always had music playing on the stereo. She'd say: 'Have you ever heard this?' That was her introduction, and then she'd rifle through their music collection and put on something, like a Beethoven symphony or a Mozart piano concerto. Incredible. And we'd just sit there and listen."

Before she went on, Blake thought some more. "Sometimes I'd page through a giant book on their coffee table. It was one of those typical books that people have, it was all about the great painters, and it had the usual Van Gogh and Monet paintings. The typical stuff. That was probably how I first became interested in art."

"That's also probably, *at least partly,* why you're right here, right now," Nick adds reflectively.

He's thinking about how Blake must have been back then. Every time she talks, more of her life slowly fills in and the corners become less dark, but his various senses of her keeps changing. He wonders over the course in her life. He wonders how she ended up right here, right at this moment.

He sees her leaving home, going to school, and eventually finding an international *something-or-other*, and eventually leaving for Europe. Working there. Studying. And then hopelessly ruining all of it.

That first night on the yacht, Nick had her pegged, and yet there was more to her story. At some point she simply figured out that she could trade on her looks, and her style, rather than her brain. She truly didn't belong here, and yet observing her as she shuffles with them through the streets, she is at ease.

"Yup," she exhales, heavily.

There is a different tone in her voice the next time she speaks. A recent memory is opened up, and suddenly it is alive again: He has heard that same voice before, but it was late one night on the yacht in the middle of the ocean, and not from her.

"Why don't you try and get it back?"

She looks dead at him, watching his expression and easily finding clues in his tightening lips and clenching jaw. The subject is grave: Money. His greed. The *crash.*

There is no preamble to her words, as if they were always on the tip of her tongue, and she has always wanted to both ask (and in so doing) state the truth. Nick has been running away from a fight. The message is clear: She knows (at least) part of him. The unhappy, miserable part.

And, sure enough, if he wants to dig into her psyche, then she will return the favor. "All of that money, your home." She feels it for a moment. "It was stolen and taken from you, so why don't you try and get it back?"

Yes - she knows Nick's story. He doesn't need to ask what she is asking about. The rocks beneath the water. Always ready to tear you apart. They both share an awkward glance. He feels a failure. Unworthy of her, or perhaps any woman. He remembers himself waking up, that first morning, on that floor in that abandoned house. His cheek rubbed red from the carpet. He remembers the cardboard boxes he came across on his long walk; someone else's place for the night. The neat little pile of cigarette butts.

"It's all gone, now," he says. He wants to innumerate all the various bank accounts run dry and unique particulars (his house, his boat, his girl) that are forever gone in the aftermath, but he resists. Remembering is also giving life to them and acknowledging his complicity in the fraud, and that is something he still wants to keep buried. All of those particulars are those things he cannot have.

She seems to grasp a final answer in his abrupt words and his unusually wounded expression, and now as they end their day together, with a sigh from her lips, she is apparently different too.

6

It is summertime and the living is pleasure-seeking, mostly.

Nick spends what time he can off the boat. He dives into the sea from the stern and pierces the water, and swims several times a day across the glassy smooth bay and then out to sea and back, where the surf is stronger and threatens and punishes him. He dawdles around the town, making small tourist discoveries: There are hidden views of the superlative coastline, and tucked away there are tidbits of history to be found in shops and in unlikely places. He walks past the inset entranceways to homes and businesses, which are curiously decorated with seemingly ancient bronze sculptures and weathered artworks, hinting at a past that is simply everywhere.

With nothing much to do, Nick ventures into a barber shop and mimes "scissors" with his fingers, and the old tough-as-nails man working the single chair invites him with a reserved smile to sit down. Strangely, Nick imagines that this man was once in the Greek navy; he recognizes something familiar in the compact and strong shape of his body and the caged manner he places his feet, as if years later he is still attempting to occupy the least amount of space possible and simultaneously steady himself against an errant wave.

Nick walks around with no destination and chats with the few locals who want to practice their English with a native speaker; he wanders along the roads that surround the village and slowly learns the complex lay of the land. He does computations in his mind, and tries unsuccessfully to convince himself that he can simply stay on this or any other Mediterranean island and live the rest of his days with the funds in his modest bank account. There is an appetizingly derelict fishing boat marooned on a beach not far away; perhaps he could return it to life and run that for few a years?

Back onboard the yacht, he finds that Santi has promised an amazing late lunch, which has drawn the whole crew and tribe home in the midst of the day. Yet there is an unexpected guest. Supposedly he is a dear friend of Radcliff's, and as he awkwardly and uncomfortably converses with the girls and Nick, they all try to appraise his story. Santi seems to know this visitor from years ago, but he doesn't seem entirely like the normal Radcliff type. Nick notices his gym-toned body; there is a thick slab of muscle forming his pectorals, something that rarely comes from anything other than serious weight-lifting or exercise.

He has a resume which includes finance and fashion work, and he has the chin, eyebrows and soft skin of a true lothario generations in the making, and also the air of someone who must attempt to prove himself at every opportunity. He says he has traveled all over and *that* particular fact explains how he got to know Radcliff, which does sound reasonable. "I'm known in Croatia and Europe as a *top* model," he says.

Nick, Blake, and the blondes share a knowing glance.

Translation: Only in Croatia.

"Well, like I said, you're going to have to wait awhile longer. He's down there writing in his memoirs," the blonde with the less-memorable nose says, gesturing below deck, and trying to end the conversation. "That's more than an hour's worth of wait time, at least."

The other blonde rolls her eyes and winks, "You mean writing in his journal. His diary?"

"I don't think so. Not exactly. Radcliff called it his memoirs the other day. I definitely remember, because you know the way he says certain words? He said it like that. *Memoirs.*"

They both smile. "Sure, it's about himself."

Normally they would send a glance to the interloper, letting him know that he is not to repeat their sarcasm to their benefactor, but in this case they really don't see the need. What they see is a man that is difficult to take seriously.

The brown-haired girl with the discreet dolphin tattoo stirs next to them and has something to add: "He's also writing a movie." Her voice is sleepy and soothing.

"You mean he's writing a *screenplay*?" The blonde with the less-memorable nose is now curious. She has visions of herself as an adored actress. "No, it's a movie. He's writing a movie."

The other blonde settles in for a long afternoon: "Naturally."

Nick knows Radcliff is sure enough down there in his office deeply engaged but probably on the secure satellite phone, arguing with someone about money or business. In fact, the appearance of the Croatian (and internationally famous model) probably has something to do with his finances.

Radcliff rarely signs his name to anything these days, nor does he explicitly own much except for the company that counts the yacht among its assets. The best way that Radcliff can ensure a private and discreet interaction are conversations and exchanges of information that occur in person. His insistence that the girls dump their electronic gadgets seemed more likely with each passing day, until it came, and then it was hard to imagine that he had *ever* allowed such external communications and broadcasts. Once Radcliff learned that people sitting in front of computers on the other side of the globe could activate cameras on computers and phones on *his* boat, and without anyone's knowledge or consent, it sent him into a tirade. Could they turn on microphones too, and listen? Of course they could.

Nick gathers he wants extra insulation and indemnity against all threats, real and imagined. The Italian government sent a shockwave through a certain group of society when they began explicitly targeting owners of luxury items, including owners of new Ferrari's and Lamborghini's for tax evasion, and found that the vast majority of new owners hid behind thinly constructed shadow organizations and fraudulent income disclosures. Their investigations were made all the easier by the electronic trails and correspondence that documented every errant step. Nick read in the paper that the sales of exotic cars in Italy fell off by eighty percent within the quarter, and a similar icy chill has run through the boat.

Even when they hit hotels, shops and restaurants it is Nick or one of the blondes who signs the bill, and Nick assumes that he himself is the go-to man for more than he realizes. Radcliff tells Nick when to call in trades to brokers and verify funds in accounts; Nick pretends to ignore the numbers and transactions, yet at this point he has talked often enough with people on the other end of the phone that his voice is now familiar to a handful of managers in banks around Europe. He (and his disengaged voice) provide half of the credentials. The other half is Radcliff using some covert system that keeps him at arm's length, one which Nick cannot identify even if he bothered to look more closely but gathers is nothing other than another minion (like Nick) somewhere else responding to messages and prodding.

So when Radcliff is down in his office, door shut, he is not only practicing his dark financial arts, but he is also writing his memoir, and writing his movie apparently. No matter the Croatian's importance or friendship, he must wait.

Yet as if on cue, Radcliff appears from below and ambles over almost as if he can sense the need for his social charm. In an exaggerated gesture he pats his fellow aristocrat on the back, and coos his *dear friend* shtick.

"Rami, old buddy, how are you? Haven't seen you in – *well* – it's been a little bit, hasn't it? I wasn't expecting you this early," and then they are back down below and into his office as Radcliff gently steers him to a friendly harbor. Nick distinctly gets the impression that, in fact, it was only recently the two old friends saw each other.

Little private oddities like this are nothing new to the girls, and Radcliff's universe, both on and off the boat, must seem disconcertingly conventional to those who have played in these sorts of waters for very long. Their excessive lunch is just about ready, but when one of Croatia's top male models appears again from down below, without Radcliff for support, he is eager to quickly leave the boat. Before he steps off into the awaiting skiff, however, he makes an overly friendly pat of Blake's backside. It seems for a moment as if he is claiming some sort of clandestine ownership of her.

Anyone who happens to remember those awkward grade school presentations, with their school's social worker, regarding *good* and *bad touch* are surely thinking this is a fine example of one variety. They definitely take note: this touch is definitely bad. An inaudible shiver goes around the group as the Croatian runs the palm of his hand along Blake's side, and then maneuvers to recklessly feel the lower quadrant of her backside.

She squirms away and gives him a withering look, and Nick is moments away from simply tearing out this man's lungs and feeding them to the fish, yet he stops short when he appraises the unknown quantity of this *friend* of Radcliff's. Since his earliest days on the boat Nick has regarded his difficult position with a bemused detachment, but lately it has taken on a new form. He looks at the Croatian, and simply hates the covetous way the man looks at Blake as he says his final disingenuous "goodbye."

Nick knows something is moving within him, and he considers the haphazard way he has followed two vastly different athletic competitions over the years: The heavyweight boxing champion of the world, and the fastest man to swim a hundred miles across open water. He has always followed the top competitors in both these fields with an intellectual interest, but that is now changing, even as the Croatian climbs down the ladder on the side of the yacht, lowers himself into the skiff, and motors away.

Nick suddenly grasps something: The first competitor is someone who can fight anyone and win. While the other is someone who can escape and not get caught. Nick feels the fascination shift. Today, he only has interest in the person who can fight and win.

•

I can't make any mistakes. Nick's girlfriend said the words like it was her ultimate truth. The problem was that she was still trying to figure out if Nick was one of those horrible mistakes. She thought there was a chance she was going to slip up and say "Yes" to him when she shouldn't. Then she would be with him, and in a way that would be her undoing.

He tried to reach for her hand as they all posed for a picture on his sailing boat. The afternoon sky blossomed an orange-yellow glow around the marina and cast everyone in a romantic light. Nick and his girl were crowded on deck with old and new friends; it was one of those spontaneous parties that always turn out better than expected, and which people talked about for months afterwards. Someone found the inspiration to capture the moment for posterity, stepped down on the dock for the complete view, and pulled an impressive camera from a bag. With some prodding, everyone assembled in a line for the photograph. Years later, Nick would go back to that photograph, as if it were an old elementary school class picture and identify everyone by their face, by their expressions (which seemed to tell everything about them all at once), and then he would smile. Or maybe frown at the way their various lives had unfolded.

And there she was. Standing next to Nick. Like all of them, his girlfriend's entire character could be found, if you looked hard enough. Still, Nick sometime ran his hand through her hair like he didn't understand the word *mistake*, or the stiffened jaw she offered, or the manner in which she tended to push him away.

Nick wasn't her first choice – clearly - but that particular fact didn't matter, because this was that particular time in his life. It was the time when he could fall head over heels for a girl, just because of the way she put on her lipstick. Or in her case, the way she pulled her keys from her purse and then curiously twirled them around her finger. It was as if she was a gunslinger showing off a quick-draw technique. It was also the one habit of hers that seemed unconsciously joyful and lighthearted. The rest of her, Nick noted, was focused on some point in the distance. Reading closely, it was doubtful that Nick would help her get there.

To his eye she wasn't even attractive in the conventional sense, which in a contradictory way made her even more beautiful. It even made Nick more certain of his love for her. She was alert and measured. She balanced people and responsibilities perfectly. One day per weekend was all he got with her, because that was all she needed to give him to keep him in her orbit. She walked out to her car early on Sunday mornings and said goodbye with a kiss on his lips, and pulled her keys from her purse and twirled them around her finger. But later, just when Nick was sitting alone in his kitchen and inattentively reading a magazine (he was sometimes sure there would never be anything lasting between them), his phone would ring and they would talk. And suddenly he was back to the same place. He was glimpsing the finishing line with her and yet unable to draw any closer.

But she *must* have made mistakes. She must have misjudged something, because long after Nick finally decided that he *had* to let her go, and he slowly dismissed her from his life, and convinced himself she was made for someone else, she called again.

They dated in a conventional manner (sometimes

spending all weekend together) and it all seemed inevitable. She loved him in her tragic and half-compromised way, and perhaps that was enough. But in truth, he needed her in a way that might have sent her running somewhere else if she ever truly saw the passion in his heart. And occasionally he let the intensity of his need show in full view.

"No," she said taking his hand and lifting it away from hers. "It's too hot out today."

Nick quieted the voice inside that said *I am replaceable; I am merely filling a role.*

The camera snapped with a flash and caught him at that juncture. The friends gathered around and congregated in line on the deck of the boat. The orange-red sky diminishing with the hours. The picture, if you looked hard enough, showed everything. And when the news of Nick's financial ruin truly impacted her in full, one thing became evident. She had made a definite decision: It was clear that Nick was, indeed, a mistake.

Now, Nick thinks, it sometimes seems Blake makes *only* mistakes. And she is now this girl whom he cannot fully run away from. Even when that is all he wants to do.

She does everything her way, and yet at the critical moment she takes an errant or provoking step to self-sabotage. But in one manner she may have smartened up and learned how to play the game. She wants to keep Nick at a safe distance, especially when it is just the two of them on the deck of the yacht in close proximity, or like today as they walk together toward the windmills. On the boat they talk frequently, and they hold conversations past a reasonable amount of time for two people in opposite corners of the ring. Sometimes they take up positions that urgently remind him of that night not so long ago with his Hungarian lovely.

Blake leans against the railing, and he minds the wheel of the boat. The breeze twirls around her. He is secretly crushed. Nick avoids looking in her direction, because he can't see into her eyes without falling into her. But thankfully, when she sits down near him, it is still always with a certain amount of safe space between them. Still, he sometimes breathes in her air, and notices that her hair does *not* smell like vanilla, but instead, strawberries. He listens to a sound she makes, a sort of "ummm" before she speaks reflectively. She gathers her words, and in her pauses he hears those little silver bracelets clinking in the wind. She has her own voice, and he is simply forced to listen to it above all else.

He notices the way she makes small confessions to him hidden in larger stories. "We weren't poor," she says about her time growing up in Missouri, and following an earlier thread, "we were destitute."

At those times, Nick thinks he understands. She is broadcasting a clear message: She is never going back to that life of needing and not having. She only wants men like Radcliff who can dispense riches to her, or more likely hold her over that pit of despair, and yet not drop her in.

Nick dissects her. He wants his critical eye to send her somewhere else and for her to stop wandering into his thoughts with that carefree walk and her sprawling stance. There is always that first touch of her hips resting against his. And that face of hers which hides something he still tries to dismiss. Freckles starting in the summer sun. He wonders over her, and how wrong he was about her.

In fact, she *isn't* near the perfectly groomed-woman that he first surmised that night on the yacht, and he wonders how his trained eye missed so much. He saw that occasional clinched smile that bared her teeth, and he observed that self-conscious brush-away of her hair which demonstrated she was new to all of this. But there was some other strange curiosity that pushed her into the rest of it.

She allows herself to spend too much currency gazing at jeweled necklaces, which shouts *Danger!* to anyone with a hint of imagination. She almost never talks about school or art, or the old masters that supposedly inspire her, but with a defiant voice she shares a story about a time she once neglected to return an engagement ring, instead substituting a fake diamond and giving the forgery back to her suitor. Apparently she eventually sold the real jewel to a dealer and pocketed the considerable money. At the time she told the story it seemed the other girls on the boat were scandalized, and yet they understood the urge to shift the balance of power; Nick wondered at her audaciousness and small-time con, and wondered what else it really said about her.

He wonders, too, over details of her appearance. She failed to grow her hair long and flowing into a modelesque demonstration of femininity, though her short little cut covers them all in confidence. Sometimes she wears her lipstick far too brightly and overtly, like another beauty with a slurring Hungarian accent once did, as if testing a boundary. Maybe she was announcing to the world that the façade was now truly over, and the truth was finally going to be revealed. Yes – he noticed that she *does* in fact sometimes hide her little tea-stain of a birthmark on her arm under makeup, and yet those are the very times when she retreats into a shell.

He thinks: She holds big pieces of herself back and shows too much of the other twilight side.

"I was a prickly little rebellious girl," she says describing herself back before she left home. Nick can imagine her clear as day. Nick guesses that she needed to pushback. She needed to fight the world before she really understood just what she was able to offer, and it was probably a difficult thing to be friends with her. She says, "The one thing I learned: Life is better for little rebellious boys."

As they leave the fringes of the village, the windmills are perhaps an hour's walk away. Together they both move forward, often in silence, Nick's mind running and thinking and filling the space between them. The road leads them to a good departure point, and so they decide to travel across the broken landscape. Ahead they see an old and barely visible path that seems to lead up towards their destination. The path flows up and away, and turns and twists, like an earth-colored ribbon.

There are occasional low-lying clouds that are waiting to coalesce into a larger single bank of grey clouds and which hint at rain. As they follow the path and gain in elevation, the climate becomes more hospitable and amenable to vegetation; soft grass and plants grow on the hill sides. The air becomes colder, and damp, almost. Soon there is a generous amount of rich-looking soil that signals a different place altogether, and which was completely unsuspected when they first regarded their expedition.

•

In the expanse they hear tin bells ringing from some unknown source.

"Goat bells," Nick says, looking across to a ridge and sighting the animals grazing on the side of the slope. The dull yet tin-sounding ring seems to carry an impossible distance in the wind. As they follow the trail, the now very distant sound of the ocean's waves breaking on rocks faintly comes and goes depending on whether they walk over the crest of a rise, or travel down into a depression. Directly out to the water from their position is a strong cliff face, and every so often a particularly large wave rumbles against it, though the sound only reaches them many seconds afterwards.

The path they follow is narrow and beaten down into the surface as if it were a century in the making yet over the last decades was forgotten. It follows a slope and climbs and falls from view so that they are never sure how close to the summit they truly are. The grass is now short and surprisingly lush, and appears like alpine vegetation that thrives in its environment but is also limited by some hidden force. After a few minutes Nick stops to survey the landscape, as if committing it to memory.

"The rocks look extra *rocky*," Blake says with a smile and with genuine astonishment. "It's just like they were made for this particular spot and then perfectly placed on the grass by someone."

She bends down to pick up a small fragment of a larger rock and she rolls it around in her fingers to judge its consistency and weight. She hands the fragment to Nick who tries unsuccessfully to ply an even smaller bit off with his fingernails, and then places the rock in his pocket as a souvenir.

"It must be the green of the grass," he says. "It's so deep. I'll bet it's good goat food, too." He turns to look at her, and she is alive like the rest of it.

At each rise it seems they must be at the top, but then there is another hill until finally they find the summit, which is plainly announced by the sight of their goal: a series of ancient windmills assembled from carved grey and white stones that stand facing the sea as if they are timeless sentinels. Up close the structures appear surprisingly large and imposing. The cylindrical bodies are rugged and everlasting, but the wood of their doors and windmill blades are weathered and seemingly near the end.

Still they have been in use at some point within the last several years, as indicated by the tattered white sail-like cloth that once captured the wind, which is now faded and torn.

It flutters and rasps on the blade's wood skeleton and announces the rolling clouds, which are perhaps soon to cover the hillside in a dense fog.

The thatched roofs of the windmills are makeshift and in need of repair; Blake finds one windmill without a door, and walks in. She examines how the sunlight shines through the roof, and how it makes breaks and patterns on the dirt floor. Inside she stays, and then takes a deep breath: There is the smell of the damp soil, which enters her like a perfume. There is also the fragrance of moss growing in the corners, and the faint smell of death and decay that says something else entirely.

Outside, now, she lies down on the grass and props her back against one of her *perfectly placed* rocks and looks out on the ocean. Nick is nearby, watching as the clouds a few miles away begin pressing against the island, but for now the view that holds Blake and Nick is expansive. The whitecaps on the blue sea are like a family to the scattered rocks and stones on the green hills, but instead, they slowly move towards the land and appear and then disappear. Blake and Nick listen to the distant waves breaking on the cliff face, which now sound like an almost indiscernible thunder; if they were to go to the edge of the round hillside and look straight down, they would find a long fatal drop to the water and boulders below.

There is neither the sight nor the feeling of another living person for miles around them, and it is possible for Blake to imagine that they are the last two people on Earth. Nick sits down and lays his head into the grass and looks into the sky. They might have been a couple, but for that space between them.

"I wonder," she says with a smile, "how long they've been here, just looking out over the sea like us?"

She turns her head to study the closest windmill for a moment, trying to judge its age. Nick turns as well to view the sight, but instantly his eyes fall on her; the only motion is her hair tossing a bit in the wind, and then his eyes fall on her neck and the color of her skin, which is fair, but changed in the summer sun. She responds for him: "Several hundred years, at least, don't you think?"

"This is one of those places," he says, answering a question she only hinted at.

They sit in silence until she finally speaks, and removes one more mystery that surrounds her, while creating another. "I suppose I should tell you. I met a Hungarian girl a few weeks ago near Portofino. She told me about your boat. That's how I knew to look for it."

Of course Nick knows instantly who she is talking about; she has never left his mind. Blake is talking about *her*. How is that possible? He tries to hide the gravity in his voice. "Really? What did she say?" He knows his voice betrays too much.

"She was going to try and hitch a ride. Earn some money, the usual."

The usual. Nick lets the information move around in his head. "But that wasn't all of it, was it?"

Blake's voice is quiet now. "No. There was something wrong. She was trying to get away from something."

"Did she say that?"

"No. Not straight out. She barely talked with anyone, but I pieced it together. She needed a sure thing. The big blue yacht with the single mast. That was what she said. It was an escape, because she, or whatever she was into, was falling apart. That much I got. And then later when I was trying to, *you know,* find something else that's how I recognized the boat."

Nick stifles his voice. It seems they are all running away from something, or maybe just trying to somewhere to land. He lets Blake's small admission vanish and apparently drift off into the wind. He wonders: What is Blake running from?

And perhaps, he wonders, if Blake is *still* running and perhaps she will soon leave again. He doesn't want to know. Not at this moment. As much as she exposes something in him, and tortures him, it is impossible to imagine his world without her in it. His mind works: What about *her*. What was his one-time Hungarian lovely trying to get away from?

He can't shake the feeling. An icy grip takes over and pulls at his ankles, from the depths below. The feeling runs a desperate, clawing hand over his skin.

He says it: "I think our Hungarian girl tried to get away. But I know she didn't make it."

•

There were many nights when Nick stayed up top, sitting on the deck of the yacht far into the small hours of the morning. The boat was anchored at such times, and it wasn't going anywhere, and it didn't need anything. He had no jobs to finish and there were no chores or seemingly endless lists of minutiae to occupy him or his mind, and then he might concentrate, and it seemed the night sky was always right there, and it merged imperceptibly into the ocean. He knew by that time of night, Radcliff had taken his way with one or two - or maybe all of the girls at once - and afterwards maybe one of them made it to the galley and fixed Radcliff a drink, or perhaps (at his behest) a stronger concoction to ease him into sleep. And sometimes, one of the girls would wander up on deck and ask Nick to fix her something special as well, and no doubt she would later drift off to a better place. And so Nick would go down into the galley and put together a little something for whomever *she* happened to be at the time. And she would smile, or not, and then disappear.

Yet often before falling asleep Radcliff would hold court, doing what he could to educate his flock as to the ways of the world, or perhaps by reading a passage from a favorite book, or poem, or often playing music on the enormous audio system, as if he thought of himself as their benefactor in many subtle ways beyond the obvious. He regularly chose Sibelius, putting a CD into the system, and Nick received a second-hand illumination many nights as well. The orchestra rose from the speakers in the bedroom, traveled through the closed door, down the hallway and then finally issued into the outside air and into his ears.

On many nights Nick thought about it: Radcliff in bed with a martini in his hand while contemplating the final movement of Sibelius, *Number Five.* Perhaps, also with one of the girls curled up adoringly around his middle. How nice for him.

Nick always stayed on deck, and always listened to the last strains of Sibelius's heartbreaking symphony powering over everything. The French horns would constantly be there with Nick, and they would always be rolling their heroic arpeggios across eternity.

And yet now, as Nick lays in the grass looking up at the sky, and views the stoic windmills next to them, he knows it is *her* music. He knows it is Blake's music as well.

The clouds are pressing on, gathering and swirling in. He reaches over for Blake's hand, which now rests beside him. She returns his touch with a clasp around his fingers that empties his soul and fills it up again. Suddenly there is her breath in his, and then a crashing down all around him. He is urgent and unrelenting, and she is simply lovely. There is the wrenching pull of a woman he desires beyond all reason, and his impossible dream.

Although his body is seemingly invulnerable and unflinching, she is gentle and caring with him. She softly touches his face with her hand; he buries his head into the crook of her neck. Around the two of them, the clouds are now joining together and forming a single mass of oppressive grey, and the air temperature creeps down many degrees and covers them in a blanket of fog and mist. She holds onto him, and her bare skin presses into the lush grass leaving an imprint of her back. He kisses her and tastes her every way he knows how, because it can't last.

He wants to take her in hand and never let go, but it is more than simply the two of them together against the world. He says her name with love: "Blake," as if *that* will somehow keep her with him. The wind picks up and urges their clutching and their embrace to last longer than either of them will ever admit to each other. There is Blake with her conflicted loyalties and needs. And what does Nick have in return?

He has only some drive that comes into focus when they lay together in the aftermath, and Blake finishes telling him the story: It is of the odd Hungarian girl, and her memorable slant of a stand as she looked into shop windows and wandered the island, and something that she once did that she wasn't supposed to do. The way she understood the end was drawing up near.

And in the last chapter of the story he hears that one particular name that makes him despair – *Johansen.*

Nick listens. He hears everything. He hears a voice now sinking into his chest in a new way; he hears the fabric tatters of the windmill's blades fluttering and rasping as a squall moves in.

Nick knows: Something has reached its end.

7

Opening a preferred *speciale* account in Italy's Pomona Banca always involves a certain amount of tradition.

After the initial introductions and back-and-forth exchanges of information are complete, you are removed from the action and kept waiting for a few minutes in a beautifully furnished office. Periodically someone appears and informs you that there are just a "few last details" to be arranged before everything is in order. Soon, a charming woman wanders in and asks if you would care for an espresso while you wait, which she makes quickly and with an expert hand. Everything else however always seems as if it is taking just a bit too long, and in Nick's case he is starting to wonder if his ruse is falling apart.

Nick is now a low-grade fraudster. One part of his life has ended, and now a new part is beginning. He is trying to *not* think about Blake, and that warmth as her hip rested so flirtatiously (even from the first) against his. He is scamming – but his target is also one of the many other scammers. He has Radcliff's accounts and numbers. He has Radcliff's birthday, pin numbers, Radcliff's mother's maiden name, his passport number, his signature, his account numbers and balances, and the list goes on. Critically, he has that same voice, which has talked pleasantly on the phone over the last several years to people on Radcliff's behalf, but whom he now meets in person. They think they *know* him, and that makes all the difference when one or two hiccups emerge.

Yet suddenly there is a small flawlessly dressed and coiffured group through the door and they are showering him with attention. His ruse must be working. He sits behind a desk with a computer prominently displaying his accounts and the various balances, transfers and trades - past and present. Voices speak and a finger points to large numbers and columns on the screen: "It is here and here. Yes?"

"Yes," Nick returns, with a pleased tone, and he is only partly acting. There are smiles and apologies ahead of time for any problems or delays that might be encountered, and also for deficiencies in their Italian-accented English, which is actually exceptionally precise and easy to understand.

Heartfelt invitations are given to Nick to please stop by and visit them whenever he is in the city again, even if there is no need for their services. "We hope you are satisfied. Anything we can do, please let us know." Whatever problems Nick imagined he would need to overcome, or that perhaps might scuttle his endeavor entirely, are nonexistent. He sees how easy this first part is, but it is the next where the danger lies. He smiles, and he returns what he hopes is an untroubled and weightless good-bye, and then he is out the door with several important pieces of paper and cards in his jacket.

The first moment of truth was inside the hotel's lobby, back on Crete. He had shown his smiling face to the same man, who did indeed remember him (even without his passport), and then that same man went directly to the hotel's safe and retrieved the same old pillowcase, which again seemed surprisingly heavy, but now suddenly momentous. Nick thanked him, and surreptitiously sent a few hundred euros across the counter. "I'll need a few minutes, and then may I purchase an additional few weeks?" And again, there was that same atmosphere of nonchalant professionalism: "Of course."

Sitting on a leather couch in the lobby, Nick pulled his own phone from the pillow case, and then all of the other devices. Surely, he looked strange to anyone who happened to glance in his direction, spreading the large assorted group of electronics to his side and pushing all of the power buttons (phones, tablets, e-readers) and everything else that Radcliff had earlier identified as contraband.

And then, on his own phone, Nick brought up Radcliff's bank of choice and his hub apparent, at least for the Zynnex accounts. The same accounts that funded the girls' ongoing retail and service adventures in shops and spas, and which he used to finance his travel with. The same accounts that funneled and channeled money for the yacht, and other basic necessities. On the screen for "username", he entered: "Dolphintattoo" (Radcliff's moniker, for at least several years) and then Radcliff's current password: "DianaJuly_1".

As expected the website responded, but there was a problem. The bank's website was duly noting that Dolphintattoo was attempting to access an account from an un-vetted source: it didn't recognize Nick's phone, and would therefore block the user.

However…

Would – perhaps? - the user care to have a confirmation code sent to the associated and *correct* cellphone, which could then be entered into the website to verify his or her identity? Nick smiled. Of course. Yes. The user would, indeed, like to receive a confirmation code.

Within seconds the brown-haired girl with the dolphin tattoo's phone was buzzing on the leather couch and the text message was revealed. Of course it was going to be her phone that allowed him to crack the barrier. Of course the brown-haired girl was the other minion (like Nick) who responded to Radcliff's prodding. The Dolphintattoo name wasn't even slyly misdirecting to someone else. He would bring her phone along with him, as well.

Nick entered the code on the screen of the phone into the bank's website, and as simple as that, the world changed. Nick had dipped his toe into different waters, and it was almost scarily easy to accomplish for someone with his knowledge and motivations.

How long will it be before Radcliff starts piecing the trail together, Nick wonders? How long until he realizes the fraud? Hours or a few days, perhaps.

This *speciale* account is only going to last one day before Nick moves the money somewhere else. What he really needs is a trusted friend, or accomplice that is unknown to anyone in Radcliff's circle. Nick considers trying to fabricate a fake ID, but he knows nothing about such things. If he was feeling even more reckless, he could always try to get ahold of some of his connections. The same people he dealt with over the years when procuring drugs, illicit and otherwise, for Radcliff. There is soon likely to be plenty of ill-will and suspicion there, however, and it is probably best to just stay away.

He will need to liquidate and turn all of these accounts into physical cash within a handful of days, and then find a safe place to store the money. With the right pressure points bank accounts and transfers can be traced as easily as phone calls, and Radcliff will bring in the heavy operators immediately - even the supposedly anonymous accounts that he hid behind shell-corporations will be quickly revealed.

The lessons Nick has learned from studying Johansen's scheme are mere stopgaps and amaturistic attempts at a larger scam. He knows that Radcliff will not approach his reprisal formally. There will be no official inquiry or legal action to address Nick's theft, which is a theft of an ill-gotten treasure trove. Radcliff cannot risk exposing his own maleficence or dubious financial dealings, even if there were to be few actual consequences to his empire. He will skirt the moored-in establishment, as he always does. He will bring in his own people, who bring in their own people, and they will use their own rules and their own methods. There is no doubt in Nick's mind that he has only a modicum of true freedom.

He takes a cab to the train station, stopping first at a few shops along the way. Nick wants to buy new clothes. He wants to shed everything, his possessions and his identity, yet again. But this time, by choice, not by unfortunate circumstance. From the racks he carefully selects a new wardrobe; it will be camouflage and self-reinvention. He finds a posh crushed-blue velvet jacket; he finds a number of flawless white shirts, which he knows he will need to rough up a touch. From the yacht, he took his beloved bicycle out of pride and out of necessity, before selling it for a pittance at the first opportunity. He found that fragment of rock in his pocket, Blake's perfect rock, and saved that as well. Again, he thinks, I'm starting from almost nothing.

But this time is different.

Smiles and acknowledgements go back and forth

between him and account managers and there is an instant rapport. Nick turns on the charm and does what he can to mimic Radcliff's brilliant social grace. He smiles; he glad-hands and assumes a familiar tone. It's as if they have been friends for years. The banks want his business. He could wrangle a sizeable loan from them, if he wanted to really leverage his position and had the time and latitude. He pretends that he indeed is more than the mere captain and crew member of that wonderful boat, and they are more than happy to believe him. Nick empties minor business accounts used to sop-up income from the boat and Radcliff's properties; accounts that Radcliff created in a vain effort to attain his lifelong goal of not paying a single British pound in taxes. All of these are Radcliff's low-tier accounts. They are the cream which Nick can skim, and which are the most obvious opportunities provided by Radcliff's tax dodges and far-flung empire.

The system is broken and weak for a short while, and he wants to do as much with the open gates as possible before they close.

Soon Nick will be in Switzerland, which is home to the last bank he will visit. Any additional subterfuge, fraud, and law-breaking with Radcliff as his target, and Nick recognizes that he is simply being greedy and taking far too much risk. Whatever form and shape his greed took last time after all, was what drove him into naïve and ignorant mistakes.

•

On the train to Zurich it occurs to him that he is becoming like *them.* He has moved away from the scavenger, and he is no longer the hyena routing in the leftovers simply to find a place to call home for a few nights. He is, also, no longer the captain of that magnificent yacht (for all of the boat's compromises and strained environment). What is he now? He is smiling and waltzing into offices as if they were a small part of *his* domain. His clothes are immaculate, but not too immaculate. His hair and appearance are clean and respectable, but not too respectable. The person he is imitating simply doesn't care that much about appearances; that person doesn't need to. He does whatever he feels like, because he is beyond social criticism. Thus, his collar is now just a small bit frayed; his pants could really use another pass with an iron; and his hair is slightly conservative and out of sync with the latest fashions.

Nick is exploiting a weakness, and he is taking some sort of revenge, but not on the person who is truly due. He plies that name in his head, again.

There is still that sour taste in his stomach, but it is even worse today; perhaps it will always be there? Out of the train's window, the landscape blurs as he catches glimpses of farm houses and large rectangular fields of wheat that are nearing maturity. On the horizon he sees some unknown city, and then the faint brown of pollution that hangs in the sky. He quickly finds a notepad and pen in his backpack; he adds up numbers in his head and then commits them to the paper and is surprised at the sums. Yes, if he wanted, he perhaps now could find that little island and buy that derelict fishing boat and survive indefinitely. But is survival enough? And *still* he would always be looking over his shoulder.

He wonders what Radcliff is truly capable of when pressed. Nick knows much of Radcliff's underbelly: the drugs, the embarrassing stories of him and his various girls, the charitable donations that are, in fact, nothing but shallow schemes to enrich his friends and save him another ten-thousand come tax day. All of this is potentially upsetting legal and social fodder, and will gnaw at Radcliff's sense of security day and night.

It is knee-deep in tourist season, and the trains in Italy are crowded and inundated by the sheer mass of humanity. There are people who don't have a place to sit, and they stand at the ends of the rail cars, amidst luggage that is piled at their feet and look out the windows, no doubt anticipating the next stop when perhaps a seat will become available. He overhears conversations and resists the urge to introduce himself and re-enter some sort of normal life. In the seat just behind him, he hears a mother and daughter recounting their favorite sights in Florence. The young girl still wants to visit Pisa, however, if only to get a picture of her supporting the famed Leaning Tower with a dramatic counter-push from her little hands, and thus keep the building from toppling over. He expects to hear pages being flipped in a guide book, but as he eavesdrops on the conversation he gathers that the mother is consulting a website for information. "*There's not a lot else there, honey*," she says, trying to change her daughter's mind.

Nick thinks back to the girls' assorted electronic paraphernalia, which are still secured in the guests' safe in a hotel back on Crete, aside from the brown-haired girl's phone that now rests in his bag. He remembers the informality and the causal way the transaction was accomplished, even a second time, and the careful way the man behind the front desk regarded him and then put Nick's face back into his own vault for use at some point in the future. Nothing else was required. Nick remembers telling Radcliff he had "taken care of it," and never bothered to mention that the location was in a hotel, not a safety deposit box in a bank. The girls' various electronic lifelines would probably sit there for months before there were any concerns at the hotel, thanks to the generous tips he shared with the staff.

Once across the border into Switzerland, the tourists recede and it is the rare occurrence when he hears English. The natives occasionally move between three languages, selecting the one right word out of perhaps dozens to make their exact point. As he changes trains at a station, he briefly helps a British couple who are flummoxed by an incongruity in the spelling of a city on their train schedule. The German name is different from the French name: it's not called *Bâle* in this part of the world but *Basel*, and he points them in the right direction. The couple shakes both of their heads at the clash in the supposedly harmonized Eurail system, and he hears the man mutter with a knowing laugh: "*The French.*"

Nick breathes a heavy sigh. This is a jumping off point.

He finds a kiosk and a vendor selling sandwiches. He lays down his Francs and remembers that handful of years past when there was no money for even just this small indulgence. He wants to commit and have faith in the enormity of his half-formed plan, but there is that doubt. He has been fighting the urge to let his mind wander to Blake.

As Nick stands there, watching the vendor bring together his late-afternoon meal, he wonders over his decision to leave without even a simple goodbye to her. He thinks he understands her allegiances and comforts himself in a paradoxical deliberation: In the weeks to come, he decides that she will certainly be yet another woman who considers him one of her bigger *mistakes*. Although in a manner, she was a small-time scam artist, and now he was showing the same nerve. (Nick abruptly thinks about the method in which Blake substituted a fake diamond for a real diamond, taking advantaged of man certainly charmed and seduced by her beautiful light.) Perhaps, Nick imagines, they now have a strange and separate balance, at last.

That realization makes him feel strangely calm, as if he were back on the yacht looking over and across the water and watching the waves move the boat as he once used to do. He can't have her in the way he needs her. The two of them will never be together. Blake desires a certain kind of person, he decides, and remembers a little aside. We weren't poor, she said - we were destitute.

It was evening, just after one of Santi's amazing and vast culinary creations had been devoured by the group, yet it was just the two of them sitting on the deck, enjoying the last rays of light in the day disappear. "Sometimes," she said, "when I was young, if I didn't have a sandwich or anything to take to school for lunch, I'd crumple up some paper and put it in a lunch bag to make the bag look full. So the other kids didn't know."

She took a big breath and remembered, as if she wanted the juxtaposition of her two lives to always be clear in her head. They sat on the deck and they shared a small laugh as their stomachs humorously rumbled and digested their food in unison and the two of them contemplated life. Around them it seemed as if the entire world was a paradise for a lucky few people. Her voice was from another place, however. "So then, when it was lunch time, before recess." she sighed, "I'd go somewhere and pretend to eat by myself. No one ever knew what I had, which was nothing."

She was trapped in a manner that Nick easily recognized; it was a variation on an age-old experience and one he had grown to know intimately.

He wonders if Blake can ever reach some different point in her life. He wonders if she will ever see that those times are behind her now. Yes - those were the tough times, but they don't have to be repeated. And, he thinks, they aren't always waiting for you around the next corner. He takes a bite of the sandwich in front of him, resting on a napkin, and tries to think about something else. He focuses on the next few critical days of his own life. This was the next step, when he would be desperately trying to out-match one particular type of man, and his various minions.

•

Radcliff, as it had turned out, was not always the shrewdest businessman, and at the beginning of the financial collapse in which world markets lost a quarter of their value, each of his positions ended up costing him tens of millions. Not only because of Radcliff's judgments, but because of the way he imagined he could brilliantly out-maneuver everyone else.

Yes. All of that was indeed the case. But yes, there was *also* the fact that Denise was the one person always answering his phone. Radcliff saw himself as the warrior-captain that could not lose, even surrounded by problematic girls. It was one of the flaws, one of the beliefs, that would later come to transform his world. And Nick's.

It started because there was a junior trader that was tracking Radcliff, like a hungry dog. He desperately wanted Radcliff as his client, his *only* client, and he had been following and sniffing around the scent for years.

His business card said "Wealth Manager" in golden font but, in truth, he did a *lot* more besides manage mere wealth and the usual trading. For one thing, he sat on people's couches and sipped tea. He made friendly and caring expressions, and quietly ate crumpets and scones in their homes. And he opened his ears. After a few minutes of his usual beginning monologue and psychological coaxing about preparing for the future and sleeping well at night (because who would deny they cared about those things?) he then listened.

He sat upright, with his legs conservatively and narrowly placed, and his well-tailored suit (in a traditionalist dark hue) showing his diminutive frame at its best, and he was even less a threat than otherwise. To the people he was talking with, he might even have appeared as the well-mannered son of some family friend. He might have been a cousin's nephew and just out of college and sincerely interested in every word that dropped from your weary lips.

He listened to once-married people bemoan the loss of their spouse, or perhaps slowly and dramatically detail the unfortunate tragedy that their children had grown into. He stirred his tea. He acted concerned. But also started to noticed trends. It seemed that more than one family was struggling. Often it was simply due to the difficulty of keeping their youngest in a *serious*ly expensive drug rehabilitation facility.

The stories started sounding alike. It was clear that money was an issue, though they pretended otherwise to the rest of the world. Each time that particular errant and drug-addled family member showed back up on their doorstep (with pinned eyes and slurred speech) the junior trader heard them exclaim that it was again thousands of pounds spent at a facility that the family really couldn't afford anymore. Sometimes, too, it was a failing business that really should have been shuttered years ago. Other times, a villa in Spain that they really couldn't afford, but kept spending money on out of some social need. There were horses and their spiraling medical bills that wives hid from their husbands. There were bad investments in real estate that husbands hid from their wives.

And each time, as soon as the junior trader heard the story, he finished his tea and complimented the fine furnishings of the house, and then he was up, and then out the door, never to return. Pleasant but abrupt.

Clearly, they didn't have the situation that he wanted to involve himself with, no matter the posh address and the Bentley (or whatever) in the drive. He wanted to pick and choose his clients differently, despite company policy, and he expected much better.

He wanted someone exactly like Radcliff.

He gleaned whatever he could from the intelligence report. A half-a-dozen residences, and *that* yacht, and who knew how much under management? And yet, this Radcliff character apparently never let anyone from the firm into his inner sanctum. This eccentric and rich headcase seemed to self-manage, which was absurd. Sure, the junior trader thought, he trades *through* us, and he uses our accountants and so on, but as the others in his firm said, "Just *try* and get in otherwise." Then they looked at each other and shared a knowing laugh.

It's been years – decades! – they said. We've got no traction. Zero. The big null and void on that all important line on your monthly report, left blank, yet again. We've had company retreats with Radcliff as our only subject of discussion. And when we come back and apply our best efforts, he still won't budge. This Radcliff fellow has seen the numbers. But it doesn't penetrate. He thinks he knows best.

Or they added conspiratorially, he is into some *seriously* shady deals, which he simply wants off the record and off everyone's radar.

But when the markets were starting their near death spiral, and yet no one seemed to gather just how bad it was going to get, the wealth manager took it upon himself to use *that* as an excuse to call and sell Radcliff uninvited, and *seriously* outside company policy. That was when Denise first answered the phone. The wealth manager dropped the well-worn name of the company. He dropped the name of the accountant. He said he just wanted to have a brief chat with Radcliff.

"I'm hoping he'll want to talk about what's going on with the economy, and how it will affect him. Maybe review his positions?"

Denise let it be known that the economy would NOT affect Radcliff in the slightest. "He's diversified," she said. "And he has the yacht." Their phone call was over.

"Yes, she's a cute little thing in person. I think she wants to be his executive secretary or something." It was Radcliff's lead accountant, relaying the facts of the situation to the wealth manager, and as he was one of the few with a glimpse into the inner sanctum, his opinion was highly valued. It hardly mattered though.

Was she, this voice answering the phone, drugged up beyond all reason? Was her frontal lobe and other brain material simply fried from too much time spent snorting up some *really* potent barbs? It was strange, because she sounded lucid. But she used the word "diversified" like it answered every question. The accountant shrugged his shoulders. Like all the managers and interested parties, he had clearly moved the matter into a different part of his thoughts.

Suddenly, the terms *sub-prime*, *loan*, and *equity* combined into nuclear waste; it had gone toxic in the markets, for good reason. The wealth manager called Radcliff, *seriously* outside of company policy, as he hoped to discuss the (perhaps) coming apocalypse and sell Radcliff on some strategies that were beyond his official capacity.

Denise answered the phone. In a pleasant tone, he dropped the name of the company into her ear. He dropped the name of the accountant. He just wanted to have a brief one-on-one with Radcliff, and perhaps evaluate his defensive positions, which he and others of his stature were surely taking up. He wanted to sit on his couch. Have some tea, and do the spiel. He wanted to find out if this Denise was simply a moron. "He's very diversified. And he has the yacht." Their phone call was over.

Other people called.

As the markets started an even greater toxic eruption, some out-of-breath fund manager called Radcliff and said he could get him eighty-five cents on the dollar for one of his positions. But Radcliff immediately dug in his heels, and said he wouldn't deal for anything less than ninety cents, and after much back-and-forth and more wasted breath, the fund manager dropped him.

A jewelry store consortium needed cash to stay afloat until the end of the year: Bank loans had dried up for even solid businesses and they were desperate to make payroll. They said they would give Radcliff his own franchise plus ten percent interest when they again broke even. Radcliff said flat out he wanted twenty percent, so they ran out on him in a panic to find some other savior.

The wealth manager called the accountant, who called

Denise. Supposedly, the accountant had straightened her out. Then, the wealth manager called Radcliff.

Denise answered the phone. "He's very busy. He's really diversified."

"Right now, you gotta grab that throttle. You gotta start that motorcycle."

Denise said, "Huh?"

The wealth manager said, "You're going to make him *millions.*" "How?" she asked, skeptically.

"Insulation," he said. "All he needs is a little bit of insulation."

•

For a change Radcliff listened. For a change he was humble. It was an emergency meeting. For once in his life, something he took ownership of *wasn't* brilliant. It was in Radcliff's London home, at 11:00 pm, while he stood there in his pajamas, and fixed a drink. And for once he set aside his pre-existing worldview, because it had gotten *that* bad.

Denise was somewhere else, and no one dared mention her. In fact, her absence in the room was felt like a ray of light between storm clouds. Radcliff dropped ice cubes into the glass with a *clink, clink* to consecrate and commemorate the occasion of this grand change. Radcliff posed standing by his alcohol cabinet, his squat and round form slightly endearing in his striped-blue pajamas, complete with funny felt-like buttons up the front, which made him seem like someone's eccentric uncle. The wealth manager finally sat on the couch, along with a few more people from the firm. Their words prodded Radcliff and hit him in the throat, and so - finally – after a near devastation, he wrested himself from the near oblivion of his highly leveraged positions. He said, yes. He would allow them in.

The near-term problem, however, was that Radcliff felt cheated.

He was owed. It seemed unlikely that markets would recover enough in time to sooth his ego and accounts, and in any event the return would be pathetic compared to where he thought he belonged. Days and weeks passed by - and then months. He kept waiting for the axe to fall on the incompetents and the corrupt that allowed this economic thing (they started to intentionally misidentify it as a "credit crunch" of all things) to happen.

He, and millions of others in similar positions, were waiting for the inevitable shakeout, but the way public figures were talking *everyone* was to blame, which was the same thing as saying *no one* was to blame. The paper ran an editorial cartoon: the bankers were pointing at the rating agencies, who were pointing at the bankrupt companies, who were pointing at the public, who were pointing at the politicians, who were pointing back at the bankers. That summed it up perfectly. Radcliff made a "harrumph." It was a circle jerk.

Radcliff had mingled enough to recognize a few things - that the wankers, the pathetic whiny little men, *were* the industry. They couldn't abide even the slightest amount of criticism or scrutiny, and so there would be none.

Radcliff knew this much: There would be no reckoning, no accounting, and no institutions, organizations, government entities, industries, businesses, or even clearly corrupt players would be held responsible. There were some secondary people and organizations doomed, but Radcliff noticed, certainly not for their participation in the great sham. The ones that fell would have fallen anyway; the market collapse just hastened their demise.

Radcliff knew something of money: The more you have, the easier it is to get even more. He maneuvered into those grey areas: offshore accounts, tax havens, and not-entirely-legal sweetheart deals from fund managers desperate to rebuild. He took advice. He wasn't particularly interested in shady deals before. Now that he had established management, it became part of his core strategy.

The wealth managers told him how to talk, if on the slight chance he ever *did* receive a visit or call from an investigative office. Be dismissive, they told him. Act outraged, they told him. Name drop, they told him – *you know who to mention.* Our friend – your friend. Wait until you actually meet one of these pushovers. It will be effortless. Park your late-model Rolls out front before they show up. Have them wait in your library. Let them see your diplomas on the wall, so they doubly know where you went to school and who you can call. Absolutely, they are embarrassingly sad. They are strivers and think they can actually be you, someday. Trust us: they are little wusses of men who pad their resumes with easy cases that they can win, and they have *no* outrage.

He listened and learned. *Insul-bloody-ation always works,* they told him, so grab that throttle. Now is the time to push! More than ever!

•

Of course the wealth managers wanted to have access to his entire empire and they wanted to see the complete picture, but he just couldn't bring himself to make that last leap. He thought: *what if they're wrong, again?* Radcliff wanted to stay involved at a certain level. They cautioned him that they couldn't be held responsible for what he didn't share. In this case, he was actually quite fine with that.

It meant that years later, and often while he was down in his office (thinking about his memoir or even writing down fragments and notes, but mostly shuffling printouts with long lines of numbers, and opening spreadsheets and tracking his returns and his losses on his own, because he didn't truly ever trust those type of men) he thought about the brown-haired girl with the discreet dolphin tattoo on her hip: Did she ever stop to examine the papers she was signing for him?

When he woke the brown-haired girl up with some Dexedrine and dragged her to the bank, did she ever wonder why *she* was the one who showed her ID and entered her pin number, and not *him*? She stayed in this dusky state between night and day, and though she didn't know it, between a member of the tribe and some distant business relation. She appeared as a useless (albeit beautiful) creature to the outside world, but could be motivated by him with simple promises, pills, and injections, and in such a way suited him perfectly. He managed her as if she were nothing but an asset to be utilized, and he teased her obvious weaknesses to make her perform as expected.

Thus, in his own amateur way Radcliff kept one piece of the puzzle to himself: several million held back and yet still earning fifteen percent, and entrusted exclusively to an oblivious and addicted minion.

Radcliff had his own little sub-empire and his own covert life raft should the impossible actually happen, and the wild storm gather and the ship sink. Sitting at his desk late one night, wearing his blue-striped pajamas with the felt-like buttons up the front, he marked the files "Tirpitz." It was in honor of the German battleship that the British kept attacking and allocating huge resources to try to destroy during World War II. He knew the story well: After twenty some missions the British finally invented and developed a purpose-built 12,000 lb. bomb, which they eventually dropped several examples of, from a high altitude.

The bombs reached supersonic speeds as they descended, and one hit the heavily armored deck of the battleship - and even then, the ship withstood the initial assault, until finally succumbing hours later with other different attacks. It was enough time for the captain to save his own skin and live to fight another day, if he so choose.

It was enough to make Radcliff smile at himself and his astute manipulation of the war. Radcliff sometimes thought: *Unstoppable*, all of this is *Un-god-damn-stoppable*. Nobody would ever guess that the brown-haired one (the girl with the recently applied discreet little dolphin tattoo, which he still didn't truthfully agree with) was the person who Radcliff anointed as his all-time most indispensable girl.

8

Blake breathes deeply and tries to rest easier. She looks out the train's window. She sees Zurich. She knows a bit: Nick is here – *probably*. And she is here because of him – *certainly*.

Radcliff has sent her to intercept him, in a sense. When he directed her and sent her, Radcliff chose his words carefully. At the time, she could see the manner he scrunched up his face in a thinking motion, the way he sometimes did, and then made his pronouncement. To her, it seemed straightforward enough, or at least as much as these sorts of messy things can be. Find him, Radcliff said. He's done something bad with some of my money, he said. It's okay, though. Just talk to him, you'll do fine. He smiled to show he was, at heart, not overly concerned. He would, of course, make it worth her while.

As she watches the city change with her approach, she keeps Nick in a certain region of her thoughts. She tries not to linger on him. She is starting to understand that Nick, apparently, is not *merely* the sort of person she imagined, but also a different sort. He is somebody, she realizes, who has some of her own characteristics, however hard she tries to justify and sometimes deny them.

Blake thinks about what she has to do just to get through this. She wonders if at some point, she has gone past a certain place in her life. She doesn't know if she can be that girl, anymore - the one who rides off into the sunset with that special man by her side. She observes and tries to approach her situation from a different perspective. It's a new city for her, but at this stage in her life she is clearly *not* arriving as a tourist, or a carefree woman with a simple agenda. Through the window, the urban area that she sees and studies is located alongside a grand lake, in a large and gentle U-shaped valley. Already, she is trying to get her bearings, but it's not quite like she expected.

Of course, what everyone who is acquainting themselves with the scene notices first is the superlative setting. And then she knows, soon afterwards, the architecture. It provides a beautiful impression, and as one of the major European cities never ravaged by war, the obvious historic prominence. But waiting for Blake, should she walk the streets and get lost, or venture past doorways and mingle around public places, is a city that is populated by an unlikely cast of characters.

There are the expected and clichéd conservative types that are easily agitated should a municipal clock display the wrong time, or perhaps by a delivery truck that annoyingly blocks a street entrance. Yet there are also a multitude of students; chemistry and other graduate students who call the city home for several years during their education. And then there are handfuls of cosmopolitan sorts who work in the many ethnic art galleries and other places of culture that climb the first parts of that beautiful "U"-shaped valley.

There are even the lowly dregs who populate the Zurich drug parks. These are the heroin addicts that flit around the edges of an otherwise steadfast culture. They can sometimes be seen lying inertly on benches and in the shade of trees.

Blake's train slows as it enters the outskirts of the city, and she sees only hints of this breadth of existence. Still, she is surprised with a glimpse into some other unruly world as they enter the rail yard, and she views the hundreds of graffiti-tagged freight cars that line the tracks. It is clear that the manicured chalets and mountain resorts are located elsewhere.

In the station, despite her better instincts she looks around helplessly. What is she to do? No answers are forthcoming from her disarrayed brain, and so she drags her bags out and into the fray of life.

A mass of taxi cabs are lined up and waiting to grab tourists and visitors, but rather than greet her with a mad dash for her fare, an orderly position leads her to the first car and driver. She gives the name of a hotel that supposedly has rooms available. This, according to a family she talked with earlier on the train. She is shuffled off in the car and begins to get a better sense of her surroundings as they cross the city. She wishes she had her phone, a computer, a handheld device, or anything to check on such things as hotels and timetables so she could plan more effectively.

But Radcliff was adamant: Cash only. No electronic trails of any kind. He wants as little "proof" of this trip of hers as possible. He even gave her some other woman's passport, with which to check into various hotels. She looks at the photograph in the passport. The woman in the photograph is close enough to her in appearance, she supposes, although the hair is wrong, and it seems (somehow) her height is wrong, and the eyes are not quite right.

One part of Blake understands Radcliff's growing paranoia, and another part questions her real role in this arrangement.

•

The hotel staff is friendly, but not forthcoming. She gets her room sure enough, but she is too insistent in her questioning regarding any information about a tall American with dark hair, who perhaps has a room here as well. Eventually, she tries another approach to get the information she wants, and attempts a more familiar tone. But (of course) the staff only answer in sound bites and canned responses. Their English is faultless and exceptionally polite, which just frustrates her more.

No one knows anything about an American named "Nick," and they look at her with an expression that says she should know better than to ask such questions. Privacy is a top concern here, if ever she ever had any doubt. She attempts to deflect them, and she asks about restaurants and then museums. She smiles and is met back with that patented neutral-staff-smile used around the world to answer the enquiries of guests like her. They are friendly but are clearly not *her* friend.

Enclosed in the hotel now, she opens the curtains to the deep windows in her room and collapses on the bed. It is near dark, and outside various house lights are turning on, and she can see the way they reveal the lay of the land as they climb higher on the other side of the city, as they follow the curve of the valley.

She rechecks the huge wad of cash in her jacket's top

pocket for perhaps the hundredth time that day. If she loses the money, which Radcliff gave her, she is in serious trouble. That admittedly large stack has to get her through all of this, and then back to the boat; in a fit of inspiration she secrets some of the cash into one of her pants' pockets and feels a little more secure.

Radcliff has sent her on a mission. And because of that, she is allowing herself to become part of something, which she only glimpses the faintest outlines of, and so she tries to trust; she tries to find her center. She knows that in this strange arrangement there are opportunities for her to exploit, if she should want to do so.

Once off the plane from the United States she had more than enough time in Paris by herself to learn the ways of a big European city, but now that seems ages ago. She had navigated the metro; she had learned the currency; she had wandered around and met people and had stereotypes smashed at every opportunity. She remembered: They weren't rude to her; they didn't take offense at her mangling of their language as she ordered food in a restaurant; they politely cautioned her away from certain places and steered her to good experiences.

But it wasn't all marvel and sophistication; there were ugly things in the shadows, and plain-old life most everywhere else. This was particularly true if you ignored the wonder of Paris, and looked at it with a more experienced eye.

It took her a few months, but she learned a few things. A beautiful and statuesque American girl with her signature style and friendly countenance made a certain kind of impact. She saw the romantic, but poverty-level standard of living in which her contemporaries wallowed, and thereafter she viewed her own priorities and experiences in a new light. She made friends. Desirable men flocked to her. She was known, without even trying to be.

Now, here she is in this Zurich hotel room, waiting and wondering. There is an anxiety drawing near. She turns on the TV and is greeted with hundreds of channels. She turns it off. The various trappings of her room are luxurious and wonderful; the furniture seems made to last thousands of years, and is elegantly functional and minimalist. She pulls a drawer open in the nightstand and feels the way it glides on its rails, as if constructed to impress even the most jaded traveler.

She remembers: In the museums and collection rooms of Paris where she studied and volunteered, she received a more skeptical reception. There, in the storage rooms, drawers were also opened by her, and they too had that oiled precision that suggested the impossible value of the contents held within. Canvases, drawings, letters, receipts, notes laid flat and protected by layers of plastic insulation and special paper, and even that paper could only be handled by gloved-hands. But still, when she looked around, it didn't feel like she belonged.

There it was, a new type of home: A room, crowded and surprisingly disorganized, at least on first impressions. Maybe she had found herself here by accident? Maybe she had been one of the lucky students that had wiggled through the cracks and found an entrance to this other world? She had to prove herself, demonstrate knowledge and competency, but as it turned out (eventually) she was rewarded with something else.

There was a sense of *growing*, slowly. She was changing and maturing, so that she could someday become equals with the true experts. She was still (naturally) just a fledgling: an inexperienced student compared to everyone else she interacted with and worked for, but she had made the trip across the ocean to be with them, and learn. They recognized her genuine knowledge and self-sufficiency within another environment. The unspoken message was clear. If she continued to follow her academic journey with the same level of perseverance, she was destined go far.

Blake knows she has found something in her travels far away from home, but always behind her she feels that desperation waiting for her to fail and stumble, just so it can catch up.

What should she do? Even at this moment, as she now moves to recline on the bed (thinking of that money in her pocket) and turning her head to watch as the lights come on around the city, she is remembering, and trying to forget.

•

Once, she sat on the floor in her little home in Paris.

Her scholarship graciously allowed for a modest single room she occupied by herself, while other students in different programs had to make do with bunk beds and crowded flats. These neighboring rooms were shared among duos of certain types. From the first days there, Blake easily recognized and spotted little pretend Audrey Hepburns. Other girls were incipient burnouts, found in equal measure to the first. One variety adopted the signature hairstyle, and feigned a ridiculous attitude of worldliness, while the other variety wasted time in their dank little rooms and demonstrated a genuine boredom with life. Even here, with all of this at their feet, they couldn't find a passion for anything or anyone.

Blake sat there on the floor in her little Paris room and listened with curiosity to the footsteps and voices moving along the hallway behind the closed door. Not only was this across the Atlantic, it was the first major city she had ever traveled to. There was a shared bathroom down the hall, which meant people were coming and going past her room at all hours of the day and night.

What would always stick with her, even decades later she knew, were the grayish bath towels for the shower; they were provided by the front desk, and one of them hung right there in front of her, over a chair. They had the same hint of stuffy mildew she had smelled once before, and even then the memory prodded her backwards. She couldn't help but think of an old hand-me-down sweater she used to wear, which had that same stuffy smell. She remembered: she was just a little child and that grey sweater didn't quite fit, and sometimes when she pulled it over her head she got lost in it, and then that mildew scent seemed to be everywhere. The sleeves were too long and the neck was two-sizes too large. It was also stretched larger by years of prior use; it was warm, however, and despite the odor, and obvious holes and tears, it was hers.

That was until one Christmas when she went to Kansas City to see her cousins. There, she observed. She saw how well they lived. She saw her cousins' mother turning up the thermostat when it was cold but without engaging in a shouting argument with their father. For dinner they sat down at the table and they ate fresh bread. She recognized, as she looked at her relatives, that she was the only person at the table who had any concept (or contempt) about sewing and mending old clothing. It was incredible. On this side of the family, when a T-shirt developed a hole, that shirt was tossed out or used as a rag. It was not patched up for another season's wearing. Yet, there she sat, in that tattered sweater.

She pretended to lose that favorite sweater of hers. When she got back Missouri and her mother demanded to know why she wasn't wearing it and where it was, she cried and told a lie. In fact, she had intentionally left it behind one day when they were out playing *hide and go seek*, but that was her little secret. That small deception was something she would always hold on to.

Blake curls up on the pristine bed in the Zurich hotel, and remembers the time past: After weeks in Paris there was an ordinary late night, and (as usual) she spent the time at the far end of the day alone in her room, thinking and wondering. She lost herself over her future and over her past.

Sometime she chewed on her fingernails and then had to plead with herself to stop. Sometimes she sat there and rocked back and forth, overcome with anxiety. In front of her, the bath towel that was hanging over a chair wafted its scent into her nose, and she was suddenly back in that park playing *hide and go seek*. She was running off so she could discard that sweater deep within a bush and then cover it up with leaves, where it would stay forever hidden.

She remembers how she sat on the floor of that little Paris room and broke down over that discarded sweater. Even now, thousands of miles away and a half-a-lifetime ago, she knows that time playing with her cousins, and that act of defiance and deceit, was her first truly horrible moment.

Yet from that time on, Blake took to life in a new way; as she grew into a young adult it was clear she wasn't like the others in school or others around the town, and her burgeoning sense of aesthetics was merely one of a thousand differences. She liked listening to music that her friends derided as stuffy and snobby. She collected and paged through magazines and tutored herself on women who seemed to possess some sort of *it* – she read their words, marveled at their different lives, and paid particular attention to their clothes, noting elements of design and color and fit. She paid attention to how she looked with differently styled hair, deciding eventually that her red hair wasn't the curse the childish taunts told her it was.

When the meanest girls sang and teased "Better *dead* than *red…*" she hardened inside, yet made the supposedly misfit hair color her own, even dying it a bolder color of red at times. She found books on art history from the school library and educated herself, for no other reason than the subject interested her. She found a picture of a self-portrait by Dalí, and the obvious humor and self-criticism of the painting piqued her curiosity much further. When she was interviewed for the scholarship years later and they asked why she was applying to go abroad, her response – "To get the hell out of Dodge" – was only partly a lighthearted joke. She simply wanted to get away from where she was.

Nick is here, somewhere, according to Radcliff.

Zurich is home to the last bank and account he will likely poach. Find him, or perhaps he will find you. Radcliff didn't seem angry when he said the words. The accounts are marked "Tirpitz," he said with apparent insignificance, and handed her various sealed envelopes and papers and gave her instructions. He didn't explain the odd German name; he didn't give a sense of gravity. He was his usual charming self, and he said that he would even let Nick keep some of the money as a sort of reward for eventually doing the right thing. At the time it all seemed simple and direct.

Aside from the passport that isn't hers. Aside from the cash-only transactions. Aside from the strange protectiveness and paranoia that is starting to make itself clear.

Blake kicks off her shoes and stares out the window as nighttime gradually reveals itself across Zurich. She looks at the lights and wonders if Nick is somehow looking out at the same view. Or perhaps he is even within one of those lights she now sees?

Radcliff expects her to check in once a day with a phone call from her hotel and with an update as to the search and her efforts. Radcliff gave her more than enough money to see her through this. Radcliff gave her bits of information to use and a series of incidental tasks to help in her endeavor. It shouldn't be that difficult, really. Yet what will she do she wonders, if she actually finds Nick?

•

He recognized her. Of course he recognized her, even from far behind as she walked down the platform at Zurich station.

He was keeping a reasonable distance; she would certainly recognize him, and of course he has done this before and knows the routine. He has often helped Radcliff and other similar people who found themselves in a bad situation or with the need for a little errand that they would rather not publicize or make known in any other company. For the time being, he was simply an observer.

He stepped into the flow of passengers disembarking from the train and kept his eyes on Blake as they moved forward towards the station's lobby, and then observed as she mingled among families, tourists, and every other type. Overhead there were the large blue train schedules and higher still the drab grey of the metal roof. People pulled luggage behind them, and she wandered back and forth seemingly without direction and with a heavy bag over her shoulder and two other bags dragging behind her. Blake, and her clothes. Radcliff had jokingly warned him, and he nodded knowingly.

He was there, in the various railcars with her, making sure that she did indeed change trains, and that she did indeed follow the correct route. He was making sure that she traveled all the way to the city and that she didn't, instead, decide to simply bolt and leave with the money for parts unknown. She was following directions, and he was watching to make sure she did as she was told, like the good girl she was.

He saw her hair and her height. That familiar quadrant of her backside, which made that shape. He recognized in her preoccupied wavering around the station's lobby that she was a woman who was perhaps out of her element, in a difficult set of circumstances, and that she was tasked with a job to accomplish that she only partly understood. How could she even imagine the rest of it?

He watched her, as she found her way to a cab and the car drove away, presumably to a hotel. It didn't matter which hotel, because Radcliff would hear from her, and he would hear from Radcliff. He didn't even need to follow her from here on out. His job was going to be easy.

So far, so good, he thought.

But the remaining steps that awaited him were both what troubled him, and when he considered the possibilities with a gorgeous and cowered girl, enticed him even further along. He imagined that he deserved part of that light that shown around her.

9

Blake leaves the hotel. It is mid-morning and the last of the working set are making their commute on trams and in cars. She has donned an urbane little ensemble that blends in with the professional population, and with her purse tightly latched over her shoulder and carried closely to her side, she could be journeying to any of the offices nearby. The streets of Zurich sometimes curve and seem to follow that old medieval city plan whereby neighborhoods come and go and meld into one another, but always pull a person into the center.

She follows her map and shortly arrives at a bank, yet she has to double-check: the building and entrance are not particularly obvious looking or in any way notable from the outside. The only signifier is an unimaginative logo displayed on the front window that plays on the red and white of the Swiss flag. Inside it is rather constricted and yet tastefully modern, and she has to gather her wits about her quickly as she is immediately met with enquiries from a woman standing behind a counter. "Guten Tag. Kann ich Ihnen helfen?" Other personnel are nearby, and their heads are bent down and their fingers are likely busy sorting papers and typing, and their eyes are focused elsewhere. To the side is a security guard standing with his legs wide apart, and even at this time in the morning, he seems weary and as if he has been on duty for many hours.

"Yes," Blake responds, smiling and hoping once again her language deficit will not cause a problem. She approaches the counter opening her purse, navigating past the wad of bills, and pulls a letter sealed in an envelope and then passes it to the woman who takes it with no apparent curiosity.

"I believe all of the necessary information is included in the papers." Blake tries to sound assured, but Radcliff did not make her privy to the contents of the letter and she is slightly worried as the woman opens the envelope, quickly scans the pages and excuses herself with a reserved smile and disappears behind a large heavy door. To the side, Blake imagines the security guard is regarding her with doubt.

Within mere seconds an older and austere man appears through the door with the woman in tow, and considers Blake from behind a bent nose, which supports his glasses. He doesn't smile and he doesn't put her at ease. "Bitte. Please.," he directs, "come around here; have a seat in the office."

Blake is navigated by a subtle hand on her back past the guard, who is now closely watching *everything,* and she is led behind the counter and through the door. She now follows the man down a hallway and finally into a cramped room. Clients are obviously not brought back here, and as she sits down at his request in a slender chair, she offers her best cooperative smile; she starts to believe that she is somehow in considerable trouble.

He begins as if she actually understands the situation.

"This is very serious," he says, "but we have already placed the accounts in what we call a *suspect* category. Yes, I believe that is the right word."

He turns suddenly and faces a cabinet and opens a drawer, removing a file to show her, as if it were earlier placed front and center for just this exact demonstration.

"Zzynex Holdings, Spa." is marked on the tab, next to the word "Tirpitz."

"Yellow folder," he says, tapping the item with his finger. His actions are loaded with importance. "Of course, we will keep a close eye on this. The first moment there is any activity we will notify you. Our administration is ready to follow the instructions per the correspondence."

He provides her with a notepad and a pen, and she writes down her contact information at the hotel. "No cellphone?" he asks, not entirely surprised that she is without one.

"No," she shakes her head, wondering how unusual this situation is, and exactly what the bank's instructions are from Radcliff.

"I recommend that you stay in your room as much as possible for the next few days. We will of course immediately contact you should circumstances dictate such." Their meeting is over.

Blake exhales heavily. It is not her, but anyone else that attempts to access this account, it now seems apparent, who is in considerable trouble.

•

The world was turning a particular way for Nick. This night it seemed it was urging him south, yet again. There was a crowd pulling him out of the bar, and they were stumbling and holding each other up, so that they looked like one strange mass of awkwardly moving legs, arms, and heads askew.

Hamburg in the early spring was still icy this year, but no less appealing. Nick had one of his contract breaks from the Athena and like any good man employed in the merchant marine for several years, he was finally succumbing to the various attractions found within the ports and cities the ship called at.

Someone had forgotten to leave their beer stein inside on the table, and a good part of its contents sloshed around and fell on the sidewalk as they wobbled and moved. In the cold night air, everyone's breath rose up and mingled with cigar smoke, and then the one other person who spoke English spoke to no one in particular, "We go now," he said, and Nick smiled in response.

It was too early to head to The Côte d'Azur and begin his seasonal shadowing of Johansen, and so he had time, yet he was without a mission. At some point he decided to take his occasional breaks and enjoy them in whatever way he could avail himself, and so here he was, out late with a group of people he was coming to know, and with his strange feeling of owed penance temporarily receding into the distance.

Back home The Great Recession was piling on in the States. In Europe it was still viewed with cautious anxiety: The press had yet to go wild and the arbiters of conventional wisdom were still consulting with people that supposedly knew about such things. The news didn't make much of an impression on him; Nick was isolated on the ship and his time on shore was lately fraught with drinking and aimless wandering.

For now the TV broadcasts, newspapers, and other stories and information featured pictures of well-presented people on the floors of U.S. exchanges with dour expressions. Other times they prominently published images of traders holding their heads in angst and inviting the public to feel sympathy for these supposed bystanders and innocent victims of this unknown thing and potential beast, which they ominously called *The Economy*. The obvious suggestion was that if these alleged creators and responsible managers of wealth were hurting then everyone else should be concerned. Surely some of the strife would attack the biggest markets of Europe, but the smart-worry was focused on the smaller countries that were already marginal even in stable times. Yet, in between the words, images, and the theater of TV news, a larger picture was emerging: The current business of fraud and self-deception was becoming unsustainable.

None of that mattered particularly for Nick, or his drinking friends at the moment. He had lost what he had lost to Johansen, and the comings and goings and tribulations of everyone else were just a backdrop, noise, and clutter. The imminent disaster for other people was intellectually interesting from one perspective, but made no larger difference to him. Johansen would profit no matter, and what could Nick possibly do about it? When he reported back to the ship the routine would be the same, and the question of "What next?" would be easily answered: "This, of course." Plugging ahead. Crossing the ocean. And in the summertime, his bicycle trips past the lion's den, merely to observe the window-dressing on a fraudster's home. And later, the sight of a gleaming white yacht and the pull of an imaginary trigger. It was the one time when the pretend world was momentarily complete.

In the cold night air, the men in the stumbling mass of drinking and smoking he was bouncing with, as far as Nick could decipher, were joking with the women. Someone had the sarcastic idea that they should see if they could exchange them for another group of females that were stationed across the street. "Look! Achtung!," someone shouted, "Kurzes klied! Short dresses!" and then they moved forward and melded the two units into an even larger assemblage of moving limbs and generally untoward behavior.

Still, there were suggestions of problems that even a few strong German beers couldn't hide from Nick. There was now a young man within the group talking about how they were running out of space to store all of the unused containers at the dock. He was barely out of his teenage years. His English had that earnestness found in people who have studied the language intently and suddenly have a good opportunity to try it out on a real subject.

He spoke alarmingly: They were literally stacking the empty containers wherever they could find a flat surface to store them. He said: It was crazy. It made him worry. He knew it was a very bad sign. His eyes were brightening with astonishment: They were thinking about trucking the containers and putting them on old airfields. They didn't have any other options or places to keep them. They were out of room! It was madness. No one wanted to buy anything, it seemed, and so there was no reason for them to ship anything.

He wasn't worried yet about his job, because he was part of a union, but he was still trying to save up some extra money all the same. If fewer and fewer of the containers were onboard the ships, there was less and less for him to do.

Maybe it would catch up to him? He promised tonight for himself "only one more drink," as if he wanted to accustom himself to a lower standard of expectation.

Nick bundled up his coat higher. The streetlamps were radiating a halo overhead, and underfoot the occasional uneven cobblestone caught some of the group by surprise and pushed them into someone else. Up ahead yet another group of *kurzes klied* were assembling and he had a choice to make.

Just when it was starting to get interesting Nick decided to hail a cab and get back to his little flophouse of a rented room.

The next morning, he kept on thinking about the enormous nightmare of thousands and thousands of unused containers piling up at docks around the world. He washed his face in the sink and wrestled the fog from his mind. He thought about the wide-eyed wonder of his drinking friend. Nick imagined the vast metal and corrugated shipping containers collecting in all of their various colors and liveries on ships, and on the backs of trucks and on train-cars. The containers were moving towards the docks like large animals migrating during the season by boat, train, and truck – but these particular vessels were empty and were supposed to be other places. Something was very wrong about that.

He called the Mazer Line; he talked to one and then another of the scheduling gurus. The whole operation was a feat of genius-level logistics and scientific management, and they wouldn't let much slip. When he finally found out that the Athena was due to return two weeks later than originally planned, he let his breath go. They were re-working the schedule. He jumped to a conclusion: Things were indeed going to change. The disaster in the U.S. was a reflection of a larger worldwide story that had yet to be understood or contemplated. It was indeed madness, or definitely headed that direction. Perhaps it was time for him to take a different position; try something else; hitch his little wagon to a different star.

He packed his bag. He again wrapped a couple of shirts around the picture of his one-time boat, and his one-time girl, and unfortunately his one-time friends whom once stood on the deck next to him, and whom he missed most of all. He appraised himself in a mirror that hung crookedly on a wall.

Whatever pleasantly open features he once had were gone; his cheeks had lost their hint of feminine softness; his jawline was now strongly defined; when he turned his head back and forth he saw tendons and muscle just beneath the surface. The fat and largess of an easy life was now clearly stripped away. Still, for whatever it was worth, there was that inherited stature which he had used as a device to prop himself up, and sometimes to coast on. And he thought to himself in a moment of truth: I literally had to toughen up.

Nick took a rambling, zigzagging route south; he was always attracted to the lion's lair. For Nick, there was a subtle urge to self-destruct - or perhaps to have fortune smile on him, and to somehow stumble into a safe haven by sheer chance. Either outcome might have suited him. There were much faster and more direct ways to get to the sun-soaked regions of Europe, but it was still far too early in the season. He bought a pass for a week's worth of unlimited train travel, and for a few nights even reversed his course to the north simply to have a free place to sleep in the seat of a train, and so he could continue moving, but without need or effort.

He stopped at the city of Dresden and saw the hulking remains of their cathedral nearly destroyed by the war, and which they preserved in its ruined state to serve as a devastating memorial and remembrance. He rode the train down through the eastern parts of the country and watched mile after mile of rolling forests pass by the train's windows. The miles of trees and grasses were a deep green, and often incredibly dense and dark. Occasionally there would be an isolated town, or even a castle. It was easy to imagine the fairytales, stories and myths that owed their existence to such a view. Nick noticed a chattery group of Germans – tourists in their own country – who stopped talking. They were silent for hours as they watched the scenery as well; they were engrossed by the seemingly endless size and tremendous significance of their home.

•

Nick remembered. The container ship went back and forth across the ocean, and the sun rose in the morning and set in the evening. Nick fought that urge inside him. It was the urge to somehow leave, even if that was possible in the middle of nothing. He was trapped on a boat and forced to comprehend the awesome emptiness of the planet.

At night, the sky was a thing that you looked up into with a sense of magnitude that you would never find on land. Out here there was only that horizon. There were no outposts of humanity or man-made lights to mask the stars or pollute your vision, and so the sky had depth and vitality. *This is the world*, he understood. On moonless nights it was pure black, except for the stars and the band of white haze that marked the Milky Way and which seemed to run diagonally across the sky with an improbable density. The Earth was an improbable thing too, of almost unbearable vastness, and Nick could imagine his ship absolutely alone on the water, pushing forward slowly.

During the day, when he took rest breaks between his various tasks, he found himself moribund; those were the times of contemplation, boredom, and futility that hit him the hardest. Much of life was fighting the elements and the relentless decay forced on the ship from the harsh environment. The corrosive salt air and relentless sun were inflicted on simply everything. Cleaning, painting, scrubbing, etcetera, over and over. Whatever metal was exposed began to rust almost within hours in such a place, and he took the gallons of paint and brushed over the same places he had many times before. His routine was simply about avoiding breaks in one part of the chain and ensuring the continued well-being of the ship. It was a habitual process learned and understood by people after centuries at sea, and there was no arguing with it.

Still, it was inevitable that nature would lay its hand down on the ship, eventually. One particular voyage would finally be the ship's last. The rust too great, the expense demanded by mechanical refurbishment too high, and the scrap value would outweigh the continued operating costs relative to the new and even larger and more efficient ships. Somewhere an accountant would make the determination after one engineering review and spreadsheet drew the final picture of *"Tina."*

The thought, which lingered around the vacant hallways, and even amongst the smallest of metal shavings left on the machine room's floor, was that it was all pointless. The sun rose in the morning and set in the evening, and in between, the day was the same as the day before. The ship was like a never-finished construction site. There were appendages and pumps and equipment sticking out of the walls, metal bars and structural elements to trip over, and places you had to duck your head when you walked through, lest you smack your skull against a beam.

It was a strangely vertical and claustrophobic thing inside with levels and narrow stairs and chambers and often poor lighting, and then with a view out of a window everything was suddenly flat and horizontal and open. At that point, it was this way, or that way, but never up or down. The containers were stacked stories high, but the ocean was broad and limitless. Nick counted off his pushups by units of "ten" and his pull-ups by units of "three," as if weighing their difficulty and responding to the simple choices he had to make. The cook, who sometimes stood nearby, taking a break from his kitchen duties and flicking his cigarette ashes into the wind understood the pointlessness of the existence, and was strong enough to disregard it. This is life; this is what you do. This is enough.

The cook didn't care about the containers being transported, or who was expecting what. He didn't care about the economics of it all, or the various questions regarding the "why" or the "where." He just wanted to do his time and get back home for few weeks, and then gather the strength to do it again.

No one was born into a life at sea, Nick imagined. They grew into it. Years of discipline and self-denial accustomed a person to it, and somehow they made it a life. Other people on the ship didn't seem to have the same urge to flee it as he did. That particular fact demonstrated they were somehow better, he imagined, and he oriented himself on the metal floor and counted off pushups adding them up by units of tens.

When Nick's train finally reached its destination after crossing Germany and much of France, he pulled his bag down from the overhead bin.

The bag was heavy and the cramped quarters uncooperative to the motion he needed in which to wrestle the object, but those sorts of little annoyances and challenges were nothing to him these days. His shoulders were effortlessly strong; his balance and frugality of movement were almost like that of a gymnast, despite his overall size. He carried the bag in front of him along the narrow margins and aisle between the seats with a deft ease. The stopping train caused people in front of him to sway with the unexpected change in momentum, but he steadied himself without a single wasted movement. He took glances out the windows and followed the other passengers down the steps and onto the station's platform.

The outside air hit him, and it seemed especially good. Mere miles away were various marinas, beaches, and for certain people, that restful life. Certainly somewhere nearby he could find a boat to work on; certainly someone would find him an acceptable fit for their little enterprise. He didn't need much. The Athena in all of its humble glory had served its purpose, and he wondered what, or who, might point him in a new direction.

10

The last bank; the last account.

As always, there seems to be that feeling in Nick's gut. It's strange and cruelly humorous to him; he can somehow taste it, and sense that it is actually sour. It is bizarrely as if he once drank a vat of pickle juice and the experience would never again leave him alone. His body is sick, it is underneath his skin, and not just in his mind. These last days, however, the feeling is often receding and then suddenly it is back and more potent than ever, and that particular fact intrigues him. He wonders if it will be like a childhood earache: Terrible, and then all at once the hurt is fading, and then suddenly gone.

Nick walks past the last bank. He is on the opposite side of the street and clearly sees the red and white logo, which is clearly an homage to the Swiss flag, splashed on the window in the morning sun; he turns to examine it briefly and then continues to walk farther on along without pause. He still has that scratch piece of paper in his pocket, and he fishes it out and looks at the sums and repeats the large numbers in his head. He breathes a long exhaling sigh. At the moment he lacks nerve, or perhaps he understands the seriousness of his quandary: jump off, or stay safe on the edge.

Perhaps he even has a faint sight of something. There is (perhaps) a hint: through the bank's windows, there is someone, impossibly familiar with a blotch of red hair, standing at the counter and interacting with a teller. And Nick decides to walk past the bank holding that little piece of paper like a security blanket.

The city is surprisingly compressed and he walks down to the lake which is not far away; there he finds a plentitude of sailing boats out cruising back and forth, and many more stationed nearby under protective coverings and waiting to be let loose and exercised. He wonders again what Radcliff is capable of. Nick wonders how nimble he is and what resources he can call upon. The day is starting to wear on. He distractedly consults the ancient watch fastened around his wrist. The leather strap is nearly broken and worn through. Every hour represents another movement of hands on that clock; each tick allows another amount of force to be organized to thwart him, and his position slips and deteriorates one more small measure. Nick tries to muster up the courage he once felt. He can't help but think about Blake. From a distance she will always be both an inspiration and a cloudy haze around him. What are those millions of things that he cannot have? Does that list include a girl like Blake? He wishes he had an answer.

Every time he seems to come to some understanding he loses the thread and he is back to where he started, and the question remains. He thinks about that unlikely vanilla smell on the deck of the yacht that one late night, and he wishes he could go back to that moment and somehow make a different decision. Perhaps compose a different set of words or simply take a hand in his for the briefest moment. The Hungarian lovely needed his help, and was also trying to help *him*, and he couldn't even see it.

On the yacht, Nick had seen enough of *the life* to make him cynical. He often observed, as the pug-nosed blonde used to stand in the galley watching the maid prepare her breakfast. "*Thinly* sliced," she reminded, and noted the peach waiting on the cutting board with a scowl. She had read somewhere that vitamin C was most naturally absorbed via direct contact with the inside of the mouth, or some such nonsense, and *that* was the beginning of that particular custom: she wanted thinly sliced peaches presented *just so* next to her cornflakes. Nick sometimes watched as she held a slice of peach for seconds too long on her tongue before chewing and swallowing it. She would then stand there and talk in her friendly way, digesting her cornflakes and peaches, and showering them all with her half-infuriating and half-beautiful radiance. "The world is *your* oyster," she used to repeat, as if it were she who coined the phrase, or was the only person who truly understood its meaning.

When she and the other blonde with the less-memorable nose talked about *whatever* life people had back *wherever,* it was with a sense of disdain. Other people had limited options. They were trapped in a rut. They didn't know how to have fun or enjoy the world's possibilities. "Ugh," the blonde with the pug-nose once said, looking at a picture on her phone, "Apparently my sister has decided to take up yoga pants!"

She laughed at her playful twist of words, and then handed the phone around to the group so they could all see the tragedy. It was a picture of her sister going out shopping in some faux-athletic garb. "Can you imagine?" she said, taking her phone back and re-examining the evidence. She was contemplating a world in which such ordinary dowdiness was thrust upon her own self, and she succumbed to it without even a fight.

What is the worst that can happen to me, Nick ponders? Surely it is much worse than yoga pants, Nick laughs to himself.

I can walk into the bank, provide the correct account numbers, enter the pin numbers, sign the slips and be done... Or I can be denied. They can say - *there is a problem with the accounts.* They can say - *One moment, please,* and then the police arrive. *Thinly sliced,* he decides, picturing the knife cutting the fruit. I will be thinly sliced, surely, and not for the first time.

He starts walking up the gentle hill and away from the lake and towards the bank. "A moment's courage and it is done," he repeats to himself over and over. It's the *principle* of the thing he imagines. To take some sort of action against the forces that Radcliff represents. Yes – that. And another hundred thousand (or thereabouts) Swiss Francs, in which to launch his final plan of action. Whatever that will be.

•

It was all fine up until that moment. "Before you go," the banker says, looking at Nick through his perfectly set glasses, which frame a bent nose (and Nick suddenly understands that he is saving all his dynamite for the very end of the transaction) "there is a lovely young woman who would very much appreciate seeing you."

Nick swallows. The scene is otherwise normal. Nick sees the printed-out check. It is marked Zzynex Holdings, S.p.a. It is just sitting there on the counter, immaculate and incredibly valuable. He should take it, put it in his pocket, turn and simply leave. *That* he thought was the last piece of *this* puzzle. But he can't help but swallow and comprehend the end of his life as he knows it, for the briefest moment. What is this clearly dangerous conversational addendum?

Nick is clearly confused and now startled. A lovely woman, who would very much appreciate seeing him? The bank manager looks at Nick, and it is *not* a hospitable look.

Nick's throat tightens. The manager now slides a piece of paper across the counter at an impossibly slow speed before Nick can respond, and Nick's eyes instantly fix on the name written in stern block letters at the top of the paper. His eyes rest on the name: "Blake."

There follows a listing of a hotel and a room number.

He meets the eyes of his inquisitor, or perhaps potential jailor, and is met back with a grave stare. The confusion is lifting and is now changing into panic. Nick wonders: How had he ever imagined that he would fight and win? He feels, again, small.

"Please accept the information," the bank manager demands. "I very much recommend that you contact her immediately." The glasses are now pushed up slightly on that bent nose, and he lets the words hang in the air as Nick tries to understand his precarious situation. Nick's eyes flick to the guard standing, feet apart, and Nick recognizes that everything is under careful observation. Overhead there are several video cameras that all seem to be suddenly oriented in his direction.

His eyes return to the banker; Nick unconsciously swallows again, gathers the cashier's check and the newly presented piece of paper in his hands, and nods his head. He tries to resurrect that familiar and glad-handing tone he has used many times over in days past, as if they are all conspirators in this together, but his voice is unsteady: "Of course, I would be delighted to meet her."

He listens for what he expects: sirens, alarm bells, the sound of doors being dead bolted and the sound of a revolver being drawn from its holster by the guard and quickly cocked. Nick is, after all, stealing money.

Instead, there is nothing. The panic moves and changes into a different kind of confused desperation.

With that, the scene is over. He turns and walks quickly from the lobby, his shoes making an unruly sound on the marble floor, and his hand suddenly thumping against the door, which opens deliberately.

Outside, he is stunned by the seeming sudden brightness of the sun; he breathes heavily; he finds his sunglasses and puts them on; he looks up and down the street. He is out of the bank, they don't have him in handcuffs, because they don't want him in that manner. He carefully folds the paper with Blake's location, which seems both like a different kind of confrontation, or perhaps a bluff, and places it in his jacket pocket. As he walks quickly away, he re-examines the check in his hand. He is holding it tightly with a pinch, so that his fingers are in danger of leaving indentations and marks on its surface.

Nick studies the check as he run-walks, splitting his attention between the other people ahead on the sidewalk, the cars flowing by, and the information and embossing on the check. The numbers seem right. The various official statements and stamping seem correct. It is signed, as well. It is a real check; he has the money. He is outside.

He realizes his heart is pounding and his upper lip is moist with perspiration. He walks fast enough to almost break into a gallop. He has completed what he needed to complete, at least for this initial stage. And yet he apparently is caught or trapped, but in a manner he cannot grasp at the moment. He is on the street, free to do what he wants, perhaps superficially. But *they* know. Radcliff's people have found him. He acknowledges it in some part of the brain that allows people to function normally despite a sense of catastrophe. Nick understands, too, that the adrenaline pumping through his veins is also making him lightheaded – not because of the danger - but because of Blake.

He admits it to himself: he might see Blake again.

•

He recognized Nick, of course. He sat in the backseat of a taxi cab, hardly noticeable across the street and in the cool summertime shadows beneath a tree, and watched as Nick seemingly burst through the door of the bank. Nick carried in his hand, clearly, a check. Radcliff said that particular check would likely include the total amount of cash remaining in Zzynex Holdings. Nick would surely follow his pattern, and drain the account just like he had the others. He could keep that check for himself, after he dealt with Nick.

He didn't need to accost him on the street. He didn't need to follow him, unless it satiated some strange curiosity or gave him some insight into Nick's mind or how he would react right there at the very moment when everyone else's plans for him became clear. He trusted that Nick would follow the carrot; he too had seen Blake, and he had touched her briefly, and had felt that radiance. She was the redheaded carrot. Yes – Nick would succumb, Radcliff was right about that, surely.

It would happen at the hotel - in Blake's room, safe and

secure and away from witnesses.

He would wait for Nick to show himself, as he walked through the doorway and into Blake's hotel room. And then as Nick closed the door behind him, looking of course at the lovely girl and losing himself in that distraction, the first hit would land. Probably on the back of his head, so the mark would be hidden. Or maybe he would use the stun gun, and simply disable him that way. Or both. Nick was a strong, physical presence. Muscled shoulders, long arms, and a deep chest meant Nick's fists would have tremendous power, unleashed. He knew that, because he had those same qualities.

That meant he would need to be fast, so he would then locate and ready one of the syringes from his briefcase. He would pop the top off the needle, and inject a copious amount of potassium into Nick's inert body and veins. Potassium, because (as it was explained to him) an overdose of this ordinarily unremarkable substance would shortly cause a fatal heart attack. And because autopsies almost never accounted for the total amounts of such an expected substance (that was in fact necessary, in much lower quantities, for the human body to function).

The next syringe would introduce a goodly amount of heroin (but not an inordinate or suspicious amount). That part, he didn't need explained to him. It would pump through the body, and as Nick's heart went into its death spasm, later show up as the red herring on post mortem blood tests. He would leave that syringe as evidence. Make sure Nick's finger prints were all over it, and then toss it unceremoniously to the side. The syringe was even the same variety as many of those given out for free by the city's drug clinics, and used by the addicts. Without need for further investigation, it would look like a pathetic but ultimately unremarkable death. And then there was the hotel room paid for with cash, by a beautiful girl who used a stolen passport and left sometime in the night without a trace. That would also steer perceptions a certain direction.

And if Blake made a sound or a wrong movement, he would deal with her as well, in whatever way he chose. For him, taking care of girls who didn't obey or betrayed their benefactors was surprisingly easy and so strangely rewarding. (He got to pretend he was like those untouchables, after all.) Those girls were lights in the world, and they could be collected and appreciated, and those lights could also be turned off. And even when they glimpsed the end - *even then* - they could never believe their fate was decided by men with such direct motivations. At the end, the big joke they finally understood was this: They didn't matter. He wondered if Nick would have the same revelation.

There were girlfriends, on the sly, who refused to have their pregnancy terminated. Former employees who held personally damaging information. Hangers on who wanted to go public with very dirty laundry. Girls who thought they could leverage their positions past a reasonable degree. Or maybe there was a relationship that had gone on far too long, and was far too deep. He gathered that this time touched on that same topic. They wanted a problem to just go away, and soon it would.

•

Radcliff knew a thing or two about love, and he saw it in Nick's face whenever Nick looked at Blake.

Over the years, Nick had kept a respectful distance

between himself and the many girls that filtered through the scene. But now there was this one. Radcliff saw Nick's eyes soften; he heard his voice reach a new place; he saw the various ways he tried to stop himself from falling further. Yet, here was this striking redhead, and things were now different. Nick walked away from her far too frequently. He kept his back to her and refused to look at her full-on. He didn't even want to say her name. She drove him mad with hope.

Radcliff imagined that Nick had sent himself to some sort of self-torture school because of the things he had done, or had failed to do, and now he was graduating. Nick had this weight around his neck, and in all likelihood, perhaps a sickness in his stomach. A cancer that he could actually taste.

Of course, losing everything (all of that money and promise) in that particular manner would tend to do that to a person. Radcliff often glimpsed Nick busying himself with some minor and unexceptional work on the yacht – maybe coiling a rope perfectly correctly, or cleaning the last speck of saltwater from a crevice. Perhaps Nick thought he could redeem himself with a certain amount of suffering and penance: Torturing himself on those long bike rides, swimming far out to sea, even when the waves were far too high. There was something disturbing in the way he seemed to court some kind of personal disaster. Nick was becoming versed at wanting and not being able to have. Maybe not even having life itself.

Radcliff laughed to himself. Nick didn't realize that there were no jailors nor keys to jail cells that needed to be earned. He didn't understand that each person was their own judge and jury, and some people even constructed their own prisons. Or, as it turned out for most of us, instead you were *none* of those people. You were just a complete and happy person. Simply put, there was no need to destroy the weak or ugly part of yourself. It didn't actually make any difference.

And then one night, this redheaded bolt of *something* landed in their midst, and apparently the simple answers were no longer satisfying to Nick.

But now, he thought, Nick was gone.

Radcliff didn't see that coming.

He didn't think the leash could be cut so quickly, and by the very pet himself, *and* he didn't predict the anger and worry he would feel in the aftermath of such a situation. He had been lulled by Nick's feigned indifference to the various secrets and financial information he was privy to. He had been taken advantage of and somehow played, and Radcliff's retribution would be swift. In fact, when Radcliff tried to nonchalantly recruit someone to help track down Nick, he immediately knew it would have to be Blake. Who else could lure him without even trying? She was *THE* girl in his life. Her name alone seemed to summon something in him.

The pug-nosed blonde wanted to go and search him out. She wanted to prove herself in ways beyond the obvious, he imagined, and she both slyly and directly asked to be the one. Little did Radcliff realize, the blonde girl with the pug-nose, was actually affected when she overheard the conversation: Nick, the wayward son, was now wayward *again.*

She heard Radcliff say it, and then there was nothing else to do but sigh. Nick's unconscious humming and singing behind the wheel of the boat, was never coming back. His kind laughter at her sometimes self-mocking jokes. Gone. Nick had apparently left them - and her! - without so much as a kind goodbye. The only one who ever *understood* her. For a moment it actually seemed as if her heart swelled to a different size, before returning to its normally scheduled programming. Difficult compromises and stifled hopes and dreams included.

But Radcliff liked the blonde with the pug-nose. He *really* liked her. He didn't want anything to happen to that little ray of light in his world. No, it would have to be Blake. She would be the one to turn the screw in Nick's gut. If she didn't return, for whatever reason, it wasn't the same sort of loss to his tribe. She was a player of her own sort. Or she had that potential, at least, and it was *for sure* that money could buy her, Radcliff imagined.

In fact, the very moment Radcliff came to understand that Nick had left the boat for good, he swallowed his pride and made the leap and called his very special friend on the phone.

Radcliff walked deliberately down the hall, and doubly made up his mind when he considered that Nick's bike was gone, as well. That minor encumbrance, which was usually lashed to the railing was gone, just like Nick. Good riddance, he thought. Radcliff entered his office, prepared his voice, and called Johansen. He called, *him*. The two friends, occasional business partners and occasional friendly adversaries talked on the phone. It was the secure satellite phone, and after the preliminaries, they talked in the same manner they always did, and Radcliff relayed the particulars of the situation, and asked for advice and help. Within a few minutes the matter was settled and arrangements were made. To Radcliff, it seemed Johansen chewed on the matter for only a few seconds and then made his verdict.

Radcliff scrawled some notes to himself in a notebook after the call concerning their plans, even using Nick's name, and then thought better about keeping any sort of a record of the conversation. He tore out the pages, crumpled them up into one little tightly-packed-ball and threw that paper ball into a trashcan.

That night, Radcliff and the girls, stayed on the boat. It was as if he were claiming it *all* unequivocally for himself. Nick's hold, already fading, was soon to become meaningless.

He wanted everyone to know: It was most surely his boat; his life; his world that he had made. Memories didn't matter. That leftover feeling could be denied. The hotel was just nearby, yet he wanted their cozy little rooms inside that edifice to wait for them till another time.

And yet later that very night, Radcliff woke up, startled, as if something else was in the room with him. There were shadows on the wall, crooked and leaning. There was an absence in the air. The waves gently rocked the boat. The air conditioning calmly hummed far in the background. It was all normal and perfectly peaceful – or perhaps...He wouldn't think it. Something, he couldn't quite grasp, horrifyingly slipping away beneath the waves.

He crawled out of bed, without disturbing the girls that encircled him. He slowly walked across the bedroom and opened up a safe with a combination lock that was set in the corner, out of the way and appropriately discreet.

Inside, he found an important key, and with that in hand he pushed through the bedroom door, and set off down the heavily shadowed hallway, and went to his office. The boat was almost completely silent. He turned that key in the lock, and then entered the code for the secondary electronic lock, and opened that door. The heavy mechanical sounds echoed in the hallway. He clicked on a light on his desk, and found the trashcan and more importantly, the crumpled up ball of evidence. Evidence, should someone ever make sense of the coming circumstances and somehow retrieve it.

Up on deck, Santi was on watch – *barely.*

As Santi reclined in a seat, his face was illuminated by the glow of a small TV screen, and he myopically stared at some show as the images flashed and changed on the screen. Radcliff harrumphed. Santi's ears were covered with headphones; it was doubtful he even noticed Radcliff appear on the scene. Still, he probably *did* notice as Radcliff stood on the deck in the darkness. That portly form of a man silhouetted and distinct. And then, when Radcliff outstretched his hands and took a cigarette lighter to the crumpled ball of paper, he probably noticed that, as well. And then, Santi certainly noticed when that same ball of paper caught fire and made a bright yellow slice of flame in the blackness.

He probably noticed the way Radcliff held the little burning wad of some-mysterious-item over the edge of the boat with his fingers, so that it burned nearly completely, and then he probably noticed the way Radcliff dropped the unintelligible remains unceremoniously into the water. And then the way Radcliff flicked his hands and fingers to be completely rid of the ashes.

Again, and so soon after the last issue, Radcliff was participating in something distasteful. Radcliff most certainly didn't like that, but again he knew it would never come back to haunt him. No one would know. It upset his sense of dignity, but soon enough it would be over, and then things would go on as usual. He knew this much: Bad things happened to other people, not him.

11

Blake sits on the bed of her Zurich hotel room. The window shades have been moved up and down by her several times as she alternates between sunlight and darkness. The TV is on and the sound is turned low, and a bizarre German-language-dubbed version of a British talk show plays on the screen. She futzes with the remote control and cycles through the seemingly endless channels yet again. It is lunchtime, thankfully, and she can justify an escape from the room and a journey down to the restaurant and a needed change of scene, even though it has only been a few hours since she returned from the bank. The maid service has already been through for the day: the room is spotless, and she feels like an interloper sullying the faultlessly creased sheets and already eating the chocolate mints that were placed on the pillows.

She wants the phone to ring, and she also wants it to remain silent and thereby delay the inevitable. The thought of going back to the yacht and to Radcliff seems suddenly horrible. Was this what she really wanted for herself?

If the bank manager or one of his associates calls her, it will possibly mean that Nick is caught or somehow in serious trouble. It might also mean that this whole enterprise has been called off. That much she gathers. It will also mean, she imagines, that her little mission, whatever its true goals are, has come to an end. She will have succeeded in one respect but miscarried in another.

She knows there is one different option available to her. It would be easy, almost ridiculously easy, to simply leave with the money. It is all cash, of course. No debit cards or checks. It is scrunched up in her purse, which is sitting across the room on a chair, and other money is folded up and wedged in various pockets and crevasses of her luggage. She has done similar things in the past. Things she justified to herself at the time as simply settling the score, or taking what otherwise should have been hers. And yet…

The phone rings. She tells herself that it's probably nothing, but her heart jumps into her mouth. She picks up the receiver and cracks an awkward "Hello" and listens. It's the bank manager. It sounds like he is calling from a pay phone. There is traffic in the background and a humming sound. She hates his voice. She listens all the same, and nods her head as she listens to him and that directorial voice, which transfers her instructions, no doubt written by Radcliff or someone else. She is paralyzed. Things are happening that she does not understand. She manages to say "yes" several times and "good bye" and "thank you," although none of those words sound genuine to her ear.

Wearily, she is off the bed and to the bathroom. Blake runs the water in the sink and splashes it on her face. She rubs her hands together and then splashes even more water on her face, wetting much of her hair as well and much of her clothing, and turning her appearance into that of a misfit. She stares at herself, judging her appearance and looking for the signs of fault and duplicity that she imagines others find constantly.

On the inside of her upper arm is her little tea-stain of a birthmark. Blake rummages through her makeup bag and finds a jar, and pries off the cap; she takes her finger and dabs it into the cream and then applies the color to the little discolored spot, moving across her skin with strokes until it is all but hidden.

•

If Hamburg seemed unusually cold for the early spring, Nice seemed unusually pleasant. As Nick walked the city he breathed easier; he had finally made the step away from the Athena and landed. This time of year the sun was still low in the sky, and shadows were still long from the empty tables and chairs set outside cafes, and also from the palm trees that lined many of the streets. But to Nick's eyes, it seemed the faces and bodies moving along the sidewalks were surprisingly less in number. True, it was still months away from the high time, but somehow too the voices seemed more subdued, and the shadows just that bit darker than he remembered.

Otherwise the air and the feeling, as he reacquainted himself with the surroundings, was simply good. The city of Nice was of course polished and unspoiled and somehow innately pleasing, and it seemed it always would be that way. He let it work its miracle on him. The world had potential. For the first time in years (he decided not to count how many years) Nick was comfortable in his skin.

And yet he couldn't help noticing there was a tension in the conversations and on the eyes that fixed on newspapers, television screens, and laptops that drew people in. He noticed it slowly, and then his opinion began to change.

The dour news of the States made constant headlines. Even here, inside the lobbies of hotels, where normally *nothing* at all was broadcast to the guests (even during the weeks when the World Cup was in full swing), the scene now featured little-used televisions propped up and fixed solidly on finance and business channels. A constant scroll at the bottom of the screens recorded the movements of various indicators and share prices. The arrows, Nick noticed, invariably tended to be red and facing downward. It worked on him, and into him.

On battlefield-like maps, which were alarmingly presented on the TV screens, the color red covered certain areas of Europe as well. It was like an invading army, or the movement of some sort of disease. The talking heads were gravely concerned, and they were now broaching the banking and debt issue as it existed on the continent. They all held viewers' attention with serious language regarding the contagion, which might easily spread to the peripheral nations: Portugal, Greece, Spain, and large swaths of Italy.

That was the word they used – contagion. It was as if the issues were a creeping virus or sickness that needed to be eradicated. They avoided certain critical questions regarding the "who" and the "how" of the situation. They kept on backing up and looking to the semi-distant past in their analysis. We have to go back to the beginnings of the EU, they said. The intricacies of a continent-wide common currency, but without a common central bank to determine policy, might wreak havoc. Debt vs. GDP figures alarmingly flashed on the screen. It would come down to the largest and most stable nations: What, indeed, would the strong economic core do to support the weak outliers? The problems in the States were replicated worldwide, and it was coming to Europe.

Various developing nations had, in the past, paid off their debt by printing more and more of their currency, which caused untenable amounts of inflation and wiped out vast amounts of wealth and progress. But in Europe, particularly Germany, the word "inflation" was something else altogether - it was a nuclear bomb. Hyperinflation, and the economic upheaval in its wake, was a disaster on an unimaginable scale. It was one of the primary causes of the rise of the Nazis state and German fascism. Nick had observed and knew enough to see *that* particular word – inflation - went straight to the center of the nation's consciousness. With the news hovering everywhere, Nick felt worse and worse about leaving the Athena, and yet what were his options? Perhaps he had misjudged everything. He had thought he could escape it, whatever *it* was, but it followed him and was waiting for him around each new corner.

He walked the various marinas and harbors, and he took scarcely used tourist busses that connected towns and resorts along the coast. He wondered if he was projecting his own uncertainty onto what he saw; the boats all seemed battened-up, the handful of people walking along the docks all seemed cloaked in mystery. It was as if they were the rare breed that had fortunately landed a secure position in the midst of an epic storm.

Nick realized that it would be the uncommon yacht owner who carried on and lived the typical carefree life in the face of the dire news. It would be a particular kind of person that triumphed his, or her, enviable position and his most frivolous assets, especially when the rest of the world veered off course so dramatically. When times were threatening, truncating a crew or a seasonal trip was the natural first response. It didn't bode well for Nick's chances in finding a position of his own.

•

He made an effort in his reserved way to connect with the scene. He was clearly identified as an American, and that both hindered and helped his cause. There was always his unfortunate language limitations, although he was starting to pick up key phrases and common questions in French, German, and Italian, and when he stopped for a beer or a bite to eat, it was *Puis-je avoir un siège?* – May I have a seat? And they were pleased to accommodate him.

Nick physically towered over most of his peers; he would need a big boat to work on if he was to have any sense of space. He was a novelty and again mingling on the margins, he realized he didn't correspond with what was expected, but at least they would remember him. He had credentials and licenses now, all he would ever need, in fact. However, aside from the Athena when she was docked in Hamburg, every person who could vouch for him in any meaningful or singular way was literally oceans away.

In large part the scene was insular and cliquish. People knew people, who knew other people. And there were the often-seen roamers who jumped from boat to boat and wandered the world. They often congregated in bars around marinas, and made their few dollars and euros stretch as far as possible. They dressed themselves in oddly fashionable T-shirts and shorts that were worn past *used,* and it was easy to noticed the deep tans on their skin, which often clashed jarringly with their lightly colored eyes and hair. These people traded names and destinations with a knowing nod. Their pay was marginal, but the attraction was clear: Working on glamour-puss boats, you enjoyed a perspective and familiarity with something that was totally unique and entrancing. You cleaned and organized. You became an expert in both the boat's equipment and the sock drawers of the owner in equal measure, and you took care of everything that was unspectacular and unintellectual in life and existence, but then you had that special entre into one version of paradise. It was a wandering life that never seemed to end.

Nick entered into easy conversations. They all seemed to be from unexpected places: Here was one from a supposedly populous city in New Zealand, which he had never heard of, and here was another person from a small place located above the Arctic Circle, and that particular village had an Eskimo name that Nick couldn't pronounce even if he tried for years. They talked about the Bahamas and the Galapagos Islands, and places they had yet to see. He noticed the way they hooked up and they spread apart, and wondered out loud about eventually settling down, although that seemed unlikely. They worked in easily formed teams and tended to set their egos aside, which was what happened when you worked around money but never had any yourself, and came from families both good and bad.

As Nick bought one or two of them a drink, he remembered, again, that these sorts were pleasant and schooled in the fine art of hanging out; the last thing you wanted on a small boat was someone who was easily bothered or insufferable in their constantly voiced opinions. They joked, and they knew when to simply not talk and listen for a change.

Nick had found one of these sorts.

He was a thin and deeply tanned fellow who flitted in the corners of the bar, and offhandedly gave Nick a tour of the scene. Again, the night was growing interesting, yet this time Nick stayed and talked. It was the middle of the week, but no one had any better place to be at this late hour. His conversational partner and tour-guide grabbed Nick's arm in a friendly manner. He directed Nick's view across the bar and past various people milling around to an ordinary man standing amongst others. Nick's guide cleared his throat and made a pronouncement: "I'm telling you, only a few people like beards, but *everybody* likes THAT beard."

Nick, looked across the room and found both the man and facial hair in question. Yes, it was a decent beard. Nick wondered and wanted to know, as with everyone else in the history of the planet, just why *that* particular clump of facial hair was so widely preferred by people.

"That's because it's not a thinking beard – it's a *drinking* beard."

Ah, yes. Nick smiled. Nick's conversational partner then tipped an imaginary hat to the hair in question, as if he were happy to share this and other knowledge free of charge.

The topic of conversation stayed on drinking, travel, and other attractions of the rootless lifestyle. Still, Nick wanted to put down some roots on a plot of land, but it seemed impossible. At least, he thought, the migrant life had its attractions and camaraderie. His new partner in crime wanted to bring Nick into the fold. Several more drinks came and went.

"You aren't going to believe it, I'm telling you. His parties, his little shindigs, his damn British charm. The game-show-hostess-women. Megawatt smiles, all of them. Christ.

I'll introduce you."

"Who, or what, are you talking about?" Nick queried.

"Let me tell you, and listen here…It's like a wedding or a funeral with too much booze. It's all encompassing. He hangs these lights from the mast, and I'm telling you, it's like a towering Christmas tree out in the bay, you hear me? But you have to be cool to get in, you know? You have to believe."

"You're right," Nick said with a laugh, "I don't believe it."

"We'll see. It's going to be early this year, so I've heard…Because of all the crazy shat. The end of the world, to listen to the news. It's like he's giving the finger to the rest of them. But of course in the most ridiculous way he can think of. Stick with me, I'll show you around. I'll introduce the two of you."

•

"That?" Nick gulped, when he saw it in full view, and said again in disbelief: *"That?"*

He laughed and shook his head. He had seen the big blue yacht from a distance once before, and in the daylight, as it made a slow pass by one of the smaller bays, and like other unschooled people that were caught unaware, he stood there shaking his head in bafflement. Now, on this night, the boat was indeed presented like a Christmas tree. And also, it was indeed, a perfectly considered and audacious middle finger to conservatism and restraint.

The various colored lights - yellow, red, white, and green - were hung from the top of the impossibly high mast on ropes that made a lovely bent triangle as they reached out to the front and rear of the hull. In the calm water, the display moved only a little against the dark sky and then Nick started noticing people wandering about on the deck, covered in that rainbow of shining colors, and then caught sight of the overloaded tables. Even from far away the amount of alcohol on hand was obvious.

Their little skiff drew closer, and they pulled up behind a motorboat that was unloading a group of casually dressed and already rowdy partiers. Nick patted his jacket's pockets, checking again to make sure he had the various documents with him; this was *also* going to be a curious sort of interview.

As if in comment, Nick's tour guide and sponsor playfully smacked him on the back: "Don't worry. He'll like you. You bring something he needs a little more of: reserved class."

•

Radcliff kept his face perfectly straight when he heard THE NAME, but still cracked a smile. It surprised him, and then seemed flawlessly right.

Nick was explaining himself in a tortured monologue that Radcliff pried from him in fits and starts.

"Tell me the story," Radcliff asked, and he really did want to know.

Nick wondered. There was something else in his drink, it seemed: the taste was chalky. His head was turning, and he wondered just where his story needed to begin in order to make this rare commodity known as "Radcliff" happy, so he might therefore land a job on this otherworldly yacht.

"I met him back in California," Nick started, and then thought. "Excuse me, but why do you need to hear all of this? What can it possibly matter to you?"

Radcliff eased back in his seat, master of his domain. He took his time. Above and outside his office on the boat, people were carousing and laughing. The noise of carefree spirits vindicated his position and solidified his character. Overhead, the Christmas-tree-in-the-bay continued to burn its candles at both ends.

"All of that," he said, gesturing to Nick's various pieces of papers and letters of reference, which were spread out on the desk, "is *not* interesting to me. Everyone who comes to me and wants this position – this coveted position - will show me the same pieces of paper, or more. The things I want to know are *not* in those licenses, or resumes or vitae. They are *not* in the things the powers that be say are important. That's one of the reasons I *don't* have my crew wear those typical stuffy uniforms, or any uniforms at all, in fact. We're more like a family."

Radcliff, thought for a moment, as if he did occasionally have a practical side that he might reference occasionally, and then spoke: "Tomorrow or the next day we'll take the boat out and you can show me one part of the job. Tonight, right now, I want to know all of the other things that matter."

Nick tightened his jaw. He felt his stomach turn. "It's not a good story," he said. "I'll sound like a fool and an unworthy dolt at best. And at worst, well…" He trailed off.

Radcliff smiled and broke into a genuine laugh. "Good," he said, "then I know I'm getting the truth."

Nick leaned forward, like he was confessing to a priest, and for the first time he told someone everything.

He covered it all; Nick told Radcliff about the first time he encountered that certain man.

There was that first hardy handshake, and then the

round of drinks for Nick and his friends. Later, there was the yacht that Nick gave his help on, and that supernatural silence as they split the waves, punctuated by the commands, and the way he felt strangely *good* at that moment. And then, there was the introduction to various business associates, an exchange of trust, and a gradual turn to greed, which again felt strangely good. There was the irritating man with the final documents who perused his house, Nick now recognized, in contemplation of how soon it would *no longer* be Nick's home.

Nick told Radcliff about the vomit in the sink. He told him about that long walk to his ill-gotten residence. He told him about the two-hundred pills just waiting there for him. Nick told his story, and for the first time in years again uttered the name *Johansen* to another person, and yet the name didn't cause the atmosphere to turn cold or the feeling in his gut to spill out and flow over everything. Radcliff smiled subtly with the name, and asked for more details about the man's appearance and background.

Later that night, Radcliff gave Nick a cursory tour of the boat, in between and amongst the revelers and dozens of people that were simply fans of the scene. It was hedonism, writ large.

Radcliff corralled one of the gorgeous girls that hung about; she was an oddly unemotional brown-haired girl who wore a crop top that showed a little tattooed dolphin right around her hip, and Radcliff had her snap a picture of Nick with her phone. The girl directed him, mechanically, into a brighter spot on the deck, and Nick tried to grin and to seem at ease around the otherwise carousing and unabashed life. He could perhaps do this, he thought.

One of the blonde girls he had noticed, with a pang in

his heart, edged in with a killer smile and put her hand temptingly on his back. Everything felt like *too much*, and yet he kept his cool.

•

Radcliff was down in his office. The door was very much shut. The secure satellite phone was cradled under his chin, and its heavy and hugely insulated cord ran from the hand piece, and then across the desk and then underneath a thickly embroidered curtain. Behind that curtain, on a sturdy shelf, he kept the body of the phone, which itself was further insulated around a lead case with a lockable cover. Did all of that actually matter? Radcliff didn't know.

Instead Radcliff's eyes wandered as he waited; soon he was considering the over large sculpture of some deeply contemplative man, which was sitting upon the edge of his desk. One of the girls had urged the sculpture on him several months ago after finding it in a gallery in Florence, and he had indulged her. "Sculpture is for sophisticated people," she had said. He supposed he wanted to be sophisticated in her view. His eyes regarded it now, as he distractedly waited for the signals through the earpiece to announce that he was indeed connected and secure to the other end of the network. He didn't like the hulking sculpture, suddenly. The problem in getting rid of it was that it was fixed to the desk with some sort of unimaginably effective adhesive, which kept it from sliding about and toppling off in heavy seas. If he had the sculpture removed, underneath, the wood of the desk would then surely reveal some sort of a hideous mark or disfigurement. Thus, if he trifled with it, he would just be trading in one problem for another.

He now handled a different phone with his other free hand – a cellphone - and it focused his attention elsewhere. It was the phone that belonged to the brown-haired girl with the discreet dolphin tattoo on her hip, and Radcliff flipped through the images saved on it. On the screen he ran across the expected photographs: the boat, smiling girls, groups of hangers on, a dress hanging in a shop window, an ordinary looking building (for some reason), and a handful of sunsets, which were all shot from the balconies of hotel rooms around the world.

Radcliff was lazily viewing the pictures on its screen until he arrived at one in particular: it was a picture that he had directed her to take days earlier, and which he then sent to Johansen. But not to Johnsen's personal phone - *definitely not.*

No, the picture in question was sent to one of Johansen's girls, assistants, maids, or whomever Johansen delegated that day. Again – Insulation. Radcliff was just barely beginning to learn the true meaning of the word, and apparently it worked. It meant you separated yourself and operated at a certain distance, even when you thought it didn't particularly matter: He had holding companies, umbrella corporations, other people signing his name so that the signatures looked different. It all added a protective cover. Deniability. Eventually, Radcliff knew that he would have to confiscate these little electronic devices, as well. No matter their usefulness, they were far too dangerous. Of course, the girls wouldn't like that.

The line woke up, and suddenly he and Johansen were networked, and he turned his attention to the most pressing question of the last several days: "Did you get that photograph and note I sent you," Radcliff asked, "it features a friend of yours, I believe?"

There was polite laughter on the other end of the line. "Yes, it is…Let's call him a former client, or perhaps more accurately, pigeon, to use the antiquated term."

"Are you absolutely sure this line is safe? I don't enjoy talking like this."

There was more polite laughter. "Please, set your mind at rest. Believe me: These are the phones the NSA *wishes* it had. They tell me these have all kinds of encryption and what have you. Can you hear that partial distortion in the background? That's all part of it."

Radcliff was still concerned. "You know, your faith in technology will be your undoing someday."

"Agreed, but that day is not now. More to the point, it is him, definitely. His face has changed and he looks different. Maybe he's lost some weight, but it's him, no question. And he wants to work on your yacht? I find that perfectly acceptable."

"Shouldn't I be concerned for you; concerned for me? A bit of a coincidence, perhaps?"

"Not at all. He was bound to turn up. Just keep tabs on him for me. I've watched footage of him riding his bike past my villa. If I thought he was any threat, I would have him dealt with. I'd just have him blacklisted; he'd lose his visa; he'd be sent home that very same day. At the moment, I can't call in any favors with what I've got going – elections and lobbying and such - and besides, he'd make a fine captain of your little boat."

"I don't doubt it. He is brilliant with his handling of everything onboard, and he seems…well…" Radcliff trailed off.

"You can't find the word?"

"Well, it does bother me, more than a little. The way his

face collapsed when he said your name. You should have seen it. I kept on pressing him, and then when he told me… He was suddenly broken. You really took something from him, do you know that, my good man? If you would allow me one question?"

Johansen was more than gracious. "Surely."

"I thought you stopped that, yes?"

"I was constrained at that particular time. I needed a cash infusion. You know, of course, that I was right about the markets – just look at the latest numbers! But my timing was off. Just off enough to make the situation critical. And there he was. It was quick and easy. He was perfect; he was the last of his family, and he was in charge of all that money. And he was more than a little naïve. But I don't like to explain myself, you know that."

Radcliff understood Johansen's motives for what he did and how he did it. He was well aware of financial stress and the benefits of a fast cash infusion of any amount, and he quickly considered his own deteriorating positions. "And it doesn't bother you that he is here?"

"Why should it? What else does he have to turn to? He was certain to eventually find his way onto a boat, and most likely a grand boat. A boat belonging to someone either you or I knew. It's much better this way."

Radcliff was slowly becoming convinced, and then Johansen closed the deal.

"If you are still concerned, just have him dirty his hands for you. Send him to some of your old friends. Have him buy some barbs. Something you and your flock need, but can't buy legally. He'll do it, and then he's in it with you. I tell you, it's *problem solved* from then on, and then you've got a line that can be cut whenever it suits your purposes."

"All right then." The conversation was already coming to a close, and other matters needed attention.

"One last thing, old friend. Have you taken those defensive positions we presented to you? I hope you're moving into cash, precious metals, or liquid assets. The markets are going to get even more brutal."

Radcliff was more than slightly miffed at the thought, but he feigned intolerance. "What? Not bloody likely, that's what! I tell you what: I'll not have my money disappear in a storm of inflation, because that is exactly what is going to happen if I go to cash. When the Bank of England is printing money twenty-four hours of every day, let's talk again. I'd love to hear how your opinion changes, then!"

There was polite laughter, "I wish you luck."

Johansen was well aware of Radcliff's reticence to take advice and didn't belabor the point, and there was more polite laughter in return. He allowed Radcliff to keep his supposed British gentlemanly effortlessness and ironic detachment unchallenged by reality.

"Let's talk in a couple of weeks."

After Radcliff was off the phone, he again considered the sculpture fixed to his desk, which seemed to stare back at him. Perhaps that particular piece of art was not so bad after all.

It was common to find rare and absurdly expensive works displayed in yachts, and he always wondered over the advisability of that particular fetish. It advertised something even beyond the grandeur of the boat in question, and seemed to make you more of a target than ever, and he didn't want any more of those kinds of eyes on his comings and goings than there were anyway. He could sometimes be practical. The yacht, which included his version of entertaining on it, was his one crazy material splurge, and he didn't need to gild the lily one more time.

He mingled with all sorts of people. He followed his interests wherever they took him, but in some dark corner of his mind he distrusted the wealth that he reveled in and understood the revulsion that some people had towards it, and others like himself. Maybe Johansen was right, and his minions were onto something as well. Maybe he needed to take a different perspective on his investments and positions. He hung his head in his hands and thought, yet the process still befuddled him. Sometimes he imagined he could literally see into the future, but not now. And not on this topic.

In several hours the New York markets were opening. Every percentage point downwards was translating into millions of dollars of losses in his accounts, thanks to his outdated and overly glib strategies. At the end of the last session the major exchanges were down nearly two percentage points. If he sold now and took the various hits, he would lock in a *loss* for the last decade or more. Ten years with nothing to show for it but a humiliating move backwards.

He thought about Johansen and the risks he took and then mitigated, and the way he perhaps literally got away with murder, for there were rumors of what had happened to people that crossed him at the wrong moment. Women. Staff. Surely, Johansen kept those two pie-faced body guards around him and by his side for a good reason. They didn't look particularly fearsome, but that was one of those big open secrets. He sent them out when needed, like errand boys with no moral compass.

Radcliff knew that Johansen didn't like half-measures. With him you were either all in, or all out. Make a reasoned decision and then do it. He apparently took a look at Nick in that picture he had sent and read something into it, and made up his mind equally deliberately. Yet Johansen could always reverse himself later and do whatever he did with those sorts of people problems. Johansen's advantage was that he didn't associate his ego with his opinions or decisions. He didn't have that sentimentality or softness when it hindered him. He cut people and businesses out, *just like that*, or kept them close and eventually rewarded their allegiance. Radcliff and Johansen had their disagreements and skirmishes in the past – what partners didn't? - but Radcliff couldn't help but ultimately trust Johansen's reasoning.

He looked again at that innocuous picture of Nick. The man somehow seemed to disregard the blonde with the pug-nose standing right next to him, and he looked straight at the camera, without any duplicity or manipulation. Whether or not he knew it, Nick needed a place on the yacht. He clearly needed a place to call home.

Johansen no doubt noticed that as well, and the two of them saw the same thing when they looked at Nick: someone who could be managed or written out as needed.

•

Nick looks up and down the hotel's hallway, and then again looks at the piece of paper he clasps tightly in his hand. The number on it matches the room number he stands in front of; there is also that name, which catches his eyes every time he looks at it, and which now has the effect of making his breathing that much shallower and uncertain. It is a name, apparently, once inspired by a soap opera character and from that inauspicious beginning, flowered a different kind of person.

Why is he here standing in front of this door, he wonders. He has the money, which is what all of this was *supposed* to be about, and now this? Over the last dozen days, he deliberately and efficiently drained Radcliff's low-tier bank accounts, and at every instance he was making a monumental choice. With each visit to each bank, and with each account drained and pilfered, there was an increasing risk of discovery and dire consequences to his actions. And yet he got away with it, over and over. If he wanted, *right now, this very instant,* he could turn away, and start life with larger sums in his own accounts than he ever believed he would have again.

He knocks on the hotel room's door, almost confidently. The sound is more assertive than he feels. This, he knows, is a huge decision and the truth of the matter is burning him up inside. He thinks he comprehends something. He is not right for her, yet he doesn't have the fortitude to simply turn away and try and forget her, no matter the consequences. She makes him both weak and strong.

There is the muffled sound of motion in the room, perhaps footsteps, and then a pause. The door opens and he sees Blake. That longed-for face. He shivers. A feeling washes over him. She is not smiling; her eyes dart to a place he cannot see - towards the corner and behind the door - and then she backs up as if she is leading him in. It is her. He cannot resist her pull. He made that mistake once before one late at night as the smell of vanilla filled the air, and he will not make it again. Nick takes a step inside, not understanding. He comprehends even less than he supposed he did.

All at once, there is a biting, horrible pain in his side. It is radiating everywhere; an electric shock.

His teeth somehow hurt, and then he is down on his knees, collapsing into a slow motion, crumpled up ball.

He is unable to bring a thought into his mind or stop whatever is happening to him. There is a smash to the back of his head. A wave of violence. He can't figure out what...

In one jump, he feels his mind cease to function.

12

There is no sense of time. Seconds or hours might have elapsed. A blurry, large figure is moving towards him; Nick is on his hands and knees now, instinctively struggling to right himself, yet his muscles are nearly useless. His body is weighed down by some huge force he tries to fight, like in a nightmare.

It is all painfully deliberate. He hears a *No!* The smaller human form – Blake? - is struggling to withdraw, but she is trapped in the room.

Nick is starting to right himself. His strength is gathering. He hears a muted cry gasping out a little sound, any sound, but she can't bring her voice to the surface.

He slowly sees…Blake is now cowered on the bed. *Cowered*, he thinks. Nick sees the other form come into focus: it is a man he recognizes and hates, and who is looming. He doesn't understand, oddly, there is a…what? A *syringe.* It is held in one of this man's hands.

Nick's power is reasserting itself. There is only instinct. Nick, lunges at the shape of the man. There is no thought. There is only the horrible emotion of seeing Blake in fear, and possibly hurt.

He slams like a sledgehammer into his adversary's body with unalloyed strength, and whatever higher-level of consciousness Nick holds onto is gone; he summons a force he has never experienced before. There is now simply rage. The fight is over in mere seconds. Nick stops hitting the face when the pain in his fists tell him how much damage he has inflicted on another person.

He feels her hands on his side now, and she is trying to gently calm the wrath in him: "It's okay...It's okay..."

She is easing him back into himself, and the sight of what he has done in seconds, apparently, is the most disturbing thing he has ever seen. There is blood streaming from this once handsome face.

This man's modeling days in Croatia are going to be curtailed, Nick thinks. Nick cruelly laughs at the view he has, because at the moment, laughing is better than thinking. He wonders offhandedly, if he killed the man. There is no motion evident in the body, and then from a nostril in the man's now deformed nose, he sees a bubble appear in blood and mucus. And then another bubble. At least the man is breathing.

Nick wonders how much noise and shouting he made; everything seemed almost silent, aside from Blake's whimper and *No!* Suddenly, he has a strange sense of mere moments ago. Nick abruptly knows that he was grunting with each hit from his fists, exhorting a cry with each blow that landed, and they all landed. Will the authorities soon be pounding on the door, demanding to know what happened in the room? How will he possibly explain this?

He is starting to feel more himself. He feels a sharp pain that is still radiating from the back of his head. He is starting to take hold of the situation, and self-preservation immediately demands that he move the inert body of this – who? – some person; some *friend* of Radcliff's into the bathroom and out of plain sight.

Without even acknowledging Blake, he grabs the man from under his armpits and drags him across the room's floor, into the bathroom, and into the bathtub. This unconscious person is now a liability. The body is absurdly lying there in spotless clothes, but with a bloodied face and limbs at disturbingly contorted angles. Again, Nick looks for bubbles appearing from beneath the nose; they are forming regularly.

Nick grabs a pristine towel and makes a rope by twisting it over and over, and binds the man's feet. He repeats the process with the man's arms, which he then lashes with yet another towel, to the hot and cold water faucets.

Nick's breathing is quieting down as he concentrates on the tasks, checking the hold of his makeshift restraint system. Another flash of insight has him looking for, and then finding, the man's wallet, and then pulling out the many credit cards, cash, passport, and then a driver's license. His name is meaningless to Nick, along with the various stray pieces of life he finds in other pockets: crumpled receipts and train tickets. He finds, horrifyingly, yet another syringe. The cap is on and the plunger pulled back and it is filled with a clear liquid, like a cross-bow that is cocked and ready to fire. Nick cannot look the man in the face, because it is now swelling up and bruising to become a sickening purple and black mess of pain.

Unexpectedly, the thought that there might be *others*, has him scrambling to the door, locking it with both the deadbolt and the chain. He looks through the peephole, and sees nothing but an empty hallway. He finds the item, which clearly sent him writhing to his knees and then into a sort of fetal crouch. It is lying on the floor in the corner, and he recognizes it as a stun gun. He must have pushed it away from his side by sheer instinct (or maybe as he collapsed, with the damage mostly done). It now waits there in the shadows and is strangely toy like, with its plastic body and snubbed proportions. Only now does he look at Blake. She is sitting and quivering on the bed. With the manner in which the situation has rearranged itself (and her intellect restating itself) she is now too petrified to move.

He wonders quickly what role she had to play in all of this, remembering in the haze of his mind, despite his best efforts, the way she seemed to lead him into the room.

He goes to the bed and sits beside her, and soon it is he who is trying to calm her. He sees that first syringe, now lying there on the bed. Its plunger is pulled back like the other one he found in the man's pocket, and inside the plastic body there is a goodly amount of some liquid, perhaps poison or perhaps a sedative?

With his hands, which Nick notices now features bloody knuckles and palms he gently grasps her arms, and then moves her into a soft and safe-embrace, which she begins to return. "We're okay," he says, several times over, although he doubts the words, even as he says them.

•

After weeks of working on the boat, Nick had decided that Radcliff was not necessarily a bad man.

He would redeem himself in paradoxical ways, Nick thought. There was the music that Radcliff put on late at night, and which issued through his over-sized stereo (over-big and over-grand, as everything in his world was) and which would serenade the entire boat. But often the music *wasn't* easy to approach, and it *wasn't* comforting. It was questioning and often unsettling. It was as if Radcliff himself was attacking and pouncing down upon his own self-created world, and in such away exposed the doubts that ran through his mind. Paradise was also tragic.

Nick contemplated: Life on the boat, and at the resorts, was becoming like a troubling waking dream. It all blurred together and happened in a disjointed sense of days and weeks flowing into each other. Nick was never the type to simply turn off the lights and listen for answers. Yet now there were those nights.

Radcliff's yacht was a home now, and the sounds that were brought to him through the stereo in Radcliff's bedroom were hallucinations and narratives, which moved and changed in all of their complexities. He sat on deck, late at night, and listened as if he had waited his whole life to hear such things. Yes – perhaps even in this stupor it would all resolve. The sounds coalesced in the bedroom, and then made their way past and through the door. The whole hull became a resonance chamber. The music flowed along the hallway, and then up the steps and into the world.

He tried to tell himself he was part of something bigger. He listened. There were the opening chords of Mozart's *Die Zauberflöte,* issuing from Radcliff's bedroom. It was worldwise and cast the boat and all aboard her in a deep nobility. And later Brahms answered with a different revelation. It was a piano concerto, another domain that was moving just off the horizon, and which Nick would never be able to reach.

Radcliff, as if in response, provided axioms. His own

answers. They were offered to Nick and to anyone else who happened to be in his vocal range. He said, "The most dangerous things in life are your wife, your girlfriend, and your car. Or, if you a very rich, your helicopter or airplane."

Radcliff liked reading about celebrity deaths on ski slopes or in violent car crashes in front of crowds. He wasn't going to go like *that*, he said. That was for other people. He didn't, nor would he ever, have a wife. He diluted the girlfriend-effect by diversifying the risk and engaging multiple providers of said service. He wanted people to assume the providers were treated like his investments: they were discarded, if they lacked an acceptable return, and set aside with little thought about their intrinsic value.

The girls assembled and dissolved according to some internal clock and larger pattern or circadian rhythm that Nick couldn't fathom. They appeared on deck for perhaps a few hours of every day, and when they were anchored at some resort the girls kept a different set of priorities. He saw less of them, until he was charged with assisting with their various errands and side trips.

The blonde with the pug-nose had made a decision about Nick, it seemed: "You need to give your adrenal glands a rest – NO coffee."

She had looked him up and down, and made a pronouncement: "You have adrenal fatigue. This is all part of *the cleanse*," she said this as she met him in the lobby of a hotel, and then she urged on him a green drink, in a clear container so that it looked extra obviously healthy. His food and beverage intake were now up for review, he gathered. "I made this for you," she offered, as if she ordinarily didn't do such things.

It tasted awful, but she nodded approvingly as he

downed it in a few gulps, and then she directed him to the shops they were going to visit that morning. The car was at the curb, with a driver holding the door open for her.

"And later on," she said while ignoring everything else, "only Egyptian coffee. My dietician says it has fewer free radicals."

Nick noticed in all aspects of life that Radcliff kept his transport traditional and impervious and measured, and when the girls and Nick and other staff were picked-up and moved around town, it was formal and luxurious. Even for little shopping sprees.

It also seemed clear that Radcliff liked Nick. Perhaps, he saw something of himself in Nick. Maybe, at times, when Radcliff considered the way Nick looked at the girls, and tried to ignore them, and then faced a kind of twisted reality. Nick was restrained and constant, and he seemed to know more than he let on. He didn't brag; he didn't actually say much at all. He seemed at home behind the wheel of the boat, and that one pleasure appeared to be enough for him, at least for the time being.

Nick had no family or home or baggage of almost any kind. He literally shouldered all he had in that well-used duffle bag of his, aside from that damn bicycle, which he was begrudgingly allowed to keep strapped to a railing in the main hallway. There also that disturbing picture of Nick's onetime yacht hanging in his room, as if he still yearned for something that didn't agree with him.

It all made him a strange case, yet one that Radcliff could parade around, and then attach himself to. *And then* he could project Nick's easy social graces onto his own charming self. Perhaps Radcliff thought the mere presence of Nick would double his own positive affect. People, after all, seemed to be strangely comfortable around both of them.

Perhaps he thought that Nick's handsome aspect reflected something positive onto his own less-than-spectacular form. Honestly, he didn't even care that much if Nick took one of the girls to bed occasionally (although he doubted it ever happened). It would have been an honest compliment to his taste; it would have been a sincere appreciation of his world. As was common, he thought that by surrounding himself with the things he, and others, admired or found beautiful, Radcliff somehow imagined he would elevate his own self.

Nick recognized, however, the moment when he was suddenly pulled into yet a different world, and was being lead down yet a different path.

It was one afternoon. It was an ordinary and otherwise forgettable day, when one of the errands he was tasked with turned him into a literal alley, complete with garbage strewn along his walk from an overflowing dumpster and rotten food that had washed down and was decorating the gutter.

As he had been directed, Nick climbed the fire escape of an apartment building. Or perhaps it was an old hotel (he couldn't be sure which it was). And once in front of the prescribed location, outside on the third floor, he rapped gently on the window, per his instructions.

This particular errand was critical. The brown-haired girl with the discreet dolphin tattoo on her hip was needing something, that much was clear. She was sleeping even stranger hours, and she was locking herself in one of the bathrooms and refusing to come out for hours on end.

Radcliff had gravely noted that she once leapt up in the middle of the night and simply *had* to get off the boat. He was afraid she was going to run down the hallway, up the stairs, onto the deck, and jump overboard, and that would have been the end of her. There was something seriously wrong with her, and the normal assortment of pills, drinks, and spa treatments didn't seem to be doing much.

Nick described her symptoms, current drug use, and condition to the man on the other side of the glass of the third-floor window. The man helpfully slid the window open and up a few more inches, which was obviously a common occurrence, and in fact perfectly suited for these sorts of consultations. The man rummaged around inside the room for a few minutes and then returned with a tube of toothpaste, which he set on the windowsill, as if they were at a drive thru pharmacy. "Two a day," he said. "Morning and night. Don't miss a dosage. And don't allow her to just stop them suddenly." The pills were imbedded in the paste - he said. "You'll have to squeeze all of it out to get to them."

"*And,*" - he said – "It would be good for her to knock off at least *some* of the drinking." It was as if he knew certain sacrifices were simply too much to expect, but like a conscientious doctor, he had to ask his patients to do the right thing anyway.

When Nick left with the toothpaste strangely resting in his pants pocket, he realized he was compromising himself in a manner that he never imagined. He didn't even concern himself about the legality of it. It was the way he felt about treating another person as problem to be managed that bothered him.

He tried (but failed) to absolve himself: It's okay. This is the price I continue to pay, he thought. I can never settle the debt I owe to everyone else.

•

The secure satellite phone was buzzing and blinking. Radcliff couldn't have said for how long because it was rare to ever receive a call from Johansen, or anyone else these days. For once, it seemed, things were at some sort of equilibrium. The markets were growing. Money was being made. Radcliff was even thinking about buying some beachfront property, and perhaps when they eventually bounced along the French coast he could investigate some options.

But that ease of life could not last, even in the midst of the summer holiday season, and Johansen sounded unusually tense, as his voice moved across the distance and through the phone: "I have a bit of a problem. Although by now, it may also be *your* problem."

Radcliff was not amused, but he masked it with a light touch to his voice. "What – or who – is this problem you've gotten me into?" He laughed to show that he was surely above such concerns.

"She's traveling under an American passport and last name. She thinks I don't know about that. But she's Hungarian - beautiful. Dark, very dark hair, last time someone saw her."

Amused or not, Radcliff must come clean.

It was rare for Johansen, after their complicated and sometimes adversarial history and disagreements, to come to him with such a direct and personal need.

Radcliff spoke: "Yes. Oh, yes. Of course. She came aboard at Portofino. She doesn't have a bomb, or something explosive does she?" Radcliff added more polite laughter, though he was unusually curious.

"No. But Portofino sounds right."

"Well, may I ask what the problem is? Want her back, do you? She's not entirely all there, I'm afraid. She can't even wear lipstick without making it a major issue."

Johansen was in no mood to joke at the moment. "Yes. Well, she's run off. She and I had a bit of a falling out, I'm afraid to say. At some point, she saw that picture you sent of your new little captain, that time ago. If you remember, I had you send the picture to one of the kitchen staff, and well, apparently they can't help but try and curry favor and ingratiate themselves by sharing everything. Part of the problem is, she knows his story. She was curious about him, and so I stupidly told her. I told her all about the way I ruined him. Took his money. Half of it was just to keep her in line, if you will…Let her know what can happen to people like him – like her."

Johansen paused as if in thought, and then continued on. "That picture. And well, your boat, the deck, the party, and all of that profligacy is on display. And one of your girls is nearby. The one with the cute little nose that you like so much. It was all very obvious: the who, and the where. Well, apparently she thinks you're harboring Nick. Protecting him from me because of our past difficulties and rivalries."

Radcliff guffawed: "Protecting him? Oh, that is brilliant. And what? Let me guess. Now she, in that addled mind of hers, also thinks I'm going to somehow protect *her* from you as well?" Radcliff laughed. "She's got it in her head that you and your boat are some sort of safety, apparently. I suppose desperate minds make desperate jumps. A sanctuary, can you imagine? God knows who else she's told."

"Brilliant, just brilliant," Radcliff added again with a laugh, and didn't even need to point out the irony. As they talked and filled in the blank spaces, he started to see the issue at hand.

The story, at heart, was very common, and he was secretly pleased that Johansen (just like all of them) clearly had his moments of insecurity and women problems.

And then, seeking to cozy up to his peer and sometime competitor and adversary, he inadvertently sealed her fate after a small pause: "There is one thing you should know," he said, meaningfully. "They were up late last night. Nick and your Hungarian beauty. One of the other girls noticed and told me. They were on the deck, talking, and they were very involved, it sounded."

Johansen was quiet while he considered the alarming news. The wheels were already turning, and then he spoke: "Was she upset? Was she under the influence of anything that would make her tell stories? Did she, perhaps, say more than she would have otherwise?"

Radcliff was starting to see what he had just done. "I wish I could say. I have no idea. But she's been fairly, well, I guess that explains it. Preoccupied."

"And what about our ruined little captain? Any change?"

"Not at all. He is both pleasant and aloof at the same time. I think he has *settled*, if that makes any sense. Is he still lurking around your fringes on his time off? Riding his bike past your little place? Observing?"

"Not near as much." Johansen thought, for a moment. "No. For a while I considered just cutting him out. Give you a chance to find someone suitable to replace him, of course, but then his painfully obvious visits past my villa waned, and he seemed to more or less stop. We barely see him, now. It seemed he recognized his place, finally. And saved me the problem, too."

Radcliff was pleased, at least about that. But the other matter was unresolved: "What stories did she tell to anyone? I can't say for sure. It would not surprise me in the least however if she dropped something. She was acting off. Somehow odd. The girls said it as well. I never knew her otherwise, so I can't say. Forgive me if I'm prying too much, but is there something else between you two?"

"It was just a fight, a mild tiff as you English might say, I thought. Until the threats started."

Radcliff saw, finally, where this was truly going. His voice changed. "They should know better."

"Yes."

"What do you want me to do? How can I help?"

"I'm sorry. I know she is beautiful and the rest of it, but she needs to go away."

Radcliff was not surprised. He tried to put on a better face than the one that suddenly descended on him, but it was useless. "Okay. Yes. She's yours, of course. Whatever you want."

"We'll talk later and discuss the details. I'll have someone pick her up, and her belongings. It will be sometime soon, early morning."

"Yes. Sounds fine."

"Where will you be?"

"Hard to say. We're still just bouncing our way up the coast."

"Are you, old chum, still feeding the cats at those crummy Italian restaurants you love so much?"

"Of course, its summertime, and what else would I do with myself?"

"The morning in question: Can you make sure that the crew is off the boat and everyone else is in a deep sleep, or otherwise out of commission?"

"Naturally, and with pleasure. I'll just load them up with something a bit stronger the night before. It won't be a problem. Who are you sending, will I recognize him?"

"Someone different, but you'll like him, at least in small amounts. He wants to help with my accounts and such, but he can't do numbers to save his life. His value lies elsewhere. He is quite taken with the ladies, although in a strange way. He actually used to be a model." They both laughed.

"You are joking, surely."

"Not at all. Give him more than a few minutes. I'm sure he will tell you all about it. *He was huge in Croatia.* Had billboards and perfume ads, according to his standard line. He's an ass, but he's *our devoted* ass."

"I understand, completely. What are you going to do with her?"

"I think you'd probably rather not know the details. What difference would it make anyhow?"

"Quite right. I'd rather not know."

The line clicked off, and Radcliff, with a surprisingly heavy heart, was soon on his way to make the few preparations for the morning when she was to go away.

13

Blake wants to throw away the second passport. It belongs to some other woman, whom she suddenly feels exceptionally uneasy about. Blake used it only once, merely to provide identification when she checked into the hotel in Zurich, and the person working the desk barely glanced at the picture, but considering what transpired there, it is now clearly a serious liability. She feels furious and yet cornered. She feels defiant but recognizes the precariousness of her position. If the police happen to find her at this exact moment and connect the various dots, what litany of charges would they bring against her?

She wants to rip up the passport, and bury it under a mile of earth, and at least do what she can to obscure that one particular *dot*.

But Nick advised differently: "Maybe we can use it, somehow?" He said this to her as he gathered up the two syringes and wrapped both of the needles in a piece of tissue paper to protect them, and they prepared their exit from the hotel. She agreed, although she still has no idea how this second passport may be of use to them at the moment, or at any other time. And so, there it sits, along with her real passport, driver's license, and various pieces of identity in her purse, which she has transferred into yet another bag.

She knows Nick is likewise compromised and suspect. His knuckles are still bruised, and perhaps there are even still microscopic remains of the other man's blood imbedded in his skin, just waiting for an investigator to swab and then run under a microscope. Then there is that ill-gotten check in his pocket. There is that stun gun in his bag. Fingerprints and other trails are everywhere.

She knows that one of the hotel's housekeepers entering the room the next morning, would have immediately found the bathroom door open and in the tub, the beaten man. Unless, somehow, he revived himself and made his own exit.

Of all the things she has ever done, she has never considered herself an actual criminal, but now, despite the circumstances, she is starting to wonder. The two of them, now traveling together, will have to be exceedingly careful, lest they attract the wrong kind of attention. At the hotel, she wanted to find an open and unoccupied room, a closet, *anything*, and drag the man there, and away from her room. But one look down the hallway showed the telltale plastic dome in the ceiling, which behind meant a camera to catch them in the act. It seemed everything was being watched and recorded. The footage would only add to their guilt. They had to start thinking like that - pay attention to everything.

Nick is now looking out the train's window with his own thoughts on the topic. He thinks about various agencies and government bodies he has heard of: Interpol, the Swiss Border Guard Corps. There may be clear and detailed videotape of him and her on surveillance cameras. He has barely spoken to her in the last hour; he has clutched her hand and has made sure she is at least as comfortable as she can be, but they will need huge distances from Switzerland (perhaps even oceans of distance) before they can allow themselves to feel relaxed, even a slight bit.

He literally crosses his fingers and hopes that the beaten man eventually crawled out of the tub, righted himself, and did what he could to clean off the blood and make his appearance less terrifying. Towards that end, Nick untied the man's wrists from the tub's plumbing, and undid the tie around his ankles.

He hopes that perhaps the man (late at night and with the hotel quiet and public areas empty) left the room. Perhaps he dragged himself along the hall, took the stairs down to the first floor, using the railing for support, and exited the building from a corner door.

Maybe it was some scarcely used door that availed him an unnoticed escape, and from there deposited him into the dark city. And from there? Who knows?

•

It is headline news, once again. Every few months it sometimes seems, it is back again. Riots. Protests. The results of economic chaos. Blake and Nick turn the pages, and this morning it is seemingly in every aspect of their view. They trade newspapers and read, mostly in silence as the train carries them farther south, away from Switzerland and now down the length of Italy. In front of their eyes, is the current and dire news of the place they are (perhaps) returning to.

The papers run with it and splash it across the front page. Another outbreak. Tear gas and cars overturned and on fire, and crowds marching down streets and clashing with police (who, the photos make clear, are armed and defended with paramilitary gear, which adds yet another sense of menace). People are throwing rocks into windows and smashing the insides of businesses with blind fury. There are pictures of men, their faces obscured by scarfs in that old time-honored tradition, wielding clubs. There are peaceful protests in front of the Greek parliament, but the world's eyes are directed elsewhere.

To Blake, it is mostly bafflement. The islands seem permanently immune from such chaos, and her reading is also a way to keep her mind on something other than her and Nick's obvious predicament. And perhaps, she thinks, the wider world's trouble may provide a sort of cover for their own problems. But to Nick, more versed in the school of fraud, it is also suddenly a hint of an opening. Another possibility. A lever to be perhaps used.

In central Athens, people observe that there is a sick variety of random vandalism on storefronts that seems to occur in the middle of the night, which is particularly upsetting. It's as if the country is sinking further into a pit that has no bottom. There is a sort of self-destruction, as a new reality deepens its hold of peoples' imagination and psyche.

The Greeks are *not pleased*, as one commentator dryly notes, trying to add some levity to the otherwise dour news. Observers and pundits record that over the last several years it appears the world's original champion of democracy is continuing to split at the seams, and complete catastrophe remains only one crisis away.

There is a division and an anger that is difficult to understand without perspective. Yet that doesn't stop the press and world leaders from scolding and playing dumb about the unfolding situation. The facts concerning horribly constructed policies and financial arrangements, which were struck decades earlier, have long been swept aside and ignored. But now, they are coming to their inevitable and mathematically destined end, whether or not other nations and organizations will truthfully acknowledge the facts and their complicity.

Austerity is the new solution bandied about (and apparently the only solution) to all of the questions about the current state of affairs in Greece, and the country's future. It is also turning into a code word: it clearly means "penance," and "comeuppance." However, it is not the same as justice.

The talking heads say yet again, with disbelief, that they can't see why the troubled nation doesn't just accept their answer with good grace.

In truth, it is easy to see: The millions of average and ordinary people have been lied to for years from all sides, and then made complicit in the fraud. The so-called experts were nothing of the sort. It is infuriating. It is humiliating. A younger generation of people have been sold out by a vile (or charitably, *incompetent*) group of largely unidentified *others.* Perhaps, it is an explosion of both humility and unfocused revenge. Economics, is suddenly also life, and they have trusted the wrong people to manage it.

Nick thinks, turning the pages and scanning the articles.

He notices that it didn't take long until the word "insolvent" started dropping from people's lips, and showing up in print. It means that the country will *never* pay back its debts. The interest owed will continually outstrip the income available. Nick notices as he holds and folds the paper with his hands that now roughly twenty-four hours later, his knuckles are returning to normal. His mind is starting to think and cover ground in a familiar way, as well.

He wonders, did Johansen read the papers and then ponder the larger situation as he did? Did he call one of his assistants, or perhaps even one of his pie-faced bodyguards over to his side, and then send them out on an errand? Perhaps they were to drive into town, and then scour the news racks and libraries so that they could return later with piles of journals and magazines rife with a certain type of information. Did Johansen read more online, did he consult with his small army of minions to form his opinions? Did he pull charts and obscure but critical financial data? In fact, Johansen probably knew the very decision-makers themselves, and had an inside line on the situation and likely outcomes. Maybe Johansen (friend of politicians and donor to campaigns) even directed some of those decisions?

Nick ponders the situation. He sees Johansen, sitting there in his estate, amongst his fine accumulations and property. He sees Johansen redirecting his focus to yet again grow his domain. (And that domain already stretched far and wide.) Again, from that particular grey haze, this time at the bottom of Europe, Nick feels that different empires will be built, and behind them, somehow, one name will be at work.

Nick knows this well. It is the time of panic and bargain selling and desperation amongst one group of people. It will attract Johansen. And among the powerless he will wield even more force.

People and businesses want *out.* Or they are being driven out. Completely. The intrinsic value is still there, but the word *desperate* captures their current reality. The debt has crushed hope. With his vast reserves and access to capital, Johansen will buy-in at the time of greatest pessimism, and the sellers will be grateful for the rescue. Hotels, beachfront property, and businesses that are sound (but are strangled in the current climate) will be his quarry. Burning cars and demonstrations in the streets are a clear expression of pessimism, which is written in large bold letters. The strategy is thus: Let a stacked-system cut people off at the knees, and then pleasantly offer them a tourniquet to ease the bleeding.

Perhaps decades later, the grand fraud will be widely understood, but by then the landscape will have shifted. The rebuilding will primarily benefit the equity holders and investors. Promises of an eventual reckoning will go unheeded. The huge prices paid to regroup will always be socialized across the broad population, and yet the greatest profits privatized into the pockets of a few. Again, the same scenario is going to play out, but on an even larger scale. A younger generation (or two) is going to have their future mortgaged yet again. Across the Americas and Europe, Nick knows he is watching the greatest wealth transfer in the history of the world unfold, and yet it is never mentioned by name.

Nick and Blake talk in hushed tones. The view from the train's window giving them something to look at besides the newspapers folded on Nick's lap and spread around their feet on the floor. To the other passengers, the two of them perhaps appear strangely focused. Not exactly as if they are in the midst of an argument, but more as if they are weighing the largest of decisions, bizarrely on a train headed down the center of Italy in the midst of tourist season. Nick schools Blake on his designs, the facts of the situation and how the larger backdrop is changing – or so he guesses. She listens, offering her observations of Radcliff: The way he once described her mission to Zurich and how he presented himself at the time, and the motives that she imagine drive such people.

It seems clear to Nick, that again, no one with any *weight* is coming to the fore to accost the fraudsters. (Johansen among the guilty.) If there is to be any justice in Nick's world, it will only be himself, and perhaps Blake, to divvy out.

He brokenly smiles at Blake, and sometimes holds her hand. But there is a burden around both their necks, and it isn't merely simple affection that makes her return his squeeze, but a need for reassurance. In Nick's mind there are years of ruminating and fallow planning and observing that are starting to coalesce. Radcliff, Nick now understands, is susceptible to certain pressures. At times, he has dangerous and emotionally destructive thoughts, and he is also intent on seeing them carried out. Clearly, there is the need for him to exact revenge and assert himself in a certain way, and perhaps (in his mind) protect his empire. Even if it means exposing himself to reprisals. Was Johansen similarly compromised and in his own way *weak?*

In this puzzle of constantly reorienting pieces, Nick hopes that there is an opportunity. He wants to bait Johansen into another fraud, and yet this time he wants to be there to collect the evidence and garner witnesses for his side. He reminds himself – he knows things. He can entrap Johansen. Nick has his intelligence and newfound strength to urge him on, and now, sitting beside him, is a particular girl. Again, he squeezes her hand. There is no way she can ever know just how much she means to him. For once, he thinks, the feeling in his gut is different.

He comes to some sort of summation as he and Blake talk, quietly. It's as if he wants to keep both their expressions low because, in the end, he still can't see a way truly forward.

And then, Blake, in her memorable voice, drops a little bomb.

She says, matter-of-factly while dejectedly looking at the papers, "There's an old saying: No one is easier to sell than a salesman."

Nick follows her gaze. He sees on the front page a picture, and it is of a particularly daft man holding court in front of a group of microphones. A sea of reporters and other people from the press and powers-that-be, are hanging on his every word.

Nick breathes for a moment.

Suddenly, he stands up, and from the overhead bin he muscles down his overstuffed duffle bag. He knows that something is locking into place.

Wordlessly, and hurriedly, he sets the bag upon both their laps, and unzips it, and digs inside.

"What are you looking for?" Blake's voice is uneasy.

"*I hope…*" Nick begins, upon finding a shirt, which is clearly wrapped around a medium-sized flat object.

He brings the item to the fore, and removes the shirt to reveal a framed photograph of his old boat. Blake recognizes the picture, of course, but the mystery deepens when Nick turns it to its reverse side and hurriedly pries the back off.

Again, quietly he says, *"I hope…"*

There, scrawled in a hurried hand by pencil on the reverse side of the picture, is a disorganized list of names of people, and perhaps organizations or businesses, none of which makes any sense to Blake. There are associated phone numbers and other numbers with arrows and circles around them. To her eyes, it's a jumble of incoherent notes. The scribbling is that of a person in a panic-induced state of mind.

Nick concentrates, scanning his many-year-old note, written at one of his lowest points. A point of desperation.

His fingers now rest beneath a clearly printed name – Samson. The man with great bags beneath his eyes, and the ridiculous affected British accent. Nothing but a salesman to the very end. Nick can imagine the man, as if not a day had past, walking around his house and holding court about art works and sculptures; things he doesn't know the first thing about. Nick's stomach turns and twists. A phone number and business, Ice Station, accompany the name.

"I hope," Nick says again, "that just *one* piece of the puzzle works in our favor."

•

They abandon the train in Brindisi, in the "heel" of Italy's boot. It is late morning, and as Blake and Nick shuffle through the station, it is clear they are in a different part of Italy. It's a port town, but a different kind of port: one that is primarily commercial and working hard for its pay.

There is a little kiosk-cafe in the station, and as Nick departs to find a telephone, Blake gathers their luggage around, and orders a pair of espressos and little cookie style wafers to chew on.

When Nick returns the news is mixed. It has been an anxious night riding down the length of the country, and his voice is weary. The number – Samson's number - he says, is *still* no longer in service, which he expected.

But, he says, he also tried a bank in Milan, eventually locating a manager that was especially helpful to him back in the Radcliff days. At least *there*, Nick says pleased, the relationship was still fine; his misdeeds had apparently not been pursued by Radcliff, which Nick also expected. Nick is pleased that he assumed correctly: Any type of official pursuit would open both him *and* Radcliff to an uncomfortable amount of scrutiny.

"I'm supposed to call back in a few hours," he says. Taking a nip of the caffeine and, for the first time in many hours, taking a close look at Blake. He wonders, touching the back of his head (which is still painful), if she is with him at this point only because she seems to have few other options.

They check into a hotel. Nick pays with cash. Nick thinks twice about using his own passport and name, but he fills out the card and slides it across the desk all the same, and then it is done. His name and this location will (eventually) be correlated in a searchable database. Are the two of them being over or under-cautious? He consults his watch. Soon enough he will need to make his return phone call, and with that, it is possible that a new avenue will open. He knows that without Blake, he wouldn't be at this juncture.

Once their luggage is in their room, and some water is thrown on their faces, they install themselves at the hotel's empty restaurant, which is alongside a pleasant little garden. Blake, he knows, is tired and mentally and physically exhausted. She stares at the flowers and notes the birdbath, which unlike their current environment, is busy with activity and the occasional happy bird "chirp" makes its way into the breakfast room. Perhaps all she really wants at the moment is a shower and a long sleep; they have traveled over 700 miles since yesterday. She reclines in a chair as Nick bothers a waiter for a phone. The waiter appears, and feigns confusion regarding Nick's request, until Nick casually pushes fifty euros his way, which is quickly and subtly placed into the pocket of his prim little black vest.

Deftly and with a flourish of unnecessary and theatrical motion, the phone is placed on a table, and its long cable crawls along the floor.

Nick dials; he waits on hold. He asks Blake to find him a piece of paper and a pen. Nick speaks and is effusive in his thanks to whomever he talks with on the other end of the line. He dials another number. Blake looks at him, questioning, and he nods his head and gives a little smile. He speaks, and diligently writes on the paper she has found for him. The waiter appears, hovering. A concerned look affects his face, and Nick removes another fifty Euro note from his wallet, and nonchalantly places it on the table. The waiter takes it, and disappears. Nick makes more notes on his piece of paper.

Nick, again, is on hold. Into the restaurant walks a small group of locals; young females who instantly find the full attention of the waiter. They smile and banter. Nick has a reprieve from the growing cost of his illicit phone rental. Nick's ears perk up with the cheery female voices that fill the room. Radcliff once called them "Imports," a term he culled from an American sleazing his way around the coast. They were small, spoke with a strong accent, and seemed to absorb an inordinate amount of attention. At the time, Radcliff said, "Look, you can't just jump in one of them and go. You have to warm them up first." And sure enough, the waiter is showering them with courtesy and thoughtful gestures.

•

"Sorry," the voice on the other end of the line is distracted, and barely paying attention, "Mr. Samson is not available at the moment." It must be the most boring call of the day for her, but for Nick, it is *everything.*

Nick's voice wants to tremble with the news he has been

given. Finally, a break in the armor. He realizes a direct assault on Johansen was never going to work. It is his small army of enablers that are his first weakness.

Instead of exerting a sigh of awareness, Nick tries to pile on the charm, and he hides his exaltation. Blake looks at him as his voice changes. For a moment everything seems possible. Nick sits bolt upright. He speaks into the phone: "Ummm, that's too bad. Will he, perhaps, be in tomorrow? I hate to trouble you."

"Oh," the voice is responding, "it's no trouble. No trouble at all. It's just been, well, a little crazy around here with the news. Riots and so forth down there. *Again.* So far away, but still. Every time we try and help, they do this. They are *ghastly.* Don't they understand? He'll probably be back in a few weeks or thereabouts. I can take a message, if you'd like?"

Nick calms himself. "He's *not* down in Athens," Nick asks with a familiar tone, "perhaps lending his capable hands with all the important negotiations? I've been reading something about it in the papers. Helping out and so forth, is he actually there? *Quite* a job, if he is."

"Well, *of course* he is." The voice on the other end of the line is adamant. They want everyone to know; they want their organization's self-effacing role in this humble rescue for the state of Greece to be fully appreciated. Hero financiers to the rescue, clearly.

Over the next several hours, there are more calls, but this time to Nice. They are made and received, and eventually Nick speaks with the Nice harbormaster and his staff. Another fifty euros is spent, and a "complimentary" very late breakfast is served and slowly consumed, while Blake stares out at the garden and watches the birds come and go, and tries to calm her thoughts. Nick is his old self, now. There is a time for glad-handing and game-playing, and it is *not* when he speaks to actual friends and associates. She hears it in his voice and sees it in his face. Things are changing.

Nick writes down a particular location. He underlines it and stares at it. He says "thank you," a dozen times into the phone. He breathes a sigh, and he looks fleetingly at Blake. Now is the time when he will have to make a considerable commitment.

•

It seems that almost everyone is familiar with the island of Mykonos. But nearby (within mere hours) are numerous other similar islands, but of course, of much different size and population. And certainly different prestige and notoriety.

The one island is a well-known tourist haunt, complete with the expected Greek culture, whitewashed and radiant architecture, beaches, and stunning Mediterranean views, and yet sometimes overwrought hotel and club-culture. Most of the other islands, however, are far less inhabited and touristed, and yet with an amazing array of simple pleasures and profound significance.

Nick consults a map on a computer screen, while Blake is elsewhere. Likely, she is somewhere nearby in the city center, distracting herself and trying to fill the time by staring into shop windows, or perhaps walking through a museum. Maybe too, Nick wonders, she has an odd little slant to her pose.

On the map, he sees the navigational beacons and landmarks, the contours of the ocean floor, the many islands, most with other much smaller satellite islands, rock formations, and uninhabited outposts easily within sight of one another. There are well-trafficked shipping lanes, and routes for commuter boats and large cruise ships, which have otherwise been crisscrossed for thousands of years. And slowly zeroing in on the location Nick has been given, he gathers that Johansen's gleaming white yacht is now anchored within spitting distance of most all of it. He consults and double-checks the numbers and finds an unlikely point on the map.

Nick sketches out the terrain and features of the water on a clean sheet of paper, improvising a map of his own. He alternates back and forth between a satellite view, a basic view and a political view on the computer, noting villages and names of various locations. He finds the phonetic pronunciation of difficult Greek words, and spells them out, for use later. He finds real estate listings, the names of town officials (where available), and looks up pictures that tourists have posted of gleaming beaches and empty bays, where – despite the beauty – it seems only a handful of people visit every year, particularly lately. Suddenly, the outrageous idea of Johansen maneuvering to buy an entire island, or at least the bulk of it, and then with his considerable influence eventually turning that island into a vacation tourist mecca doesn't seem far-fetched at all. Or perhaps he might simply hold it, and wait long enough and then quadruple (or more) his investment. He imagines this as just one of Johansen's many pronged approach.

Clearly, Johansen has his boat inconspicuously moored many miles away from the nearest harbor, and decently far out at sea, but still protected by one of those many rock formations and sandbars, all in order to keep the native eyes from it. No doubt, the intent is to hide his wealth, but still have access to one aspect of it, should the circumstances dictate such. He may want to entertain on his boat, or prove a point with it (as he once did with Nick many years ago) or simply enjoy it. He may want to follow some of those ancient sea routes and partake in the history of the location.

Nick makes a leap in his head. Sure enough within the opportunity of financial chaos, Johansen is there to buy, to scam, to leverage his position, and doesn't want to tip his hand, or provoke an untoward response.

•

Nick and Blake share a strange, lightly tortured and chaste romance. She imagines that he questions her motives for staying with him, and he is perhaps afraid to completely avail himself to her. He holds her hand, and is amazed when she does not remove herself from his clutches. Here, in the deep south, where Italy flirts with becoming an different country than most people know, the summer is simply hot and sometimes oppressive.

In another time perhaps they would have smiled together at the beautiful way the plaster in their little hotel room cracked and made an abstract design on the wall. They might have taken a small joy together, as they playfully fought over the scant space in front of the bathroom mirror, or in trying to find a place to stow their luggage. This time, however, they have but one night in their small room alongside the garden, with the air conditioner rattling away in the window, and the bird chirps waking them in the morning. All that transpires is Blake placing her head on his chest for comfort as she falls into a much needed deep sleep. And, as Nick slowly drifts away (the exhaustion finally taking complete hold) the weight of her head and the way her arm rests across his shoulders, becomes the most gentle thing that he has ever felt. Perhaps it is because they have made a decision. He told her, "It can't be me."

He told her: Blake, *you* are the one who will have to stay in Athens, once we get there. You are the one that will have to find Samson, and drop the name of the island in front of him, *and right into his ear,* and at just the right time. And then read the expression on his face. It can't be me. He would, of course, recognize me.

"And even then," Nick added with an attempted laugh, "I'm not as good as you at those kinds of things."

She cringed imperceptibly. She thought: He thinks I'm a manipulator. He thinks I play people. He thinks I'm a con artist. Still, she nodded her head "Yes." She said, "Of course, I will do it. Anything for you to get your money back." But inside she was breaking a little bit.

As they stood in the bank's lobby, Blake wondered (again) if they really had to do this right now. As awful as it was, she wondered if they could live in this uncertain twilight world for a few days longer, because the alternatives could be so much worse.

It's so primitive down there, he explained. Radcliff's money, the bait, has to be in place. We have to be nimble. We have to move fast. We have to misdirect his attention, and make Johansen spread himself thin. I just want him to be alone – *unguarded* - for a little while. Down there, we won't find banks to do this sort of thing. He held her hand. The unspoken message was: I'm trusting you with everything I have or will ever have. Don't let me down.

He said, "Have you ever underestimated someone? And then been bitten by them?"

She smiled in her eyes, "Yes."

"That's what we're going to do."

After it was done and all of Radcliff's ill-gotten money was grouped together for the first time, and then transferred into a business account that Blake had complete control over, she tried to look strong. She brushed her hair away from her face, and her little silver bracelets jingled in the air. She looked at the deposit slip. She shuddered that Nick trusted her that much.

"If this doesn't work in the next few days," he said, "you'll have to get the money out in cash. You'll have to simply hide it somewhere. You'll have to leave the city. Maybe just go back home." He said, with worry, "We're starting to leave a trail, and it might all fall apart. I don't know."

She looked at him, an expression of fear and then hope crossed her face. They stood together in a far corner of the bank's lobby. Sometimes the swinging doors opened to the street, which allowed the hurried sound of traffic and buses noisily making their way around the city to echo inside.

"And what about you?" she asked. "How will you find me?"

"I don't know where to tell you to go. Or where, exactly, I will be. We'll figure it out. We'll talk." He searched his mind. "We can use our phones again. In fact, we *should* use our phones."

People wandered by, barely giving them a look, and oblivious to their gravity. It was getting closer to their final farewell.

She sked, "Remember the windmills?"

He smiled.

"That's not too far away from where you'll be, is it?"

"No, he said. "Not too far at all."

She fumbled around in her purse. "I nearly forgot, I bought this for you," she said. "While you were looking up maps and so forth. But I think I got the wrong size. I just liked the color so much."

She handed him a new leather watch band.

He laughed. "It's a woman's size, I'm pretty sure." He removed the band from the plastic packaging and he temporarily wrapped the new leather band around his wrist and showed her.

"Oh, yes!" She laughed. "Too small."

He smiled and said, "You can just ask. If you want me to give you my old watch. I'd be happy with that."

He removed the watch from his wrist. And then she helped him detach the old torn-up and nearly threadbare band, and together they affixed the new one. He noted, the color she chose *did* look wonderful. And after pushing aside her silver bracelets, by moving them farther up her arm, he buckled his old watch securely around her wrist, so it was now hers.

14

Blake looks around the terrace on the third floor of the Athens hotel. There is a random mix of locals, tourists, and business people, and then every so often one of these obnoxious caricatures. They are easy to recognize: they are all men (or so it appears to Blake after a few scans of the area) and they wear dark three-piece suits with ridiculously overdone pinstripes, as if they were somehow attempting to resurrect the zoot suit. In truth, it's a reference to the 1980's bankers' uniform, but the irony has been lost, and thus transformed into a parody. The suggestion is that these people are incapable of really seeing themselves when they look into a mirror, which is an unsettling thing to see ad nauseam.

Nick had said that Samson was ageless, he could be 30 or 60-years old, and that description she has noticed, seemingly applies to all of them. They're like man-babies, or strangely aged boys playing dress-up in their grandfather's clothes. Instead, she ignores the overall person and looks for the revealing bags under the eyes. But like this one specimen standing in front of her, they all have painful complexions from their sudden exposure to the Mediterranean sun and it's difficult to for her to remain impassive.

The scene is unnerving for other reasons too. Days ago the very streets that surround the hotel were clouded with tear gas, and anyone unlucky enough to be caught outside was running, and trying to hide their faces and breathe through their shirts. It seems every so often there is another flare-up, like a forest fire that refuses to simply be put out. Sometimes it makes the news, other times it is just background and ignored by the larger world. Today, there is an armed force on the streets, keeping the status quo and dispersing any groups larger than a set of four.

Inside, and up and above on the terrace that overlooks this tightly packed part of the city, Blake considers the view, and then her many conversational partners, which she needs to engage and coddle. She thinks: In the 14th century no one else produced repulsive, inbred, and humanity starved like the European gentry. And she can clearly see the lineage while listening to the droning and insulting conversation. Her mind can't help but wander and then follow a thread. Offhandedly, she imagines the thousands (maybe tens of thousands) of portraits that aristocratic families commissioned during that age, and she marvels over the artistic skill that it took to produce pictures of these people that were recognizable and yet not hideous to behold. How do you make *that* seem honorable? And now, due to the Mediterranean's strong sun, the otherwise sheltered thing (standing far too close to her) is a pinkish-white.

Blake is fully deployed, however. And like the artists of past, she knows how to coax, flatter and bait what is in front of her.

"It's so unfair," she says. "They're blaming people like you for the crisis. Can you believe the audacity?" She stirs her drink with the little straw letting the ice jingle, and feigns a look of concern, indicating that the thing may resume its sermonizing, and casual affronts to her intelligence. They never seem to get tired of talking.

In the early evening the offices across the city are turning off their lights. People are starting to think about food, and every so often another small batch of speculator types and zoot suites unloads from the nearby elevator (and hence from the conference rooms below) and deposits itself at the bar. It seems no one up here is keen to leave the building. The earlier marching in the streets, and the chaotic events that followed, suggest that, yes, the hotel is indeed a *very* closed arena. And that, eventually, Blake's eyes and ears will find that one special person.

The representatives from various governments, those few from the International Monetary Fund, and bureaucrats from central banks (and so on) have the good sense to at least maintain some sort of formal distance from these hangers-on, and thus have closed meetings and an otherwise highly selective guest list at other locations (usually undisclosed) around the city. But that doesn't mean they don't mingle afterwards. That doesn't mean they don't engage in side deals and invitations to different meetings to *gather opinions*, and see how the bond markets and traders are going to react to possible decisions. In fact it's an absurdist feedback loop, one where businesses and individuals that would otherwise be ruined, toxic and permanently ejected from the economy (after years of catastrophic decision-making) are instead consulted with, and then advise leaders on public policy, so that the very organizations that have demanded bailouts are also the ones weighing-in on economic strategy. Again, the irony has been lost and transformed into parody. Everyone is supposedly a ruthless capitalist during the good times, but then suddenly pivot towards socialistic altruism (but only for privileged groups) in the bad times.

The immediate concern and person for Blake, who is still standing far too close to her, is now starting to imbue his voice with a new timbre of victimhood. It's upsetting to see such a strong and sour correlation between internal and external appearances. Blake knows that if she were to shake hands with this item, she would feel the baby-soft skin of someone who has never lifted a shovel, changed a tire on a car, used a broom, or otherwise engaged in the bitter business of manual labor even once in his life. He would find it beneath himself.

In her heels, she is several inches taller than he is, and most of the others gathered around the terrace. It gives her something of a wide view of the proceedings. Looking around, as if in complete interest, she says, "Oh, that is *quite* fascinating. I had no idea." And then changing tack slightly, "Although it reminds me of something I heard someone say here the other night. I'm trying to remember his name…"

Her conversational partner is all eyes and ears, now. She places her hands on her hips, as if to draw attention to her shape, and moves one leg in front of the other, revealing even more thigh beneath her mid length skirt.

It's the second night of this, and Blake has adapted and improved her game, and yet it is apparent that time is running out. "Mr. Sam-*something*…," she says, studying the reptilian expression of the man in front of her. The hint of the name doesn't seem to trigger any recognition in his face. Another zero, she thinks, hiding her frustration.

"Will you please excuse me?"

Even leaving him, he seems to not understand. "I think

I see my friend," she says, touching his arm in a friendly way that makes her revolt the smallest bit inside. He turns to watch her walk away and then plant herself at the bar, as two other men immediately engage her in conversation.

•

From the moment Nick departed Blake's side, he was trying to refocus his thoughts. She had her role to play in this trap, while he had his.

It seemed likely, even definite, that Johansen was down on the islands, perhaps on one island in particular, buying real estate. Or rather, Johansen was forcing himself and his empire upon an already compromised prey. His beloved gleaming white yacht was anchored right in the heart of the cluster. His focus, was doubtlessly trained on purchasing some otherwise disregarded asset, and at an incredibly discounted price. Blake, with her world-wise grace and charm (and coy manipulation), could confirm that small but critical point. Perhaps she could even narrow it down to a single location or venture? And in the days that followed, she would knowingly play a different role.

It was a role that Nick had played, unwittingly years earlier. That of dupe, chump, mark, pigeon, and fool. To succeed, she needed to seem like a certain variety of person: overly eager to work her position, and with just the right amount of naïveté and misplaced confidence. Those same attributes he had displayed years before, and horrifically drawn in Johansen. He tried not to consider her motives for joining him.

One time, not long ago, she had said, "Why don't you try and get it all back?" And now here they were, trying something similar.

She never once said to him, "Be happy with what you have." She never said to him, "Let's just leave this place, and start again together."

Instead, she looked at him and ran her hands through his hair. She tugged at his shirt collar, and then looked into his eyes. She knew the truth and so did Nick. Very rarely had she seen his real self. Nick had moved from one person into the next, and perhaps she was still waiting for the time when he would safely make it to that final shore. Maybe she would be there, waiting for him in her entirety as well.

Until then, a handful of smaller tasks await him. Stores to visit, purchases to be made, travel arrangements decided, and tickets to be bought. And then he must travel back down to the islands himself. Once there, a much larger and more dangerous undertaking will loom for him.

•

"I didn't catch your name," this one says to her, as if sizing her up, and attempting to bait her into a flirty conversation, that will eventually end in his hotel room's bed. The overly Britishized inflections in his voice are almost too much to endure.

"You didn't catch my name?" She replies, without missing a beat. "Well, that's because *I didn't offer it to you."* Her face is posed in a half-smile, and the hint of a challenge towards his very being.

He looks at her and nearly cracks a laugh, unsure how to proceed. There is an awkward silence. She turns her head more than slightly away from him, as if uninterested in continuing the conversation with the likes of him. She knows the baggy-eyed man is starring at her. She can feel his eyes tramp over her body. For the hundredth time, her intellectual capabilities have been underestimated because of her looks.

It is the last evening of this, and the hotel's terrace is at its most boisterous and crowded. To the side, someone of an equal disposition is droning on, in an agonizing conversation to yet another one of these types. He is holding court regarding the outrageous taxes he is forced to pay in the United Kingdom, and he says he is thus considering moving himself to Monte Carlo, where there is of course no personal income tax. It's *this* exhausting barrage *again,* which Blake has heard several times now. Although, he wants his conversational partner to know, there are additional strategies he can adopt to lower his tax rates even more. Clearly, both he and his bankrupt industry will surely take the rescue handed out, but not the economic accountability or debt they owe. Apparently there is always too much money going the wrong direction, and nothing else matters.

"It's the reason so many Formula One drivers call *Monte* home," he states with pained emphasis. The exchange is embarrassing to all within earshot. "But, for people with certain freedoms, there are other aggressive measures available."

There is, then, the inevitable sound of the voice to Blake's side, once again. She looks over with indifference, and a hint of irritation painted across her face.

"Are you part of this?" he says, his baggy eyes gesturing around the room and elsewhere, while holding his drink in his paw. He continues to require her attention. "Part of the show?"

Blake narrows her expression, as if not comprehending. "No," she says. "I don't think so."

He explains it to her, clearly expecting her to be impressed. Every last one of them, according to his version, is rescuing Greece and the Greeks from themselves.

"Well," she says, brightening a small bit, "maybe you are a person to talk with. I'm actually down here looking at real estate."

"Oh, are you?" he says.

•

Nick holds on to the railing as the small craft launches from the dock. At early evening, he will yet have enough time to locate a room for the night at his destination. Mere hours on a small boat, or minutes, are all it takes to travel from one island to another. The skipper nudges the throttle open, the diesel engine wakes up, and the propeller churns the water at the stern, and a copious amount of diesel smoke billows from the exhaust and then diffuses in the wind. The railing vibrates in sympathy beneath Nick's hands, and the boat pushes out and speeds up. The few tourists and locals on the boat look ahead and across the water in order to judge the distance and character of their short crossing.

Soon across, Nick moderates his anxiousness. He allows his fellow travelers off the boat first, taking time to help an older lady with her few parcels and belongings. She is weathered and dressed traditionally: darkly colored clothing that drapes her body in a conservative silhouette. This place, he reminds himself, also serves as peoples' longtime home.

And then, after he sets himself on the island, there it is. After only a short walk. A sort of white beacon on the blue water.

He has walked along deserted roads, and not much more

than a half-hour to find this view, and out there, unnervingly far, is a gleaming white yacht. The setting sun dramatizes its distant shape, and he can barely see three, perhaps four, navigation lights in the growing dusk. A quarter mile to the side, a group of towering rocks seem to look over the boat.

Nick knows what awaits him, sometime in the coming nights. He will have to plant a sort of "gift" on that yacht. It is something he has come to think of as an Easter egg, a little discovery for Johansen, or one of his crew to make, seemingly by accident in the following days. The item is nothing but an older cellphone, with a text message viewable across its screen, but it is something critical, if Nick is to have any chance against Johansen and his small army of support. That message (Nick now imagines) will provoke Johansen in a manner like nothing else.

It will take Nick half the night to swim out to the yacht and back. He could perhaps rent a boat himself, and then abandon it halfway there, and swim the remainder, but the boat would later be discovered floating and drifting. He has experience with the little harbors and the people who occupy them, just like those here. Word would spread. It would be clear giveaway that something else (something out of the ordinary) was being perpetrated. Nick can't take that chance. There can be no doubt, or other alternative scenarios at the moment of discovery, or later on, circling in Johansen's mind. It must appear that the phone is part of a larger separate story, which Johansen cannot afford to allow to continue.

Instead, Nick reconciles himself to the task ahead. Although, he knows that if Blake cannot find Samson, if she cannot succeed in her undertaking, all of this final effort will perhaps be for naught. He finds a rock to lean against, and contemplates the view and the distance in the fading light, which he must eventually cross. Many times he has set off into the ocean, swimming, and wondering if he would ever return; sometimes acknowledging that a small part of him hoped he would never make it back. This time he knows he must. For the first time in years (he doesn't dare count the number) there is something at stake that matters more than his own life.

•

She takes a remaining sip of her drink, and finishes it off, while the man with the great bags under his eyes insists that he get her another, and so he makes a spectacle of attracting the bartender's attention.

He is now doubly intrigued by her and dying to prove himself of use and importance. "Real estate? What part of the country? Here in the city? It's a good time to buy property, actually. If you're smart about it - and thinking long-term."

Blake looks at him. She knows that she needs to slow her pace. Or, perhaps even push him further away. "Probably no place that you've heard of…No place that you would know."

He says with affected concern, "It's going to be quite difficult for you to get a loan these days. Money is tight. The Credit Crunch and all, which never seems to go away, at least in these parts."

He wants her to see that he knows more than her: "Down here, I'm afraid, it's a different business. Where, again, were you looking?"

"I'm thinking of paying with cash, actually. No need for a loan. It's an investment. And I have a decent amount to spend."

His appraisal of her is clearly changing, now. She notices him check again, and make sure her ring finger is indeed bare, although it probably wouldn't matter either way. He is silent now and thinking, perhaps maneuvering in his mind.

"You know," Blake says, filling the space momentously, and without a trace of jest in her voice. "You would be a decently handsome person if you just learned how to dress like a man."

What? The baggy-eyed man stumbles in his thoughts. All at once, he is suddenly fuming. He tries to laugh. Is she joking?

Without looking down at his shoes, Blake states matter-of-factly into his face: "You shouldn't wear little Italian shoes with a suit like that. *Didn't you ever learn that?* (She looks dead at him.) You need to wear shoes with some good-sized welts. There is nothing worse than some little meek and dainty feet at the bottom of a strong pant line. It's weak."

His face is turning even another shade of pink. He looks to the side, nervous that someone else has heard her take him apart so easily.

Again, he is at a loss, but cannot disengage from her; he must prove himself.

"Yes. Okay, I see. So real estate? Property, homes, commercial, resort?" He re-enters the conversation, trying to steer the two of them back to safe ground, and ignoring her dismissal of him, once more. "I know a great deal about such things. Part of the reason I'm down here, as well, in fact." His face is returning to what passes for normal, although his breathing is heavy.

Blake's drink shows up, set in front of her and looking especially appetizing. "Thank you, for this, by the way. And to answer your earlier question, I'm considering buying something on one of the islands."

He is clearly drawing in.

"Well," she says and continues conspiratorially, "I will probably have to transact the purchase through a trust, or some such intermediary. Foreigners and beachfront property. I'm sure you know the drill."

"*Oh*," he says. "One of the islands?" Almost imperceptibly he leans in closer. Trying to tempt her, he helpfully offers that he can easily refer her to any number of people who can assist her with buying. Trusted people that can act as intermediaries. They can draw up papers; do the homework.

She delicately drops the name of a few of the islands in his ear, almost as if by accident. There is no change in his expression. She saves her dynamite for the last one.

She reads his face perfectly as the final name explodes, quietly.

"Oh!" he is suddenly concerned.

He is stalling for time. "I might think twice about that." She sees him glance up and to the side, searching his mind hurriedly for an excuse as to why she should purchase elsewhere. She is targeting one of Johansen's islands, and if there is one thing a con artist hates, it's competition. Another bidder to raise the price. When his deflection finally arrives, his lie is as transparent as they come. "Bad water there," he says.

"The ocean? I don't understand."

"No. No. The drinking water. Completely contaminated. Poisonous, perhaps. That island has a horrible reputation. You can buy cheap, but you wouldn't want to. I'm sure of it. It would be a disaster." She's dumb;

he's smart, apparently.

"That's good to know!" She takes a sip of her drink. "I'll certainly pass that one by, then. I might have made a huge mistake. *Thank goodness I met you.*"

He sticks out his hand. "Everyone just calls me Samson. They don't even bother with the *Mr.* these days." He says this with a manipulated laugh. It's the kind of laugh that attempts to say he's including her in a brilliant inside joke, and that in fact everyone regards him as a beloved old chum.

Sure. Of course, everyone thinks you're a beloved chum, she thinks. Right up until that ugly last moment.

Blake smiles, and offers her hand, and lightly grips his child-soft skin.

"Miranda," Blake says. "Very pleased to make your acquaintance."

•

The real estate broker looks nervous. He has the telltale signs of someone who would rather be anywhere else than where he is right at this moment. His brow is sweating (it's a hot day, but *still*); his eyes keep looking at the entranceway to his little office. And then his eyes look through the door's window to the Athens street, as if he is expecting someone to suddenly show themselves.

Directly across the street is one of those ugly and horribly aging cement buildings, which seems to define the leftover parts of the city. Blake notices that his conversation keeps bending towards a certain purpose.

She really doesn't want that little stretch of land, does she? What possible use could it be? Again she hears the lie repeated. Bad drinking water. Samson coached him on that point, and many others.

From the very beginning, he was a certain way with her. Steering her to property she didn't want. Treating her with a condescending attitude, and underestimating her observational skills. He didn't even try to hide his agenda. Before she walked in he already had a map laying out, and brochures and pictures scattered across his desk. All for locations *far away* from that particular island. It would have been humorous, if it wasn't also so sinister.

But then there was a change in mood.

Together, Blake and the broker look at the map, with parcels marked out and identified by strong lines and clear demarcations. She puts her finger, again, exactly on the same parcel she has several times before. She won't be dissuaded. It's a narrow little stretch of land, and not unlike a finger itself, which seems to almost bisect two other much larger and clearly attractive pieces of property. Both of those, along with numerous other pieces of the island have apparently been taken off the market within the last few days and weeks. Strange, she notes, and the agent ignores her.

It's as if someone is buying up the whole island she states, intentionally sounding naïve, stupid. If she (or anyone) happened to look up the buyers (a difficult process at any time, but especially now), what would they find? Merely a listing of anonymous-sounding people and entities, which just happen to have the similar goals. Ostensibly, none of them connected.

But this piece of property. Well, perhaps if someone wanted to run a road connecting beachfront locations and little coves, they *would definitely* want to have that spot. It would be critical, in fact. Maybe if they were trying to develop a resort. Create some sort of new tourist mecca.

There's a scarcity of undeveloped (or under-developed) property that could serve that function. Or maybe a completest, someone that wants the whole thing just for its own sake. Otherwise, it's not particularly noteworthy, with its rocky outcroppings and steep slopes.

And yet, Blake has offered roughly sixty percent *over* the asking price. The real estate broker is incredulous. Blake says: she just wants to make sure it's hers (this little piece of land, which is not much of anything to the casual observer). She just wants the seller to accept her offer, and to take it off the market, so no one else can bid on it. The broker sees her confidence; he sees the way she focuses in on that little stretch of land. He sees the way she is becoming irritated at his deflections and the way he tries to reset her expectations: It could be weeks, he cautions her, before we hear a reply. That's just the way things move down there. Slowly.

Frustrated, the agent says, "You've been warned about the water, so why do you persist? It's not right for you!" He is getting angry.

Blake stands to the side of the table. She lets it be known that she is not pleased with his attitude or the snail's pace; she brushes away entreaties to consider other, apparently more attractive pieces of property on different islands, far away. She rests her hands on her hips in that way that she does when she is on display, and adjusts the sunglasses in her hair. It's pure Blake. The broker will not look at her full on nor meet her eyes with his own.

Then he says, out of nowhere: "Can you do this? Please, hold up this map of the island for a picture. I need to send it." He says, awkwardly: "When the map is laying down on the desk the light reflects on it too much, there is a glare."

He urges the decently sized map on her. "Here!" He

seems to say, as he holds it out to her, and she plays along. With his phone at the ready, he steps backwards, taking many more steps than are necessary to get a full view of the map. Clearly, what he is really doing is taking a picture of her.

An electronic sound produces its version of a "click." He fidgets with the phone. There is the obvious electronic sound of a message being sent. There are some papers on his desk, which he rearranges, and he then takes the property map and sets it aside like it was suddenly the least important thing in the world.

A few minutes later, he checks his phone. He reads a message. He pauses for a moment.

He then says, "Maybe, we should set up a meeting?" He doesn't look at her. He says this resignedly. Outside, on the busy street, a tour bus rumbles by. A street vendor, a man pushing a rickety cart selling what appears to be baked potatoes, despairingly fills the view.

He says, "Two men who represent a local concern, these agents, they can expedite the process. I'm sure they can be here within a few days, maybe earlier."

"We can all meet here, at the office," he says, but then modifies his words. "Or perhaps sooner, at the very property in question. I can take you there. Yes? That would be better. You'd surely like to see it in-person. Not just on a map?"

His eyes are on hers for a second, and then elsewhere: "You should really see the property, before you make up your mind. These men represent the seller," he says, looking elsewhere. "I think it would be good."

Blake breaks inside, but her face stays calm.

She says, "Of course. That would be wonderful."

•

The details concerning many different contacts and alleged experts that Samson helpfully relayed to her consume approximately a full page, and their names and numbers are seemingly innocuous and surprisingly ordinary. She wonders if this was the way it was for Nick, when they scammed him out of his families fortune.

Here is one from a midsized city in Wales; here is one who has the first name "Delilah," which was also the name of an old professor who once taught her color theory. But there are also people that provide types of esoteric functions, which are not entirely clear to her.

There is one that deals (Samson had said days earlier) "primarily in late-stage due diligence."

She remembered the way he allowed the last word to leave his mouth. Samson had a strange tone in his voice. *Diligence,* he said, as if she were supposed to be impressed by the word. *Late-stage*, on top of it. Yes, it was *all* so official and formalized, imposing and trustworthy.

"Although he can be put to use in many other ways," he also suggested. She thought, pretend to be Samson's friend. Just for a few more days.

But now she is talking with other people. There is a voice on the other end of her phone, asking her to do things she is not sure about. The voice says, "We need to verify funds." It is late at night, but they are supposedly making a rare after-hours exception for her. The office that Samson works with is always available to help.

That is, until there's a change that does not accommodate their wishes. Then the phones go unanswered and messages go unreturned. Blake has talked with Nick, she knows this was coming, but her reply still betrays the smallest bit of anxiety. Only a few days from now the two "agents" are supposed to be meeting with her and the real estate broker. It will supposedly be on a lonely piece land, several hundred miles from here. Nick had said, "This is good. We can use this. This is what I want." But for the first time, she thought about just running away.

"Yes." Blake replies. "Verify funds. How shall we do that? Will a letter suffice? Something official from my bank?"

The voice on the other end of the phone is easy and effortless, as always. It is perhaps business as usual to them, but after Nick's stories, and after the other things she has seen and heard, every exchange of information appears as a battle that cannot be won. It's an engagement that presupposes a titanic amount of trust, but is also a one-sided transaction. She cannot tell where "normal" ends and deception begins. Because, clearly, she is starting to think, they are leading her down a certain path. There was that awkward picture of her. The sound in the voice that said, you've been warned - *why do you persist?*

"That would be fine," the voice says. "Although, in the interim, and to speed up the process perhaps you could email me a computer image? A screen shot of your holding company's bank balances?"

Blake thinks: Yes, but there will be other information on that computer image. Names. Numbers. Dates.

They *know* or think they know.

Soon enough, they will see that I am pretending to be someone else, with a different agenda. She wonders. She tries to imagine the other side.

Perhaps they will think that I have over played my hand?

But Johansen, Samson, and the rest will *still* defraud us, and they will try to do it so well we won't even have a single piece of evidence in which to bring charges. She imagines a ruthless smile on the other end of the phone, though the voice sounds measured and effortless.

"Certainly," Blake answers. "I'll send that over to you just as soon as I can."

The screen capture of the account (should she and Nick decide to send it along) will show the collected total of all the money pilfered from Radcliff's illicit dealings. It will of course appear to prove she is a serious bidder on the piece of property. There will be an account number that can be confirmed with the bank. She, or rather the holding company, can purchase what they say they want, even without external sources. Thus, saving weeks of bureaucratic drag, and perhaps more critically overcoming the impossibility of securing financing at a time like this. All of that is true.

But it will also disclose that her name is not actually Miranda. A name she chose days earlier with a sly smile of her own.

Miranda - it sounded romantic and exotic. It sounded like a name someone who was a dreamer might chose, if she had to invent one for herself. Maybe it sounded like an invented name chosen by someone who thought she could naively step into the tiger's lair without a plan, and fight unarmed and win. She wonders if that possibility is enough to spur Johansen into his final course of action.

It will (hopefully) be a course of action that will have Johansen either playing them for a couple of fools, or a hopelessly outmatched adversaries. Either way, it doesn't really matter, as long as Johansen thinks he's the one with the upper hand. She imagines Johansen as Nick has described him. That estate in that valley, a summer home, in which to contemplate and enjoy both life and business. Two things, which for him were inseparable. After the handshake "sale," they will deliver a false deed to her. Or direct her to transfer money into a corrupted escrow account. Sure enough, there are any number of devices that they can bring to bear on her and Nick, and simply fleece the money away without granting her the property.

And what of these two so-called agents? There might be even worse consequences to this than she and Nick expected, if things go wrong. Tens of millions of dollars are at stake, maybe more depending on Johansen's plans for that property. People will do a lot of horrible things to protect such an amount. One thing is certain: She is *not* going to meet those two agents, no matter what.

Blake was starting to feel and understand what Nick had once been through. There was the feeling of powerlessness, should events turn a certain way. She and Nick were playing a dangerous game. She wants it to be over.

•

Tonight, Nick can barely view the navigation lights on Johansen's yacht. He stands on the beach, he removes his t-shirt, so that all that remains on his body is his swimming suit. His skin looks grey in the darkness. He stares out across the inky-black surface, and reminds himself, again, of the distance he must cross.

Things were different earlier that day. During daylight, when the sun shone down with all of its intensity, the distant white of the yacht provided a perfect target. He could sit on a small rise near the beach, and view it clearly, even those many miles away. When he brought the binoculars to his eyes, he could almost see those old familiar aspects: the rigging on the two masts, the polished railing, the perfectly ordered deck, the long and proud bow, and the rakish tilt of its cabin. It was a unique design, seemingly combining elements of a racing yacht with a more traditional cruiser. And on the stern, pulled up out of the water with an intricate wench system, was that small tender, which was used for back-and-forth trips from the yacht to the land. It sat transversely, decently far above the waterline.

Now, miles and miles away in the black night there are apparently only three white dots, which are nearly invisible to his eyes.

He knows that out there, the water is churning and choppy. Thankfully, he can't see the turbulence. It would warn him away, without hesitation, and farther out on the water a haze is hanging low. An impossibly hot African air mass from deep inside the Sahara has moved north. All this way. Tonight it is pulling water up into the atmosphere and disturbing the ocean with its push. On this night, there seems to be only a few colors: black and the many dark reflections and variations on the surface. As he stares out at his objective, he knows part of the reason for the haze are the few whitecaps, smaller waves breaking in on themselves, which produce an extra amount of water vapor. He can barely see those faint dots of light on the yacht, and none of this makes him feel any better about the miles he must cross.

Especially at a moment like this, Blake simply couldn't be by his side. Not when he stepped into the ocean. It is better that she is so far away. He would feel grief and love, and a different kind of need with her looking on. Maybe, he thinks, he wouldn't even be able to turn his back to her, and then wade into the water. He has dreams of a life with her, which he doesn't want to test against the ocean.

The moon is nearly full, and ordinarily it would be bright, even casting shadows in the darkness. Instead there is deep halo and glow around its perimeter. And instead of Blake on this many-hour long journey, he thinks, the moon will be his companion. He readies himself.

The sea can change in an instant. At the moment, the bone-white circle in the sky is providing a diffuse light, which dramatizes the beach and the waves as they roll in and makes them look even stronger and bigger than they otherwise are. He reminds himself that he knows these sorts of things, and he understands the way they will move him and sometimes fight his progress, and he again reminds himself that he has swam this sort of distance before.

Nick half-wades into the ocean. In the darkness, it always seems particularly incongruous when the water is warm, as it is now. It surrounds him, and both welcomes him and threatens him.

He is not familiar with this beach, but even so, the pull and unrest seems particularly energetic as he carefully places his feet, checking for sharp rocks. Fixed around his head are a small pair of goggles held tight by an elastic band. He pulls them down over his eyes and his view is suddenly narrowed and clouded that additional bit more. His swimsuit provides an internal pocket alongside his right hip, and inside that pocket (zipped firmly closed) he can feel the bait, the Easter egg – the cellphone.

It is tightly wrapped within three layers of watertight bags. Stuck to the reverse side of that phone is a looped-length of electrical tape, somewhat-sticky and ready to perform its small but important part in this trap. He feels the sand beneath his feet, and each step takes him further out, and then the floor of the ocean becomes that much deeper. And then, with one final step his body is no longer supported by his feet, and he begins to swim across the blackness. In a moment he is through the crashing waves, and then it is open water, which is rolling and lifting him up, and then sinking him into a valley. As always, it is at first difficult and then effortless. There is nothing but a space to be covered.

15

Hours in the water, kicking and pulling and keeping his mouth and nose free, means a certain type of endurance. It also means a certain type of preparation. He has applied liberal amounts of petroleum jelly between his skin and where the tightest part of the elastic band of his swimsuit meet. A similar amount of the jelly covers his thighs where they broach the lower legs of the suit. Over the thousands of repetitive kicks and movements his body will make, that thin layer will protect his skin, which could otherwise start to abrade and turn horribly painful as it continually rubs against the material. He has fed himself; he has consumed enough water to add pounds to his weight.

Around his wrist, is strapped a new timepiece with a new particularly tough leather band, thanks to Blake. She found it for him at the airport, paying too much, but neither of them cared nor made any mention of it. He said, "This watch looks just like my old one," and they matched them up, wrist to wrist, and laughed.

One thing he knows with certainty, is that he can't swim directly towards the navigation lights of Johansen's yacht.

Whomever is on watch will likely sit near the cabin on the deck of the yacht, and will certainly be scanning the sea towards a certain direction. They will perhaps be occasionally skimming the water with their eyes, looking for another boat or even a raft. And their attention will tend towards the main island. Nick knows the lights of the nearest village will draw their eyes, and that area would be, after all, the most direct route anyone would likely take when approaching the yacht.

The question is whether they will even consider the possibility that someone might approach from the opposite side, and *not* in a craft of some sort.

The key is that the yacht is anchored far away from the main island, but relatively close to a forbidding group of rocks, and is the sort of towering formation that has surely wrecked many vessels over the ages. Pinpoint-accurate GPS systems will sound alarms should the boat wander too much from its anchored point, but even so, a good crew member will double-check and make his own visual confirmation. Additionally, that group of rocks *could* serve as a base for someone approaching the yacht, but it would be unlikely and difficult. The waves no doubt break powerfully on its side on this sort of night, and there is nothing to serve as a natural launching point. Nick has studied the charts; there is a submerged sandbar that runs many thousands of feet from those rocks, and that is surely what has secured the yacht's anchors.

Nick looks up from the water; he aims himself roughly to the front of the yacht, perhaps over one-third of a mile in front of his final goal. It will mean *that* much more swimming and effort, but it will also mean that between the haze and the water's roughness, he is all but invisible.

He is now past the point at which he considered it a free

part of the swim, the early time when he inevitably feels made for the water, and his body impossibly strong and resilient. It is the first thirty or so minutes when he imagines the possibility of actually attempting a super-human feat of distance, swimming from Cuba to Florida, or some such miracle. It's like coasting a bike downhill, he often thinks, as he allows the mechanical sameness of his stroke to become a sort of mantra. Occasionally a wavelet surprises him, and breaks his concentration. The ocean plays tricks on his view: In a trough it seems that he is in a deep gorge, with black walls moving towards him, which he then rides up. And then on top, it seems he is far above the fray, as if he has climbed a little mountain and is looking down on the surface from a surreal height. There is a supernatural distance from life, but also a siren call to the depths below. Come to me – take my hand.

Sometimes, the walls push water into his nose and then nearly into his upper nasal passages. His mouth is full of the raw taste of the sea. Now, he has to watch the surface more carefully. Nick has to raise his head another fraction with each breath. He has to spend more energy; he has to focus his mind.

•

Even through the bandages, and the haze of pain medication, he recognized who was being described. Of course he recognized her.

He had decided to keep his face almost entirely wrapped and his eyes partly obscured, so he still couldn't look directly at people, nor they at him. Neither could he fully see their expressions, when they regarded him and gauged his injuries by the few hints, which they could discern and imagine. The nurse who first treated him tightened her jaw when she came up close. He certainly *did not* want to have an unobstructed view of himself in the mirror.

The nurse had said he could remove the majority of pieces of gauze and soft cotton like material on the third day, but he decided to wait, although he was unsure how long it had actually been at this point. After the swelling subsided they might look at a certain amount of surgery. He stayed down in the cabin of the yacht, the TV constantly on, even as he slept.

But then Johansen's voice roused him. Johansen was always precise and the way he used words cut through the fog.

He recognized her description. Of course he recognized her. Yes, he nodded his head. Tall. That red hair. Worn like she didn't care, and yet somehow as if she cared all too much at the same time. He cringed at the word *beautiful.* Yes, she was. Very.

He wanted to ask Johansen, why are you here on your boat? Is your business down here in Greece finished? He also thought, maybe eventually he could help Johansen with his accounts. After this was all over. He could do some numbers, maybe later identify investments for him. Do that sort of work, whatever it was. In a week or so, he would make overtures.

Johansen sat down nearby. He glimpsed Johansen's hands, which he tapped on his thigh in agitation. That was unusual. He saw that mane of silver hair move and seem to gesture more than anything else. The precise voice started, again, as if it was already halfway through an idea: "So, it's this girl, Blake. Apparently, she and him, together. Now they think they can block me. Lure me. Keep me from buying a piece of property I need," Johansen said. "*That part* is ridiculous. Perhaps they think that they can negotiate with me? But it is worrisome, don't you think, that she and certainly your friend and mine, Nick, should suddenly appear? And they seem to have intimate details about my new venture."

He agreed. He tried to shake and nod his head in assent, but the gesture was barely noticed. The TV continued to drone on in the background, and Johansen seemed to talk to himself. "In this line of business, you have to know the other side's information, *and* you have to know the people you're negotiating with. *That's what they don't understand.* If you have neither of those, you are blind. If you announce your bottom line, then you have no room to move. Instead you talk about flexibility. You find out what motivates someone, and then you have a lever. The good thing is, it's only partly about money."

"What are you going to do?" he asked. The conversation seemed like a dream. His voice was disembodied. It seemed like someone else was speaking the words.

"Let me ask you this. You didn't, perhaps, tell them I was going to be here, did you? Maybe you accidentally let something slip? Maybe while he had you knocked about in that hotel room? Tied up and bruised. Helpless. Something about an island? A hundred-million dollar deal? Did you say anything?"

No – he shook his head strongly, but then the blood pounded, and the agony when he moved caused his vision to blur. He reached for another pain pill, and Johansen took the bottle from his hand. Again, his own voice sounded wrong, "No. Never. It was just like I told you, before." He thought for a moment. "I would never…" He shook his head, even though it made him woozy.

Johansen twisted the top off the bottle and placed two pills in his own hand, he thought a moment, and then he placed them on a nearby table. Johansen watched as the bandaged man fought to move and retrieve the pills. There was a shaft of hideous purple making its way down this man's neck, from beneath some of the white gauze.

"Of course you would *never*," Johansen said.

Johansen stood and walked away, with the sound from the television mingling with his voice, as he said again, "Of course, you would *never*. You know your place. And what I am capable of."

•

The three white lights are now close enough that Nick can see the way they illuminate part of the bare mast and rigging in the darkness. The haze is still there, and the white yacht seems like a ghost ship in the black sea, rocking on the waves and abandoned. Nick tries to deceive himself, and he argues in his thoughts that no person is on deck. He imagines that there are no eyes regularly scanning the water for a boat, a raft, or even an errant piece of debris tossing and turning in the water and reflecting in the moonlight.

The time has worn on him. The water has seemed both heavy and thick; the waves broad and tireless; the wavelets small and mocking. His shoulders are painful, and it seems his left foot is mere seconds away from cramping in the arch, with a laser bite of torture that will leave him floundering. And yet every stroke and kick, he knows, brings him that much closer. And so he turns, to finally move the last leg of his journey, generally toward the lights. He will approach from the "backside," close to the formation of rocks, and then navigate around to the stern of the boat. It is perhaps the least likely approach. He glances at the watch strapped around his wrist. Fifteen minutes, he thinks. He can do that. Fifteen minutes. And then he is down in a trough and then riding up on a peak. Come to me, something says. He won't listen.

•

With perhaps only a hundred yards to his goal, he quiets his swim yet another measure. There is only his head above the black churning sea. He pulls the googles up and onto his forehead, giving him the clearest view yet. In the moonlight, he sees the tender, raised from the water. He catches, too, the faintest glow from a cigarette. He sees what must be the murky form of a torso, reclining on a chair just beside the wheel, and perhaps only a dozen or so feet from the rearmost of the yacht. An arm in the darkness moves the tiny red glow of the cigarette in a slow arc, and then it is gone. And then, it is returned.

Many times, Nick has glimpsed this boat through Radcliff's prized high-powered binoculars, and more than a few times from a much closer distance, as it sat berthed in a marina. He knows the details of its external design; he recognizes everything, although this time from a much different perspective. As with Radcliff's yacht, and others, approaching as a swimmer does from such a level gives the impression that it is actually a giant thing. Nearly treading in the water now, so as to make no noise or splashes, Nick hears the muffled sound of a TV, so perhaps someone else is onboard, down in the cabin. He hears too, the semi distant breaks of waves on the rocks, as if they were a reminder of a tragedy from a time past. His breathing has calmed. His mind is recovering from the exhaustion.

His hand rises from the water to touch the boat. Suddenly, he feels his heart racing, again. He finds a grab handle, in the form of a cable used to secure the tender. Above it is an actual handle, and so he pulls himself up, out of the water. His muscles are weak and straining, and crying for rest. He hears, faintly, the water drip from his body and back into the ocean. In the moonlight, everything seems half-real, half-living. Even himself.

Like a strange animal, he works and pulls, fighting to keep his breathing quiet. There is still the drip-drip-drip from his body and swimsuit. His muscles are barely there (his back, his arms, his chest) they feel simply *spent.* His body, though, remembers the many thousands of pull-ups, the paint ground into his palms. There is the feeling that he is simply a physical thing, with blood and fibers and electrical impulses that he can control. It functions like a machine. He recruits the muscles.

Another handhold is reached and then he slithers into the tender, waiting, breathing, listening to everything in the otherwise near silence, aside from the breeze, and aside from the sound of the TV somewhere not far away. And too, aside from the distant waves crashing on the rocks like a dire warning. Overhead, he looks at the bone white circle in the black sky and waits. And yet, there is nothing.

He delicately unzips the pocket in his swimsuit. He delicately removes the tightly wrapped cellphone, and drops the three bags over the side; they catch momentarily in the breeze and then disappear in the night. The piece of electrical tape is still stuck to the back of the phone's body, so he simply lays it face down on the floor of the tender, where it will no doubt slide around in these and other heavy waves, eventually making its presence obvious to someone on the yacht as it begins to thump into the side of the hull or a structural member.

•

He remembered: Lowering himself back into the ocean, he felt different. He could still hear the TV playing faintly in the background; he could still imagine that unknown form on the deck taking slow dramatic drags of the cigarette and the hot red dot moving like a disembodied light in the blackness. The night was still that same color (*charcoal* he now thought) and as his feet immersed in the water, and then his legs, and finally his torso, it seemed he could sink to the very bottom of the sea. Surrounded by it and by everything.

And yet, he floated on the surface. He aimed himself to swim away from the stern of the boat, and his gentle pulls through the water were rewarded with motion. He constantly looked over his shoulder, and the faint and tiny red dot of the cigarette was farther and farther behind him, until it was gone. He remembered aiming himself roughly towards the lights of the distant village, knowing that his initial steps into the water and launching point were not far to the side of those lights. He didn't look at his watch; he gave a brief glance to the moon, now further across the sky, and imagined that it would be gone when - *finally* – he stumbled back ashore, and collapsed in a heap of nothing on the sand.

He remembered his toe touching the sea floor as he approached the beach. He was simply exhausted. It was too much to even cry out in ecstasy that he was still alive. He remembered emerging from the ocean, with no one else to see him, like a bent and twisted creature that was somehow still breathing. He knelt there on the sand. His chest finally calming down. He turned to look back again at the three navigation lights barely visible those many miles away.

When the sun began to show on the horizon, he lifted himself up and walked away.

•

Blake talks to Nick on the phone. They try to share pleasantries and discuss business, such as it is. The sun is now shinning; it appears as a fresh wonderful day, completely oblivious to the previous night. "Did you do it?" she asks. "How far was it?"

"It was far," he says. "I did it," he says. How can he explain those moments to her?

She wonders: is something wrong? Is he somehow mad at her? His voice is clipped and brief, yet her voice is gentle, and it embraces him. "Are you okay?"

"I will be," he says. "It may take a little while."

"Tell me," he asks, trying to return her warmth with his tone, "what happened on your end? Are they still going through with that meeting at the property? The two men?"

"Yes," she says. "First, they want to 'verify funds'. As we expected. They want a screen shot of the bank balances."

Nicks laughs. Nick shudders. "Along with all sorts of other information, which will also conveniently be included in that same picture."

"That's what I was thinking, too," she says.

There is a pause. She says: "Don't forget. The real estate

agent. He took a picture of me."

There is another pause.

"So, there it is. *Maybe.*"

Nick thinks as he speaks, but he refuses to truly address the danger. He wonders if she really understands, but he needs her to hang on, and be brave. "I want you to leave your hotel. I want you to find another one. An ugly one. Pay with cash. This might sound absurd, but perhaps not after what we've been through. Make sure you are not followed. Look behind you. Use a completely made-up name, and if they ask for an ID, instead leave a hundred Euro note on the counter."

Blake whispers, "Yes."

"Hopefully, Samson's intermediary will soon email you with forged documents. We'll be there, ready to capture the evidence. Whatever you do, don't move the bulk of the money to any account they give you. Are you recording all your phone conversations?"

"Yes."

Blake speaks, trying (and failing) to sound calm: "But we know that they might just run the deal entirely legal! Johansen might simply outbid me for the piece of land. In that case, we'll have no evidence to go to investigators with; no proof of anything gone wrong. Any hope of luring him into another fraud is gone. And then that will be it, nothing we can do. You'll never get your money back."

"Yes. Even if they know who you *really* are, because he needs that parcel. He'll just pay the extra money, and probably laugh at our plan."

She sighs. "And all of this will be for nothing. So we make him pay an extra sixty-some-percent, and that's it? He will still be so far ahead. The owner of that little parcel makes some extra money, and *that's it?* Nobody else will ever do anything. Unless that cellphone, and that message prods him."

Now it is Nick sighing, with a big breath. "Yes. Perhaps it was always going to come down to that." He thinks of the words on that phone, waiting for Johansen. He thinks of *her.* The terror in the water.

The feeling in his gut twists, and it is like an acid, burning. "Yes," he says, again. "If it seems like there is something beyond that one little piece of property. If, *maybe,* it seems like there is something beyond some extra expense, which he can easily afford. If his faith is shaken in a certain way."

Blake speaks. "If this seems like a fight for survival?"

"Yes," he says, "something like that."

•

The truth is too awful for him to think about, so he doesn't.

He had her picked up from Radcliff's yacht. It was early in the morning, and good to Radcliff's word, the crew, and the girls (and, of course, her as well) were all in a deeply medicated state. They slept through it all. Now, he has her loaded up with enough alcohol, drugs, and tranquilizers so that she will die no matter what, and probably within hours, but somehow he still has her disposed of while her heart continues to beat.

Her eyes are instinctively darting around (she's fighting against the chemicals in her blood, perhaps) and then, in a moment too sick to recall, her face makes that expression – *understanding* – that he doesn't want to see.

Of course, he won't be there when it happens. He will

be far away. But he will still know that it *has* happened. The Croatian, with the insatiable need to please and impress, can be trusted, and so it will be finished. Johansen will feel it, and then perhaps ten minutes later, he will see the confirming text message - "Done."

He wonders about the sound of the rusty chains dragging on the floor of the rubber boat. They would be far out at sea, and the rubber boat would be tossing, perhaps. And the chains probably made a scuffing sound, every so often, as they moved. Certainly at the very end more so. And perhaps they even left an otherwise imperceptible mark on the orange material of the little inflatable boat. Maybe, a so-faint abrasion that it would seem to be nothing except an unremarkable wear mark. Even if a person knew what happened, they still wouldn't be able to recreate it by the evidence.

Old rusty chains. The kind that are lying around every harbor, in every part of the world, if you know where to look. They have that smell to them. The metal oxidizing and whatever paint was on them leaving its own remnant in the air.

And if you viewed them wrapped around someone's ankles like a reverse noose to carry them to the seafloor, even then, you might only think about their fragrance. It's the sense that something powerful is decaying and succumbing to the harshness of the sea. But once they hit the water that would be the end. The scent in the air would fade, and then be gone. So in other words, there would be nothing to view in the aftermath, and nothing to sense. Looking out on the ocean, where it happened, there would just be the waves moving over and over as they always did.

No matter, he would still have the rubber boat destroyed

– perhaps burned. A funeral pyre on the water, days afterwards.

Johansen was sitting in a movie theater. His two bodyguards beside him in the darkness. He wanted to be seen and viewed by many different people in a public place before and after, just in case.

It was a little extra bit of insulation, deniability and security. It really didn't matter, but it made it easier for him. The movie played, the movie dragged. He never took these sorts of entertainment breaks for a reason. Then, he knew. The feeling was uncanny. He was sitting there trying to involve himself with the images on the screen, the music, the words spoken back and-forth between characters. And then that *certainty* was there. Like it had just washed over him. Several minutes later, one of his bodyguards slightly touched his arm, and in the darkness of the theater, illuminated on the screen of the phone, he viewed that one word.The bodyguard had no idea what the significance of the word was. He just gently touched Johansen and showed him – "Done."

"Erase it," Johansen responded with a whisper, and the text message disappeared from the phone. Because a person could never be too careful.

•

Johansen stares at a different phone, these weeks later. Why should his doom show up like this?

He can't see the date or the time stamp of the message. He can't see any sort of larger identifying mark. On the cellphone's screen is just a phrase, which seems to appear as the first part of a much larger message.

The words and numbers show in a sort of half-light, and

then when he taps the screen, the phone's screen instantly replaces the message with a number pad, requiring a keyed-in security code, in order to access anything further. He alternates between the two views. A finger tap brings one frustrating view, and then a second finger tap brings the other frustrating view. He struggles with the urge to simply disregard what he cannot completely comprehend.

This phone belongs to *whom*? He can't tell. *When* was the message sent? There is nothing to tell him anything more about the message. It just stares at him. Taunting him. Maybe tempting him. On the back of the phone is large piece of black tape, looped in a circle, as if it had been earlier used to secure the phone in a hiding place, and had since ceased to function as intended. Perhaps someone didn't realize that the salt air would play havoc on something as flimsy as electrical tape.

He had heard something sliding around in the tender. He ignored it, and then in the rougher sea that afternoon it started to annoy him. That occasional, and barely discernable, *slide* and bump. The late-day winds usually picked up, and so did the waves, and this day was no exception. His boat was supposed to be *perfect*, and a lose piece of equipment meant a problem. And when he peered into the tender, there it was, every so often sliding into the side and making a sound. A phone. In a very strange place. If he hadn't found the item himself, he might not have been so dismayed.

But whose phone? And what about that message – who sent that?

One of his staff; one of the girls; *her?* The tender went back and forth to land, so that opened the range of possibilities incredibly. There are people who can investigate and perhaps tell him these vital things, he knows, but at the moment they are hundreds of miles away and the answers would still require a serious amount of work. And so for the time being all he has to contemplate is a cryptic message: DEATH BY WATER.

It is followed by a series of numbers. A pair of double-digit numbers, each extending to a decimal place seven digits long. Possibly a very specific GPS coordinate. He thinks: X and Y. Latitude and longitude.

Within moments he has brought the apparent coordinate up on the navigation system. He is pleased with his detective work. It is on a nearby island, and not on the water. It is here in the Greek group, and the exact point is close to a cliff-face. But still curiously in the midst of nowhere. Maybe more than an hour's walk from the closest village. A satellite view changes his perspective: a small structure is built on that point. One of several apparently identical structures all lined up in a semi-formal order. There is simply not enough detail to make a better determination. He thinks: Only half a day's sailing to get there. Death by water.

Tomorrow morning his two body guards are going to be off the boat, heading to the property in play, and to accost his inept rivals. He laughs at the fake name: Miranda. He had viewed the screen shot with the account balances. What pathetic lever do these low-level scam artists imagine that they have in order to pry money from him? Maybe they actually think that he will attempt yet another illegal maneuver, and then they will be there, this time to document the fraud step-by-step? Turn him into the authorities? Blackmail him? He laughs to himself.

He still doesn't know what he will do with them. Perhaps have their visas revoked and force them home, chastened and humiliated. He can make sure their names are front and center in a very serious *watch list* so if they flee, the repercussions are enormous. Or perhaps there will be an opportunity for something even more aggressive and permanent? He can bat them about; play with them at his leisure, if he wants. But eventually, he will lay his hand down on them. He will protect himself and vanquish his rivals.

Tomorrow, after the bodyguards are on their way, the Croatian can sail with him to this other island, and he will be the one who takes the tender to the shore, and walks up to that point, investigates, and then reports back. Maybe, there is stashed evidence there, but what? Johansen can't think of a thing. He was always smart. Over the years there have been perhaps hundreds of major and minor events and actions, but with each one he had distance and insulation. A few extra pain pills should see his lackey through the climb and journey. Johansen knows just the right amount. Only an hour or thereabouts walk for the injured man. The false promise of a promotion in the coming months should push him along nicely, as well.

While he – himself - can remain safe, and stay isolated on the yacht out in the bay. Still, he feels just a touch demoralized. Maybe there are consequences to his actions? No - he quiets the thoughts. He refuses to engage a feeling. He reminds himself, instead, that he will remain untouchable (as always). He can put an end to this whole unpleasant and wrathful chapter in just one day.

16

The white yacht is gliding. It is beautiful on the blue sea. Even at a time like this, Johansen pilots the boat with all the sails up until the last moment. As if the view of it, proud and dauntless, was for some unknown audience. His mane of silver hair tussling in the breeze.

The afternoon's winds are dying down, however, and as he makes a sharp cut with the yacht (he deftly spins the wheel and the nose turns obediently) the sails collapse in the suddenly dead air. The motion of the boat is brought nearly to a halt as the energy is dissipated in the turn, and a near-circle is transcribed in the water. The white sheets, now rumpling in the mixed air, are quickly lowered. Unusually, the boat is still thousands of yards from the shore, and well outside the borders of the cove.

There is little-to-no activity on the deck, as the boat gently rocks in the waves. It is merely Johansen bringing a pair of binoculars to his eyes. He sweeps back and forth. And then his gaze continues on, across the rocky slopes, on the buildings that radiate up and along much of the amphitheater-like surrounding of the cove, on the road that crawls in and out of the village, and on the beach where a handful of late day loungers still laze around. Their tan bodies and beach chairs seem to form a new and undiscovered variety of animal. At this time of day, the sun is low in the sky, and shadows are starting to dramatize the figures. Johansen, checks each one as best he is able.

He drops the front anchor. It makes a rat-a-tat sound that can't quite make it to shore. He drops the rear anchor. It, too, is silenced by the distance.

And then his gaze crawls much farther up the slopes and far away from the village. Up he climbs. He finds one structure. It is a windmill that is almost occluded by the cliff face and the contours of the green hillside just in front of it. The skeletal wooden frames of the blades are only hinted at; the door on its reverse side is unseen. The grey-and-stone cylindrical body stands starkly, and passively, on display. He stares at it through the binoculars, often setting them aside, and staring at it with his naked eye only to bring the binoculars up again and continue his study.

The time is wearing on. The shadows have grown a fraction longer. To the west, the sun is piercing. The waves and ripples on the water are solid, like a series of knife blades in the sharp light. Johansen wants to touch the surface. Just to experience the manner that it will *give way* beneath his fingers, and remind himself that it is not actually metallic and unforgiving. For reassurance, he pats the pocket of his windbreaker. Even though he can feel the heavy weight of the revolver as it rests there, he double-checks, all the same. He notes the shape and length of the barrel. He wonders at the sound it will make, should he fire it (and whether that distinctive report will *still* be distinctive, should people hear it that distance away in the village).

Another figure appears on deck. His head is a bizarrely wrapped form. The bandages are indistinguishable from a distance. It is as if his face and head are covered by a strange and heavy white turban that has slipped down, and which is also making his entire posture sag. It is incongruous with the tall and athletic shape he otherwise possesses, and he steadies himself with a clutch of a nearby railing.

Soon, the two men are busying themselves. And within minutes the wrapped form has climbed into the tender at the rearmost of the boat. Slowly, the tender is lowered, until it settles into the water, and then it bobs and moves much more enthusiastically than the large yacht, which seems almost immobile in comparison.

The tender is pointed to shore. The motor revs and it begins its brief journey. It heads for an area of beach to the side of the sparsely gathered tourist grouping. Johansen brings the binoculars back to his eyes and watches its progress, as it finally runs itself partially aground on the beach. The tender's rearmost portion still lapped by the waves, its front secure enough on the sand.

Johansen watches as the bizarrely wrapped form climbs delicately and cautiously from the tender and slowly walks up the beach and into the village. Johansen notes that the tourists' eyes follow the progress as well, and then seem to share a baffled, disturbed, reaction with each other at the bizarre man they have just seen. Their peace and tranquility has been memorably broken for the briefest time.

•

Through the binoculars Johansen can sometimes see the figure climb and leave the more arid lower elevations of the island. There are green slopes; there are sheep that wander around and congregate. They look like little puffs of white in the afternoon light, and are slightly larger than the rocks that seem to randomly populate the hillside. And then, he notices the walking figure is down into a depression and once more unseen.

Johansen glimpses the windmill. He scans the hillsides and sees the sheep, the rocks, and the green grass.

Time, again, seems to wear on. His cellphone, apparently, cannot connect to a network. (And the secure satellite phone can only be used with like devices, unfortunately.) The topography on the far side of the island is blocking the signal from the towers, in all likelihood. *More problems with the Greeks,* he scowls. What about his island? Down here it is always one or another hassle, he reminds himself, and something *else* to fix and invest in. But only after everything else is settled. He thinks about the future. Look up, look ahead, he prompts himself. All of the possibilities that still lie in front of him. But now the shadows are starting to seem alarmingly long.

The beach population has dwindled to almost no one. They have other places to be; people to meet for dinner. The summer air seems unnervingly warm, even at this hour when the night is approaching. Rarely is he ever completely alone, as he is now. There is a creeping sense (for once in his life) that he has made a titanic error from which he will never recover. He sees that the yacht's silhouette is darkly cast in the waves.

There is a figure moving down the beach. A bandaged head in the half-light. Staggering, almost. There is a breath of relief. The figure is carrying with it a duffle bag, it seems. He watches the figure place the bag in the tender; he watches the figure push the small craft the few feet down the beach, so that it is free enough to move in the waves; he watches the figure struggle to climb aboard. He wonders if he should have provided a few extra pain pills.

•

Johansen eyes the duffle bag obsessively as it is thrown on board. It flies over the railing and onto the deck, as the tender briefly parallels the yacht and makes for the rearmost quarter. The soft-sided bag lands with a heavy thud. And in the moment, Johansen attempts to judge its contents. He is no different from a person evaluating some strange package left on their doorstep, with careful consideration of the sound it made as it was dropped there.

"What is it?" he practically shouts while launching and scrambling for the zipper, undoing it with a rushed, focused movement. Immediately, digging in, his eyes fall upon a bag half-full of laptops, cellphones, e-readers, power cords, and external hard drives, but cushioned by a mass of clothes and wadded-up newspaper. "Stupid to throw it," he says, fixated on the possible solution to his mystery (death by water?) as he begins hurriedly pushing buttons and watching as devices turn on and beep and buzz, and vibrate with energy.

Little green lights appear, and screens show images. "You should best hope that none of these devices were damaged with that throw," he states angrily.

And then something dawns on him, and he turns just in time to notice he can see a length of neck beneath a mound of bandages. But the skin is not purple and not bruised, as it should be.

•

"Money," Johansen says. "Is that what you think you can get from me?" It is the first time Nick has heard this voice in years, the first time since the *crash* and the rocks under the water. The fraud, which Nick once thought cost him nearly everything.

Nick holds Johansen's gun on its owner, who sits on the deck. His legs splayed and his torso uncomfortably leaning against the railing. The strong blow to Johansen's jaw, which knocked him down and thwarted his attempt to retrieve the gun, is leaving a bruise. Johansen tenderly touches it with his hand and fingers, apparently unused to the sensation and abnormality of physical pain.

Nick takes a syringe from his pants pocket, which also happens to be the exact same pocket, and the exact same finely-pressed linen pants, which the one-time bandaged Croatian was wearing earlier. He sets the syringe on the wood deck, and in the growing darkness it seems just as lethal as the gun. The needle is beyond Johansen's reach, and his eyes contemplate its possible meaning. Does he know at one time there were *two* syringes?

Nick, breathing heavily, crouches down in front of Johansen and from around his head begins to unwind the bandages, which cover his face. He removes blood stained gauze, which is more black and violet than red. With every twist and pull, more of the bandages fall off, more of his face is revealed, and more of the world comes to his view. He smells the sweat and sickness from some other man, which slowly disappears, and is replaced by the soft air. He looks straight at Johansen, saying nothing as the bandages undo. They fall on the deck in front of him in a pile. Nick is still unsure (with this abrupt opportunity) what he finally intends to do. From another pocket, Nick removes the stun gun displaying his captured arsenal in full.

"I suppose," Johansen says, "we might be able to work something out." His voice is tempered and calm. Nick wants to laugh through his fractured nerves.

Nick speaks. Adrenalin is rushing through his veins, and his voice betrays his heightened state. He is no Johansen, or even Radcliff, capable of dealing with near or imminent catastrophe with a measured tone no matter the internal struggles. "Can you imagine," Nick gasps, "my surprise upon seeing *that* particular man push open the door to the windmill?"

Johansen shrugs, but only with his expression; complete nonchalance follows. During his long walk down from the windmill, Nick had time to gather some thoughts, and to come to some hard-wrought conclusions.

When he first removed those bandages inside the windmill and saw *that* face, which lay bruised and beaten, he understood that Radcliff and Johansen knew each other: they shared people and they shared crimes.

Certainly, this whole time, Johansen knew that he was captain of Radcliff's yacht. This whole time, while Nick imagined he had been anonymous and stealthily slipping past Johansen's life and observing here and there, it seemed likely that Johansen had instead been keeping tabs on him. Perhaps waiting, again, to cut into him with those razor sharp instruments of his, should he chose.

Johansen is amused, or perhaps fittingly dispassionate about the change in their balance of power. "Did you really think it was going to be *me* walking through that door?" Any confusion or questions that surely preoccupy Johansen are hidden behind a mask. Nick realizes that Johansen is studying him, and that Nick betrays too much with his own eyes and voice.

"No," Nick answers, "but neither did I realize that you and Radcliff apparently share the same thugs. It makes me wonder what else you have shared." Johansen flinches just a touch at the word *thugs*; he doesn't seem to grasp the reality of his own methods.

Suddenly, a thought occurs to Nick. And it makes perfect sense. He knows the Croatian was there at the very end. *The very end*, when the Hungarian lovely had her life…he can't think the words. He knows, somehow. Drowned. But the horror is not here; it is somewhere else.

Just an hour earlier, the missing syringe was *not* missing. It was emptied into the body of that same person who was there at the end. His resume extended, apparently, in other directions besides experience as a famous model, and so he would pay the price for that, if not other things. The man lay there, disabled by the stun gun. Nick had fished out one of the syringes from his pocket, sank the needle into the man's arm, pushed the plunger down, and emptied the vessel. It had all happened as they were hidden inside that windmill, out of view of anyone else who might have chanced across that unlikely place.

Nick did whatever it was the Croatian had failed to do to him, or to Blake. Whatever that clear plastic cylinder contained, it was now flowing in that body and doing its damage.

He now looks closer at Johansen. He sees up close that he has aged but that the years have not diminished the considerable force - or the disarming charm - which he still seems to possess. The mane of hair turning darkly grey in the twilight is one of many things that physically separate him from any other person he might meet. There are the intelligent, narrowing eyes that meet his, the compact and still athletic body, the deeply tanned skin earned from months spent out in the sun and on the yacht. There is also the indifference to other people's suffering, which Nick can now recognize as a trait of a particular type of predator.

Nick sees that he has always been outmatched relative to Johansen. Nick could be hurt and wounded, and slowly cut apart. But Johansen could only be destroyed, and nothing less.

It is now, *this moment.*

Nick doesn't want to put the world back as he imagines it should be (even if he could); he doesn't want to retrieve whatever tatters remain of his old life. Those people are *gone*, and so are the places and feelings, in all meanings of those words. He wants to make something new. Start again.

•

"Take the boat out to sea," Nick says.

Johansen immediately rises from his seated position, as if he expected as much. Nick keeps the revolver carefully trained on him, his eyes studying every move of his body and nuance of his expression, which stays eerily flat. The remaining syringe sits there on the deck, perhaps a particularly strong gust of wind might blow it off the side. The stun gun lies there temptingly, which is perhaps just as well.

Nick follows Johansen and stands behind him; Nick presses the barrel of the gun between his shoulder blades. The safety is off. A mere pull of the trigger, and it will all be over. It is *not* the impossible shot he once imagined from a great distance that would pierce Johansen's forehead, nor the shot with the two bodyguards looking hopelessly on, viewing a sniper's riffle scope somehow reflected in the bright sun. But can he do this instead, Nick wonders?

"Where are we going?" Johansen, now behind the wheel, pushes a button and the front anchor begins to ratchet up; another button brings the rear up. He wakes up the diesel engines with another push of two separate buttons, and on the instrument cluster, gauges spin on their axes, and a muted tremor carries through the boat. The tender, still in the water and tied to the yacht with a single rope, will trail behind them.

"We will know when we get there…Navigation lights," Nick reminds, and another switch has them turned on, and with the wheel turned and then straightened, the boat heads out to sea and into the early evening.

•

"How much do you want?" Johansen expects to negotiate. He wants to know Nick's position. The darkness is falling all around. The radar tracks a few vessels many miles away. The diesel engines turn, the bow cuts into the waves, and the boat rolls and heaves at times. Johansen's cellphone begins ringing. "Where is this boat's transponder?" Nick replies. He keeps the gun pushed into Johansen's back. He finds the ringing cellphone in Johansen's pants' pocket. A name and number that he does not recognize light up the screen. He places it in his own pocket.

Just to the side, in a storage locker, Nick finds a length of bungee cord. And with his free hand he loosely binds Johansen's wrists to the wheel of the boat. It is an awkward and difficult maneuver, as he keeps the gun to Johansen's back, and so the knot is not tight as it should be but it serves its purpose well enough. Johansen acquiesces, perhaps, because he still thinks he can buy his way out of this situation.

"Where is the boat's transponder? That's the last time I'm asking that question politely."

"There are several," Johansen answers with a measured tone. "Just to insure *against* this eventuality. One of them is in a nearly indestructible case, which is welded into the hull. It has a one-year power supply, should the primary fail. With the tools onboard, you'll never break it free."

Nick cannot view Johansen's face or see his expression. But he imagines he is contemplating, thinking, maneuvering. Nick *does* see that he tightly grips the wheel, as if the bungee cord was not needed at all to bind his hands to the boat.

Johansen is now silent. Instead, his cellphone begins ringing again. It sounds like an alarm, suggesting that whatever time Nick has is coming to a conclusion. Even now, Johansen's forces are marshaling themselves. He is being missed, already. Perhaps it is one of the bodyguards, alerting him that Blake was not at the meeting.

"Then sell me the boat," Nick demands. "Sell me the boat so it's mine. Or trade me the company that owns it. Whatever manner the deal takes." Johansen remains silent, but then speaks, mildly amused.

"At gun point? Sell you the boat? Do you know how much it is worth?"

"Probably as much as you promised to make me all those years ago."

Johansen, huffs in response, he is not impressed with the naïve irony.

"You'll get some money," Nick continues, just to make it

legal. "Whatever is up against that piece of property. And I suppose, then, *that* too. You can build your resort unencumbered. Whatever you want."

Johansen remains silent for several seconds and then finally speaks. "How did you find out about my resort? My plans? Who talked to you? The deal is structured all through intermediaries; my name is nowhere."

"First tell me, Johansen." Nick presses the gun harder into his back, so that Johansen flinches, just a bit. "Tell me about a tall Hungarian girl with jet-black hair." Nick thinks for a second, before crying out, "Which smelled like vanilla."

Nick lets the words hang there in the air, before they disappear in the breeze. "Tell me, Johansen, do know what you have to answer for? Do you know what you have done?"

•

Nick knows that Johansen has finally shed one layer, when he hears him ask, "So it's not *just* about your money, is it?" And Nick shakes his head, and simply says, "No. It's not."

The boat has pressed farther into the distance; they are starting to thread other islands; Johansen's cellphone has rung incessantly and each time Nick has let it continue on. It now sounds like a calamitous warning, which Nick refuses to acknowledge. It rings and he lets it ring. Perhaps it suggests that Nick is beyond thoughts of self-preservation or rational decision making. Each time it rings, Johansen flinches. But soon enough, however, they will likely be beyond any cellular signals and the prodding ring will cease.

And so Johansen tries to tell him a story, to appease him. It is of a Hungarian girl whom he once met at a symphony concert, years ago. He saw the way she sat there, listening and transfixed. He saw the way she stood there, in the intermission, with that strange slant to her body as she sipped her drink and ignored who she was with, and then, of course, he introduced himself to her. Nick imagines the steady gaze, the confident handshake, but wonders if it was somehow different with her. Nick notices the way he talks about her, in the past tense.

Johansen tries to leave out details or his motivations, and yet Nick fills them in with his imagination and with his fractured knowledge of both her and him.

Reluctantly, Johansen tells Nick about their little tiff, and how she ran off. It wasn't the first time. But even with the gun pushing hard into his back and between his shoulder blades, he remains evasive. Nick expects acknowledgement; he expects some form of contrition. He expects a change in Johansen's voice. "Did she threaten you?" Nick demands. "Did she somehow want to shake you from your position? Make you just the smallest bit accountable to some other balance in the world?"

All that Nick receives is a small moment of unadulterated anger in Johansen's voice when he confronts his present situation. Johansen will never repent.

"Sell me the boat," Nick repeats.

Johansen begins to see. "If you kill me, afterwards the sale will be suspect. The sale will be voided. You'll get nothing."

"Then *maybe* I won't kill you. I won't do to you, what you did to her…into the sea."

Then they come to the part of the story where everyone understands who they are.

"How do you know? How do you know?"

•

From a distance, she had first glimpsed the big blue yacht. It was there, in the marina, just as she had heard it would be. She viewed it behind and amongst other boats, their masts and cabins partly concealing its size and grandeur. She knew the boat. She had seen pictures, including that particular picture sent on, from a time past. The gleaming wooden deck. The blonde grabbing hold of that man. That polished smile on her face, and that cool and removed expression on his. Later, she would hear why. Johansen had told her about him, perhaps to warn her, or to demonstrate his power over people. It was the way he could just cut people out.

Still in the picture, the party was continuing on all around them, as if nothing else in the world mattered.

Sure enough, as she surveyed the marina, she saw it. Maybe a home, for at least a little while. The hull was that easily recognizable rich, royal blue. The single mast climbed far above everything else on the water, and was an unreal height.

But, unexpectedly, the boat *wasn't* moored along a platform. And then she contemplated the facts of the situation. The green hills, scattered with villas, climbed almost immediately from the water. The tight and intimate setting of the town and harbor were not to her advantage. It meant that there would be no flirtation with an attendant to receive access to a particular part of the marina; no walking amongst the other boats; no simple wave to whomever was on deck, followed by an inevitable invitation to come aboard.

She couldn't go back to where she came from. She wouldn't. The façade of her life was now truly breaking apart, yet there were only a few alternatives that she could see. From her handbag, she distractedly retrieved her lipstick. It was red, a shade too bright and wrong for her natural colors. With her jet-black hair mirroring back at her from a shop window, she drew around her lips. A few tourists and locals waltzed up and down the handful of streets, oblivious to the state of her mind.

She would have to ask around. Radcliff, *that* yacht. Someone would know something she could use. She couldn't miss this opening and opportunity. Soon, there would surely be some sort of get-together, which Radcliff would host. Or some social occasion that she could ride in on.

She walked along the streets a few moments longer, looking into shop windows, wasting her time. Thinking. She had spent herself needlessly on people and on arrangements. She had spent herself in millions of ways that would never return what she had given up. This was going to be the last time she made that bargain with herself.

And then her head turned a little bit, and out of the corner of her eye she saw him. She recognized him. He was sitting there, alone, outside at a café. His face seemed to have that same expression, which she had contemplated in that picture that time ago. Removed. Alone. Distant. Qualities she realized that applied to herself. There was a cup of coffee waiting for him on a table, and a newspaper, which he had set aside to focus his attention on her.

She turned away and continued on. With a shiver she thought, she was getting closer to something.

17

"Here," Nick says. "Cut the engines."

Johansen complies. The barrel of the gun, pushing into his back, speaks in the same tone as Nick's voice, and Johansen has no other recourse but to look out and around, into the growing darkness that surrounds the sea and his boat. Here, on the water, this little piece, which is constantly recycling and flowing and moving, will be the place. The weight of *her*, covers this night. In the dusk, the stars are starting to decorate the sky. The horizon is blurred into the subtlest shift of color. Behind them, the tender trails, like a small shadow. The rope, which binds the craft to the yacht, will soon enough go slack as the two boats slow and come to a rest.

Nick removes the lazy restraint, which tied Johansen's hands to the wheel. The gun still against his back. Nick again finds Johansen's phone in his pocket. Although it is not ringing at the moment, a signal is still available. The islands are close enough, the only outpost of humanity.

"What is the name of the company that owns your boat?"

Johansen, apparently, accepts the bargain he is presented with. "First United Relief Foundation."

"A charity, a nonprofit?"

Without a hint of shame, "Yes."

"Are the organization's accounts and audits available? Can I look them up online?"

Johansen hesitates. "No. It's incorporated in Germany. There are no public disclosure requirements."

Nick has time to digest the information, such as it is. "Then I'm sure it's only you at the helm; do you even bother with a board of directors?"

Johansen starts to see that Nick has learned something over the years. His voice is growing enraged, but the feeling of some unmentioned loss, perhaps makes an appearance. "No," Johansen answers.

"So, there is just an auditor and *you*."

Johansen is trying to accept what he thinks is going to happen. Nick, explains it to him.

•

Johansen speaks on the phone; faintly, Nick can hear Samson. The inflections in the voice, even heard second hand, are as distinctive and irritating as ever.

No. She wasn't at the meeting. She checked out of her hotel. I don't know what happened. What do we do now?

And then Johansen speaks. Precise, measured, direct.

There has been a change, he announces, as if he had always intended such. The holding company is to take full ownership and executive powers of First United Relief Foundation. Miranda's holding company, and whoever else is on those documents (he scoffs at the name.) You have the information, so use it. Forge my signature; sign as a witness yourself. You'll find the files in the usual place. Same password. It won't take but five minutes. Email them to her, and don't argue with me about it. I'm told they will withdraw her bid on the land.

In the background, Nick can hear Samson. "Are you okay?" Nick presses the gun strongly into Johansen's back. The reply is unweighted, "I'm Fine. Get to work."

And then the phone is passed to Nick. Blake is soon on the other end, and her voice is suddenly in his ear, worried, upset, trembling. He steels himself against her need for reassurance or further explanation. This *isn't* what they had planned. In front of Johansen, he must remain impervious. Unaffected.

Still, his voice does crack.

Johansen: Observing. Waiting. Tensing.

Nick speaks. "I'll see you as soon as I can. Don't say the name of the place; go there, now. Just hold on. Please, just hold on."

•

Without the forward motion of the boat, the only breeze across the deck is from the dark warm air, which now pushes gently from somewhere seemingly many miles away. They have been at a dead stop for minutes now, and the yacht is starting to drift. The ocean is beyond vast at such times. The huge distance in human terms to anything else is impossibly obvious and enormous. The tender is dangling behind, and they are both starting to slowly rotate to come broadside with whatever wind has gathered force. The stars overhead have twisted. In the rich yellow light of the instrumentation of the control board, Nick can see a pair of hands continue to tightly grip the wheel.

Johansen is speaking, "Pull that trigger, and you will never keep this boat. *You'll have to let me go.* Unless my death is worth tens of millions of dollars to you." It is as if he is saying: you can have justice or wealth. But not both.

Nick prods Johansen in the back. There are no words to speak. There is just the horrifying end that Johansen is starting to see.

Nick pushes him towards the edge of the boat; Johansen starts to struggle. His walk is that of a condemned man. Can someone hate him that much? Johansen makes a sudden dash for the place on the deck where the syringe might still be lying, where the stun gun might still be waiting, as if either of those items could somehow help him, but in the near darkness there is nothing to see. The duffle bag sits to the side, open and taunting, the electronic debris that baited him, visible. Otherwise, there is just the wood of the deck, the well-ordered equipment, the cabin that stands proud but is raked far back, like the windshield of a sports car. There are tie-downs and lengths of rope tightly bound, and therefore unavailable to him without a certain amount of effort and time, though what good they might do to help him escape is not clear.

Nick clarifies the situation, while advancing on him. The gun leveled at his chest. "I don't own this boat; nor will I ever own this boat." With an ironic laugh he says, "My name is nowhere near the holding company, which you've just sold the boat to. A trick I've learned from you."

Johansen is retreating. He is looking behind him, and at the figure moving forward at him. The bend of the hull, announcing the prow of the boat is nearing. Nowhere else to escape. "I've trusted Blake with all of it, and she is hundreds of miles away from this particular place on the water. It's hers. I've no connection to it. Everything I have, in fact, is hers."

Nick pauses for a moment, and then begins in a different tone, walking more slowly. "In fact, you might find this funny, Johansen. If she wants, right at this moment, she could be leaving me. Taking it all. And again, I'd have nothing. So now do you see? I don't really care. You have nothing to bargain with."

"How do you know I deserve this?"

Nick throws the gun overboard and into the sea. He no longer needs it with what he intends to do; the weapon makes a surprisingly quiet splash. And mere seconds afterwards, with a sudden sprint, he has Johansen by the neck. The fight is *now.* There is a thrash, a panic of flaying arms and kicks, and then he has lifted Johansen up and over the railing. For a moment, the two men are inches apart, and then they are separated. There is a larger sound, as the man himself lands in the water. Nick is standing tall in the unmoving boat, and seeing him from above, starting to lash wildly in the water.

"How do you know?" In the voice, there is a sound that Nick has never heard before. Shouting and baffled. But some other sound is present in the cries.

Nick quickly runs the perimeter of the boat, there are no ladders over the side. There are no ropes dangling as a hold. There is simply the clean line of the boat. The exception being the tender, which Johansen is now swimming towards.

Nick rushes to the wheel of Johansen's boat. He presses those same buttons; the engines wake up. The exhaust burbles. He moves the throttles to their farthest ends, and the noise sends the final message to Johansen. The water churns. The slack rope between the tender and yacht tightens and the rope lifts from the water, and immediately pulls on the nose of the tender, which straightens and follows. The two boats move forward and accelerate. The sea is a dark blue and he glimpses Johansen swimming alongside in the gloom, trying to reach for anything.

Nick thinks he sees Johansen's hand touch the tender. A motion filled with panic and yet focus - the revealing moment of someone who has spent so much time at sea - someone who knows the terror waiting, but has refused to let it overwhelm him. He thinks he hears, "How do you know?" over the deep powerful thrum of the engines.

•

Nick kept a light reversed and on the tender all night. He saw the way the little boat trailed behind the yacht, bouncing in the waves.

He directed the searchlight with different beams, and with different focal points, looking intently at the prow of the tender as it cut through the waves, but mostly inside, at the rear compartment. As if he would see a hand reaching up over the edge and grabbing hold, and a head with silver hair coming into view and brightly reflected in the light.

Sporadically, he averted his gaze. He checked his watch for some reason; he checked the radar; he checked his headings and the map. He found Johansen's phone in his pocket and threw it far into the distance. But then his eyes were back on the bouncing tender, and he was convincing himself that in the brief time he had removed his eyes and the contemplation of it, the man had silently crawled into its hull, just as *Nick* had once done, and was hiding in the shadows.

Waiting.

•

The sun rose in the east. The water was consumed in that glowing brilliance of life. The tender bounded behind in the wake, vacant as it had been at night. It pulled on the line. It trailed and fought against the force; the ocean moderately passing, and waves turning.

Down in the interior of the yacht, near the engine compartment and neatly and perfectly stored *by the book*, he found a secured container of diesel fuel.

In a survival pouch, he found a package of water-resistant matches.

He brought the pair of items to the deck. He went to the stern; he found the cleat, he untied the rope that connected the two boats, and watched as the tender dipped and fell behind. The rope dropped into the water and snaked around the edges. At the helm now, he pulled the two throttles back, and turned the wheel of the yacht. He made several slow circles of the small craft. If his eyes were not on it, they were near to it.

He made a scan of the surrounding water. By radar and by sight, not another vessel was within 20 miles.

He cut the engines. Suddenly there was near silence - the waves quietly beating on the hull, and the absence of the moan of power.

He told himself that no one could possibly hold on, being dragged in the water all that time. Still, he would not have been surprised to see the man suddenly standing beside him, dripping wet and somehow driving a knife into his stomach. A real knife this time, to replace the other knives and blades, and that sick feeling that was slowly abating in his gut. With trembling hands Nick coasted the yacht closely aside the tender, so that they were within mere inches, and looked again at an empty craft. With the morning's light he saw clearly. Nick viewed the vacant interior piece by piece; the fiberglass forms of seats and its bottom, the storage lockers, the wheel and controls. The two boats were now next to each other, stationary, but bobbing in the waves.

With a clumsy motion he emptied the container of fuel into the tender, the many gallons of diesel smelling that predictable way, and sloshing around in the open hull. With a panicked swipe, a group of matches suddenly became a flame. He tossed that ball of flame into the tender and near instantly it became a raging fire. The engines back to life, he throttled the yacht forward and away. He stationed himself, as he judged it, at one-hundred yards, and watched for several minutes as the fire grew enormously. The fiberglass and plastic burning with an intensity that startled him, the thick inky black smoke carrying up and then diagonally with the wind.

And then there was a point, when it was clearly at its peak. Yellow and red flames mixing with blue. All of the surfaces consumed; but the hull had burned through, and water was now flooding in. It was sinking. Every second it was lower in the water. The engine compartment must have flooded because suddenly the rear sank and the nose came out of the water. It was several feet above the surface. A death throe.

It then slid under and disappeared almost immediately. Nothing but waves, the smoke in the air already turning into a haze, and then gone.

Without a body to see and contemplate in its lifelessness,

Nick wondered if the feeling of dread would ever pass.

•

A different beach. A different view than he has ever seen before. Sitting on the sand, far above the tidal zone, is a vibrantly red structure. It's an open air restaurant, pillars supporting a roof that is likewise red, and visible for miles away. Behind, he sees an apron of palm trees, as if framing it for just this view.

From this distance, Nick does not need binoculars. He can see the beach-goers relaxing on the beach, most with wide-brimmed hats, and sunglasses. There are umbrellas expanded, which are shading couples and families, and in the surf there are children playing. A few sandcastles otherwise decorate the scene. He lets the front anchor let go with a rat-a-tat-tat. He lets the rear anchor go with a rat-a-tat-tat. He stands on the white yacht and looks across the distance to where the water finally meets the land.

He sees a figure leaving the red structure. It is a woman. She is walking down the beach. He sees that same hair, those silver bracelets on her wrists apparently collecting the sun and then radiating the light back out like a mirror.

He readies himself. He jumps from the rear of the yacht, hitting the water with the merest splash of an expert diver, and begins swimming to shore.

The End.